# THE INCONVENIENT ELMSWOOD MARRIAGE

Marguerite Kaye

MILLS & BOON

First Published in Great Britain 2019
by Mills & Boon, an imprint of HarperCollins*Publishers*
1 London Bridge Street, London, SE1 9GF



ISBN: 978-0-263-27279-6

MIX
Paper from
responsible sources
FSC C007454

This book is produced from independently certified FSC™ paper
to ensure responsible forest management.
For more information visit www.harpercollins.co.uk/green.

Printed and bound in Spain
by CPI, Barcelona

# *Prologue*

*Elmswood Manor, Shropshire, April 1820*

Kate glanced nervously at the tarnished mantel clock. Like everything else around here it had seen better days. It told her that it was fifteen minutes to the allotted start time of what she hoped would be her life-changing appointment. One minute less than when she had last checked.

She adjusted the blotter so that it sat perfectly in the middle of the desk, then straightened the ledger so that it sat square on the blotter. Next, she placed the annual accounts summary she had drawn up on top of the ledger. Finally, she ran a hand nervously over her hair, which she had pinned tightly up in an attempt to project a mature, businesslike demeanour, though her bedroom mirror had reflected something more reminiscent of a frightened rabbit. Then she glanced over at the clock again.

It didn't seem to have moved. Had it stopped? But she'd wound it up yesterday evening, as she did at the same time every night, as Papa had been in the habit of doing, and she could hear it ticking slowly and softly, just as it had always done.

She felt sick. Was she really going to put her outrageous proposition to a virtual stranger? No, not outrageous. She mustn't think of it in those terms or she'd come over as an irrational fantasist. It was actually a common-sense suggestion rooted in practicality, one she had evaluated from every angle in the long weeks spent awaiting this much-heralded return, while her future, her father's security and the fate of every one of the estate's tenants and those few staff that remained were left hanging in the balance.

Pushing back the worn leather wing-backed chair, Kate edged out from behind the huge desk that dominated the Estate Office to risk a glance out of the window. The office was located at the far end of a row of outbuildings, behind what had once been the kitchen gardens, with an excellent view in all directions. If he was coming from the stables, walking around from the front entrance or any of the rooms that opened onto the terrace at the rear, she'd see him approach.

And he would turn up, she reassured herself, he had asked for the appointment himself, hadn't he?

Though the appointment had actually been made with her father—for the new Lord Elmswood seemed to be uniquely unaware that his lands were being managed by his estate manager's daughter.

Kate returned to the desk and retrieved the note from under the blotter, but the brief informal scrawl told her nothing more than she already knew or had surmised.

*Sir,*

*With regard to the settling of my late father's estate, which I have perforce returned to England to oversee, I anticipate that I will have completed all necessary business with my lawyer in London by the sixteenth of this month. I will then travel to Shropshire, arriving at Elmswood on the seventeenth.*

*I assume it will be convenient for you to meet with me on the eighteenth in the Estate Office at ten o'clock that morning, with a view to formally resolving the issue of your continued stewardship and any residual outstanding business.*

*I would appreciate it if you could do everything possible to expedite matters, as I am extremely eager to return to my own pressing business abroad.*

*Yours respectfully,*
*Daniel Fairfax*

Fairfax, she noted. He didn't use his new title. He had clearly returned reluctantly, for the briefest period possible. How would he feel, knowing he would never see his father again? There was no trace of any emotion in that note save impatience. Her own dear papa's slow decline over the last few years had forced her to face the reality of his mortality, but she didn't for a moment imagine that when the time came it would be anything other than a terrible blow to lose him. It seemed to be a very different matter for Daniel Fairfax, who could probably count on one hand the number of weeks he'd spent as an adult in his father's company.

He was twenty-eight years old. She'd known him—or of him—all her life, for, like him, she had been born on the estate, though, unlike him, she had never had any desire to live anywhere else. He was six years her senior. Though she knew from her father that he had been a sickly child, and educated at home as a little boy, by the time she'd been old enough to perch in front of Papa in the saddle as he rode around the estates on his regular inspections, or sit here in this office, drawing happily while he attended to estate business, Daniel Fairfax had been a boarder at a prestigious school.

As a result, for most of the year, Kate had been able to pretend that the grounds of Elmswood Manor belonged exclusively to her. When he came home for the school holidays she would catch the occasional glimpse of him, swimming in the lake or setting out on his pony from the stables, but those encounters had been rare. She'd had no idea what he did all day, or where he went, and his awareness of her had been confined to an absent, uninterested nod as he'd passed purposefully in the opposite direction. Though he was, in effect, like her, an only child, he'd seemed perfectly content in his own company. She couldn't recall him ever having friends to stay, save once, and that hadn't been a school friend but some sort of tutor.

During the last school holiday he had spent at Elmswood he'd left, before it was over, when he was sixteen to Kate's ten, not to return to school but to go to London to take up a position at the Admiralty. When he'd next returned, on reaching his majority, after an absence of five years, he had left both the Admiralty and his youth behind. The deeply tanned young man she had encountered one morning, staring grim-faced at the lake, had been a rather intimidating and fiercely attractive stranger who'd left Kate embarrassingly tongue-tied.

Where he had been in the intervening years not even Papa knew, and it had only been after he'd left—a long time after he'd left—that Lord Elmswood had revealed his son was off 'exploring the world'. And, the world being a very big place, it had seemed unlikely that he would return any time soon.

'Any time soon' had turned into never. If there had been letters, old Lord Elmswood had kept the contents to himself. On his death, it had seemed like a minor miracle when his lawyer had revealed that he knew how to contact the heir, and a miracle of considerably larger proportions when he'd sent word to Elmswood to inform Papa that the man himself had actually arrived in London.

But, regardless of the fact that he'd inherited

an estate and an earldom, Kate was willing to stake her life on Daniel Fairfax, nomadic explorer, heading back to his life of wandering the far-flung corners of the world as soon as he possibly could.

In fact, she thought wryly, she was banking on him doing exactly that, even though she knew almost nothing of him. She was taking a leap of faith, but he was Lord Elmswood's son, after all, and she'd heard nothing to suggest he was in any way of dubious character or unsavoury temperament. In any event, if her plan came to fruition she wouldn't have to put that assumption to the test, since she was unlikely to see hide nor hair of him for the foreseeable future.

'Excuse me, I have an appointment to meet Mr Wilson.'

'Lord Elmswood!' Kate scrabbled to her feet.

Daniel Fairfax, for it was unmistakably he, stood in the doorway, eyeing her quizzically. 'This is still the Estate Office, I assume?'

'Yes, you are in the right place. I am Mr Wilson's daughter, I—'

Kate broke off, blushing. Dammit! Cool, calm and collected was what she needed to be, not a simpering miss! Daniel Fairfax might be a self-confident man of the world, and she might be a country hick, but she was a country hick who knew his estates like the back of her hand, and he needed her—even though he didn't know it yet.

'Lord Elmswood. You clearly don't remember me. I am Kate Wilson. How do you do?'

'Miss Wilson? Well, I never! The last time I clapped eyes on you, I'm sure you had pigtails and freckles.'

'I was almost fifteen the last time you were home, and I have not worn my hair in pigtails since I was ten.'

'Really? Good Lord, that makes you—what?—twenty-two? How did that happen?'

'By the simple process of aging. It affects us all, unfortunately.'

'Well, the passing years have certainly done you no harm, if you don't mind my saying so. I hardly recognised you.'

'Since you have, in all the years I've lived here, barely acknowledged me,' Kate retorted, flustered, 'that is not really surprising. I've not changed so very much in seven years.'

'You're quite wrong. But I can see I've touched a nerve. I hadn't thought myself rude, not even as a sulky youth, but clearly I was. Please accept my belated apologies.'

'You were not rude. It's not surprising that I

barely registered with you, given that you were six years older than me and—'

'I still am.'

'The gap is more of a chasm when one is younger.'

'True, but I apologise for my ill-mannered younger self all the same.' Daniel Fairfax glanced at the clock. 'I thought your father was expecting me? Didn't he receive my note?'

'He did,' Kate said, belatedly remembering her carefully rehearsed plan for this meeting. 'On behalf of my father and myself, Lord Elmswood, may I offer our condolences on your loss?'

'You've already done so—or your father has, in a letter. I understand I have him to thank for organising the funeral too. I'm told it was very well-attended. I'm sorry I wasn't here, but by the time I had word of my father's accident he was already dead and buried, and it took me the best part of six weeks to get myself back to England. Is Mr Wilson intending to meet me this morning or not?'

'I'm afraid he is indisposed, but I believe I can settle all the necessary business on his behalf.'

'Without wishing to be rude, Miss Wilson, my business is with Elmswood's estate manager. Perhaps it would be better for me to return when your father is feeling better—tomorrow, perhaps?'

'Lord Elmswood, when I said my father was indisposed, I'm afraid I did not mean he was afflicted with some minor ailment. Would that it were so! Unfortunately his condition is both long-standing and irreversible. I take it you are unaware that I have been acting in my father's stead? Clearly you are,' Kate continued, in response to his blank look. 'In fact I've been helping out for some years now, but in the last eighteen months or so I have been obliged to take on almost all of my father's duties as his health has failed.'

'I am deeply sorry to hear that. But, with respect, I am surprised to learn that he delegated the management of the estates to you. No matter how competent you are, you are a female, and that alone, in my father's book, would make you quite ineligible. Your father must have known that.'

'The arrangement was of an—an informal nature.'

'Ah. So my father was blissfully ignorant of the fact that his estate manager's daughter was running things.'

Kate bristled. 'I was born and raised here,

and have been helping my father ever since I was old enough to ride a horse. With the greatest of respect, and with no offence intended, my lord, I know your estates a great deal better than you do.'

'That would not be difficult, for even the cows in the fields could claim that.'

'I love this place, my lord, even if you do not.'

'There's no need for those raised hackles. I am not questioning your competency. In this, as in everything else, I have nothing in common with my father, and I have no issue at all with having a female estate manager.'

'In that case, perhaps you would care to take a look at the summary of accounts.'

Kate pushed the ledger forward, but Daniel Fairfax gave it only a cursory glance. 'I won't pretend to have any grasp of the financial ins and outs, but I know from that London lawyer fellow that the lands are in good hands.'

'Relatively, all things considered. Unfortunately your father was reluctant to invest either his time or his money. Frankly, he seemed uninterested in his estates.'

But once again Daniel Fairfax seemed to have no interest in pursuing the subject of his lands.

'I really am sorry to hear that your father is so gravely ill. If there is anything I can do…'

'As a matter of fact, there is.' Kate wondered fleetingly what he would say if she simply blurted out the outrageous proposition she had for him, and was so amused by the idea that it calmed her. 'If you would care to take a seat, Lord Elmswood…'

'I really wish you wouldn't call me that.'

'It's your name now.'

'No, it's not. I don't plan on making use of any of it—the lands, the title, or indeed the house, which my father seems to have allowed to go to rack and ruin.'

'Yes, that is one of the topics I wish to discuss with you.'

'Only one? I have a list of my own, you know, and a limited amount of time.'

'Of that I am perfectly well aware.' She hadn't meant to snap, but her nerves were stretched to breaking point. 'Please, if you will sit down I will explain everything.'

Kate indicated the seat on the opposite side of the desk from her own and to her utter relief he did as she'd asked. The legs of the chair had been shortened by some shrewd previous estate manager, intent on ensuring that he loomed over whoever sat opposite, but Daniel Fairfax was very tall and her own stature so diminutive that when she sat down she was still looking up at him.

She straightened her back. He stretched his long legs out in front of him. His hair was cut very close to his head, as if he had taken a razor to it, showing off a slight widow's peak. His face was tanned to the point of swarthiness, strong-featured, with sharp cheekbones and jaw, a nose bordering on the assertive. Despite the fullness of his lips it was a very masculine face, and one that bore testament to a life lived in a very different climate. The grooves which ran from his nose to his mouth, the fan of lines at the corners of his slate-grey eyes, spoke of a life lived at a pace that made hers seem positively sedentary.

Those eyes were now focused intently on her. She resisted the impulse to check her hair for any escaped locks.

'How long had my father been living as a virtual recluse?' he asked. 'From what I've seen of the house, he seems to have been living in two rooms, with only his manservant and a couple of kitchen staff to look after him.'

'His withdrawal from society was gradual. It

was only in the last two years or so that he became almost completely cut off from the world.'

'Making it easy for you to take over your father's duties without his realising?'

'We did not hoodwink him,' Kate retorted angrily. 'Once a month Papa submitted the books to Lord Elmswood, via his valet, and if your father required to consult him on any matter he sent Papa a written note. The authority remains formally invested in my father. To be perfectly frank, I don't think your father cared who actually did the donkey work and—without wishing to offend you, Lord Elmswood—'

'You offend me every time you use that title. I wish you'd call me Daniel.'

'Daniel.' It felt strange saying his name…intimate. 'It wasn't only that he was uninterested in the detail, he seemed indifferent to the fact that only the bare minimum was being done. I'm afraid that you've inherited an estate in dire need of modernisation.'

He dug his hand into his coat pocket to retrieve a small, brightly coloured precious stone, which he began compulsively to turn over and over in his hand. 'I made it perfectly clear the last time that I was home that I wished to relinquish my claim to Elmswood.'

'Relinquish! You mean you wanted your father to disinherit you?' Kate exclaimed, shocked to the core to hear the place she loved so passionately dismissed so summarily.

Daniel smiled thinly. 'Don't worry. As ever, he completely disregarded my wishes.'

'But—but can you really mean you want nothing to do with Elmswood—ever?'

'Never. Though that does not mean I am pleased to see the place so run down. I could barely locate the door into the walled garden.'

'I know, and that is a subject close to my heart, believe me,' Kate said, diverted. 'It's been a dream of mine for years to be able to restore Elmswood Manor and the gardens to their former glory.'

'To say nothing of modernising the farms? It's a strange ambition for a female to have.'

'I have inherited my father's love of Elmswood.'

'Is Mr Wilson likely to recover? Forgive me for being blunt, but…'

'I would much rather you were. I'm extremely aware that time is of the essence to you. Papa is frail, and, while not in any immediate danger, his days of estate management are well and truly over.'

'Does he have everything he needs to make him comfortable? You said there is something I can do for him? What was it?'

It was the perfect opening. Kate's throat was dry, her heart thumping in her chest, but she might not get another opportunity. She owed it to Papa as much as herself to take it. And of course to Elmswood itself.

'My father is concerned about what will happen to us now that he is not fit to continue serving you.'

'I'm not sure what you mean?'

'I mean, where will we live and how will we survive? Our house is tied to your estate, as indeed is our income, save for a small legacy your father left in his will. Our circumstances would be severely straitened were you to appoint another estate manager. I don't mind for my own sake, but Papa…'

'There's no need for that. You are currently acting as *de facto* estate manager. I see no reason for that situation to change. I will formalise the arrangement before I leave—you have my word. I came here with the intention of investing complete authority in your father to allow me to resume my foreign travels. Circumstances have changed, but now I shall invest my authority in you instead. You are clearly trustworthy—better still, you obviously cherish this place. I consider you a very safe pair of hands.'

Daniel smiled, looking as much relieved as pleased.

'There, I hope that puts your mind at rest. So, let us turn our minds to what I need to do in order—'

'I'm very sorry, but I'm afraid it won't work.'

His smile faded. 'You don't want the position?'

'I'm extremely flattered that you should offer it to me, and I can say, hand on heart, that I would do my very best to ensure that you would never have any cause to regret placing your faith in me. Believe me,' Kate said earnestly, 'if I thought for a moment it would work in practice I'd leap at the chance. It's not that I can't do the job—the accounts prove that—but the reality is I'm a female of modest background, and you would not be here to underpin my authority, or indeed be available to make important financial decisions. Though it pains me to admit it, that is a fatal combination. It would be doomed to failure.'

'But what is the alternative? I don't want to employ a stranger and throw you and your father out onto the street, and even though I don't give a damn about this place, I don't want to let it go any further down the road to rack and ruin.'

'You could look to offload it. I'm sure you could find a willing purchaser.'

'That would make your situation perilous.' Daniel began to turn over the stone in his hand again, frowning down at it. 'No, I need a caretaker I can trust implicitly. My sister in Ireland has a son. It seems to me that he is the obvious person to hand the place over to, when he comes of age. Lock stock and barrel, as they say. Of course I can't pass on the title, but I see no reason why my nephew shouldn't make use of that too.'

Kate's mouth dropped. 'You have a nephew!'

'So I've been informed.'

His tone was one of insouciance, but he could not possibly be indifferent to such news. Or perhaps she'd misunderstood.

'You didn't know that your sister had a son? His birth is a recent event, then?'

'I believe the boy is seven or eight, so it will be a good few years before I can hand the reins over to him.'

'Seven or eight! Did your father know of his existence?'

'I have no idea. There was no mention of the boy in his will.'

'And your sister? What does she think of your plan?'

'I don't know. I haven't discussed it with her,' Daniel answered impatiently. 'I am no more interested in her life than she is in mine, and I would be obliged to you, Miss Wilson, if you would resist asking the many questions I can see you are desperate to ask, because I have neither the time nor the inclination to discuss the matter further. I would rather my nephew did not inherit an encumbrance. You are the ideal person to ensure that he does not, and yet you're telling me that, much as you'd like to take on the job, it's impossible. We both want the same thing here. Surely there must be a way of making the impossible possible.'

There was, and she must speak now or for ever hold her peace, but her head was swimming with the revelations Daniel had so callously announced. But they were all grist to her mill, she reminded herself.

Her hands were clammy. She wiped them surreptitiously on her gown under the desk. She cleared her throat. 'I do have a plan, as it happens, which will restore the fortunes of both this house and its lands, and make them a fit inheritance for your little nephew.'

Daniel set his turquoise stone down on the desk. He sat back, his hand curling around the crudely polished stone. He smiled suddenly. 'What a very surprising young woman you are. What is this cunning plan of yours?'

His teeth were very white and even. When he smiled, his eyes lit up. It was a very infectious and unexpected smile. The kind that she suspected one would do a great deal to earn. It changed him, that smile, and it made her uncomfortably aware of him as a very attractive man.

Kate allowed herself a very prim smile in return, but now she was coming to the point her stomach was starting to churn again.

'It's a little radical.' Perspiration prickled her back. 'In fact it will take a bit of a leap of faith on both our parts.'

'Now I am thoroughly intrigued. Take a deep breath and spit it out.'

'Very well. What I'm proposing resolves both our dilemmas—your desire to live abroad unencumbered by responsibility, and my desire to live here with Papa while he is still with me. It would provide me with the natural authority to make whatever significant decisions need to be made without referring to you, including financial ones. It would allow me not only to maintain your lands but to improve them, and to restore the house and gardens too, while you'd have nothing to do save return to your life in darkest Africa, or wherever it is. And then when the time came, you could make the lands over to your nephew and I could—well, I don't know what I'd do, but we can worry about that when the time comes. What do you think?'

'To be honest, I think it sounds too good to be true. And when something sounds too good to be true, it is my experience that it usually is.'

Kate shuffled her feet under the desk. She picked up the polished stone, turning it over in her hands as Daniel had done. It was elliptical in shape, smooth and not quite flat, and had a very soothing effect. 'Is this turquoise?'

'Yes, it is, Miss Wilson.'

He held out his hand. Embarrassed, she surrendered it. 'Kate. You may as well call me Kate, since—if we are to—and after all I'm already calling you Daniel.'

'You've come this far without equivocating. Don't falter now. What is your devilishly clever plan, Kate, and what is the catch? For there must be one.'

'I suppose you might say *I* am.'

'You really have lost me now.'

She took a deep breath. 'I think we should get married.'

He looked as if he wasn't sure whether to laugh or have her committed to a Bedlam. 'Right! Anything else I should know?'

'There is, as it happens,' she said breezily. 'In order to protect my father's pride, I'm afraid it has to be your idea.'

# *Chapter One*

*Elmswood Manor, June 1831*

With a heavy sigh, Kate pushed aside the letter she had been attempting to compose to Eloise. Her husband's eldest niece, she had just learned, had given birth to a daughter. She had, it seemed, embraced motherhood with an enthusiasm that was staggering, considering that she had originally wed Alexander with no intentions of consummating the marriage, far less of conceiving a child. But Eloise's marriage of convenience had turned into a true love match.

Her obvious happiness leapt off the page of the letter Kate had just received, and she was desperate to accept the invitation to her home in Lancashire to meet baby Tilda for herself. For the moment, however, that was sadly completely out of the question.

She had missed so much while she'd been away. How long would this very strange state of affairs continue?

Pushing her chair back from the desk, Kate prowled restlessly over to the window. The morning room faced out to the back of the house. The expanse of lawn had been neatly mown and trimmed, revealing a vast swathe of verdant green. Leaves covered the huge, ancient oak which Eloise had been so fond of climbing when she'd first come to live at Elmswood. On the still waters of the lake a pair of swans were gliding effortlessly.

Had it really been last October when those two distinguished gentlemen had turned up unannounced on her doorstep? 'Colleagues of her husband', was how they'd introduced themselves, and she'd thought they were bringing her some long overdue letters. She'd served them tea and cake, and they'd talked about the weather, and the shocking state of the roads, and there had been mention of them having met Eloise socially, she recalled, before they had revealed the real purpose of their visit by informing her that Daniel's wellbeing was a matter of grave concern.

She'd still been wondering what connection the pair of them might have with Eloise, and why Eloise had never mentioned it, when she realised that their polite smiles had been replaced with another expression entirely.

Then the interrogation had started, with questions being flung at her one after the other in rapid succession, until finally she'd startled them by demanding that they stop bombarding her with demands for information and start providing her with answers. What they told her and what they had proposed had sent her reeling.

They'd given her no time to recover her composure before the younger of the two, Sir Marcus, had started issuing her with a series of concise instructions, including what she was permitted to say to Estelle, whom she'd had no choice but to press-gang into holding the fort. Within three hours of their arrival they had been gone, taking Kate with them, on the start of a journey that had taken her through the end of one year and well into the next.

In the end, she'd been abroad for all of winter and spring, arriving home yesterday with the beginning of summer.

Looking around her now, smelling the sweet perfume of the rose she'd picked only an hour ago, Kate had to remind herself that she really was home, for Elmswood Manor didn't feel in the least bit familiar. The Elmswood Coven was no more.

For the first time since her husband's nieces had arrived, more than nine years ago, she was alone, all her beloved wards gone, embracing their own lives without any further need of her.

Eloise had a husband and now a child. Phoebe had not only opened a restaurant in London while Kate had been away, but also married a man Kate had never heard of, never mind met. A man she would not meet for the foreseeable future, and a restaurant she wouldn't be able to visit, no matter how much she longed to.

For this next, wholly unexpected and hopefully brief stage of her life she would be without the company of any of her husband's nieces, for even dear Estelle, who had stepped into the breach and held the fort at Elmswood for nine long months, had been obliged to leave.

Not that she'd objected, thank goodness. Quite the contrary, in fact. She'd embraced her freedom and the chance to embark on a long-planned Continental trip, loyally refraining from asking awkward questions or from making what in

Kate's opinion would have been perfectly reasonable demands under the circumstances.

And what circumstances!

Kate sank onto one of the chairs, leaning her head back and closing her eyes. Had the last nine months really happened? She had told the girls only the bare bones. Not the story that Sir Marcus had constructed for public consumption but the truth—or a fraction of it. What they truly made of it she couldn't begin to imagine, but they were fiercely loyal, and she knew that if they talked it would only be amongst themselves.

Now it was over, and it felt like a dream—or should that be nightmare?

However she chose to describe it, it wasn't over yet. Upstairs, in one of the guest bedrooms, was a very real, lurking reminder of that fact—a simmering volcano which could erupt at any time.

Daniel, her husband of eleven years. The girls' nearest living relative. A man Kate barely knew and whom his nieces had never met.

The sound of the handle of the morning room door being turned made Kate's eyes fly open. She was on her feet when the man in question appeared, larger than life and, if not actually bursting with health, very far from death's door and most certainly not a figment of her imagination.

'So this is where you hide yourself away.'

'Daniel!'

Instinctively, Kate rushed to help him, but the fierce frown she received made her sit straight back down again. He was dressed oddly, in a somewhat exotic-looking tunic and loose pantaloons, over which he had donned a rather magnificent crimson silk dressing gown emblazoned with gold dragons and tied with a gold cord. A matching pair of slippers covered his bare feet.

'Chinese,' he enlightened her, noting her stare. 'It seems the powers that be managed to get my luggage back to England ahead of me. Considerate of them, don't you think? That they moved heaven and earth to make sure my effects were delivered? A small consolation for you, dear wife, in the event that you'd been forced to return here alone.'

'Don't say that!'

To her horror, tears welled up in her eyes. Kate blinked them away. There had been more than enough opportunities in the last nine months to shed tears, but she'd rarely taken them.

'Well, at least you'll have something to wear, then,' she said, forcing a smile. 'I don't know how long it would take to send to London for a new wardrobe of clothes, and you'd struggle to find anything more sartorial than a fleece shirt and brogues in the village. There's your father's clothes, of course, they are packed up in the attic, but—'

'I would rather dress as a farmhand,' he snapped.

There were so many questions raised by that one sentence—questions she'd asked herself over the years since they had married—but now was hardly the time. Perhaps there would never be a time.

The last time he'd been home, eleven years ago, Daniel had remained at Elmswood barely long enough for her to promise to love, honour and obey him. They'd married by special licence, because technically, he'd been was in mourning, though she had known he hadn't been able to bear the thought of waiting another six weeks for the banns to be read.

This time she hadn't exactly dragged him back to England kicking and screaming, but if he'd been strong enough to do more than protest weakly then she doubted he'd be here—despite the orders he'd received.

How long would he remain? Lord, look at

him—he was hardly in a state to go anywhere. The florid dressing gown was far too large for him. He had, she suspected, put it on in an attempt to disguise his loss of weight, not realising that it merely drew attention to the fact. He had shaved too. She wasn't surprised. As she had tended to him on their protracted journey from Cyprus to Crete, then on to Malta and Gibraltar, Lisbon, Portsmouth and finally home, one of his biggest bugbears, in the intervals when he had been lucid enough to have bugbears, had been his unkempt beard.

He had not permitted Kate to wield his razor for him, and she had not allowed him to try to use it himself, having visions of him accidentally slitting his own throat, so she had been forced to beg the services of a weird and wonderful assortment of stand-in barbers on his behalf.

'What? Have I nicked myself?' he asked her now.

She realised she'd been staring and shook her head.

'Then you're thinking that I look like death warmed up.'

'I'm thinking that you look remarkably well, all things considered.'

Which was true, and if anything an understatement. He looked gaunt, and there were shadows under his eyes, new lines on his brow, but somehow they suited him. It was unfair, for the lines she'd acquired in the last few months simply aged her, while with Daniel the changes served to accentuate the fact that he was a lethally attractive man. Dammit!

'I didn't expect to see you up and about so soon,' Kate said, her tone made acerbic not by his presence but by her reaction to it.

'You can't keep me secreted away in my bedchamber, no matter how much you'd like to.'

As he closed the door behind him and made his way carefully over to the chair opposite hers by the empty grate Kate remembered that behind the attractive façade there was an extremely infuriating man, and gritted her teeth.

'I don't know why you are so convinced that I want to imprison you here.'

'Not you—them.' He showed his teeth. 'The irony is not lost on me that I've been sprung from one gaol only to be forced into another. I will concede that you are a reluctant warder, but you are charged with keeping me here nonetheless.'

'I trust you won't put me to the test. Having travelled halfway across the world to bring you home, I'd rather not chase you halfway across Shropshire to drag you back.'

'Would you really do that?' He grinned. 'I'd rather like to see you try.'

'I won't have to,' Kate replied tartly. 'Go on—why don't you leave right now? Walk down to the village...hire a post chaise.'

'I have no need to do any such thing. I have horses and a post chaise of my own.'

'Actually, you don't. There's a carriage, but it's not been used in heaven knows how long, and aside from my mount, and the pony who pulls the trap, and the farm horses, the stables are empty. So you'll just have to walk. Please, don't let me stop you.' She smiled sweetly at him.

For a moment she thought he might actually call her bluff, but then he gave an exasperated sigh.

'You know as well as I do that I'm under orders to remain here. Hopefully it won't be for long, for the terms of our marriage did not anticipate any form of cohabitation. I'm sure you don't want me here, getting under your feet and treading on your toes, and I assure you that I have no intention of doing so. This is your domain, not mine.'

'This is your home, Daniel.'

'No, it's your home and my gaol, albeit a considerably more comfortable one than the last. I wish to hell they hadn't embroiled you in this diplomatic mess.'

'I'm your wife,' Kate said tightly, 'the most obvious person to become *embroiled*, as you put it.'

'My wife in name only. I married you to look after Elmswood, not me.'

'You were at death's door, for heaven's sake!'

Kate gazed down at her hands, counting slowly to ten. It was the same refrain he'd uttered on and off since he'd first recovered consciousness in Cyprus almost two months ago, and it was beginning to grate. Seriously grate.

'I won't apologise for doing what was asked of me. You're my husband, and it's my duty to take care of you to the best of my ability. That's what I did, and as a result you are alive to berate me for it. If that is the price I must pay for what I did, then so be it.'

A tense silence followed, in which they both glowered at each other, and then, to her surprise and relief, Daniel laughed. 'I've married a despot! And I should know—I've met a few!'

She didn't know what to make of that, so instead said, 'If you would be a little more co-operative and conciliatory then I wouldn't have to fight you every step of the way.'

'Ah! So you admit that you have been imposing your will on me? In my book, that's a despot. Or a tyrant, if you prefer.'

'I prefer—' Kate stopped short, narrowing her eyes. 'Are you teasing me?'

Daniel grinned. 'Only a little. Do you mind?'

She smiled reluctantly. 'I suppose if I say yes it will only encourage you.'

'Which would be extremely churlish of me. I rather think it's me who's been the tyrant.'

'You've been very ill.'

'That doesn't mean my temper is obliged to follow suit. You're a diplomat, as well as a despot. Have I said thank you at any point?'

'There's no need to thank me. We are married, I was doing my wifely duty.'

'And your duty to your country, as they doubtless pressed upon you,' Daniel said, rolling his eyes. 'But there are very few wives who would have done what you did. Diplomat, despot, whatever other qualities you have, you are a very remarkable woman.'

'Thank you. I think.'

'Oh, it is a compliment—you must not doubt it. And as to thanks—it is I who owe you profound gratitude,' Daniel said. 'I wish you had not been involved, but I do understand that the powers that be gave you little choice in the matter. I wonder—' Daniel broke off, shaking his head. 'It doesn't matter.'

'You wonder how they came to decide that I could be trusted to do what they asked? I have wondered the same myself. I had plenty time to fill, after all, as they shifted me from pillar to post to preserve my cover story. I decided that they must have sounded Alexander out. He would be the natural choice. I presume I am right in thinking his previous position at the Admiralty masked the fact that he was in the same line of business—do you call it "business"?—as you?'

'What do you know about my line of business?'

'Next to nothing. They told me you were incarcerated. They did not tell me why or even where you were being held.'

'Good. The less you know of that business or any future business of mine, the better. I won't be here long, Kate. Before you know it I'll be off and you can resume your life as if nothing has happened.'

'That's all very well, but while you're here,

Daniel, what on earth are we to tell people? What are you going to do? How will you occupy yourself?'

His expression hardened. 'I won't be here long enough to have to worry about any of those things. They'll come calling, Sir Marcus and his sidekick, believe me.'

'You've only just got here! I'm surprised you made it down the stairs without help. They can't possibly expect you to return to whatever duties you perform for them already.'

'I've no idea what they expect.' Daniel slumped, looking suddenly tired. 'Do you think I could have a cup of coffee? I could sorely use one.'

'Of course you can—this is your house. Only—do you think coffee is a good idea? Why don't you go back to bed and rest? I could bring you…'

He shuddered. 'No more healthy, nourishing broth, I beg you. And I'm not going back to bed. Just coffee, please.'

'I'll fetch it myself.' Kate jumped to her feet. 'I won't be long.'

She was gone before he could suggest ringing the bell for a servant, and on reflection Daniel was glad of the brief respite. He felt as weak as a kitten. The act of dressing and making his way from his bedchamber to the morning room had been a comically exhausting struggle. Until he'd put his clothes on, he hadn't realised just how much weight he'd lost. Shaving had almost defeated him. He'd had to stop and start so many times due to his shaking hand that the water had been cold by the time he'd finished. But he'd done it.

It was a small triumph but a victory all the same.

He stretched his legs out, wriggling his toes in his boots, for they had gone quite numb. He was cold. He could see that the sun was shining outside, and he knew it was June, the start of summer, but he'd become accustomed to much warmer climes. He would not ask for a fire to be lit, though. Kate would be bound to blame his chill on his various sicknesses. Gaol fever, the ague, and heaven only knew what else had laid him low. She would doubtless be right, but he was damned if he'd admit that to her.

She was so capable! He'd thought her unflappable too, until this morning. He'd enjoyed teasing her. She had a reluctant smile, but when she did smile—yes, it was worth waiting for. He'd seen it very rarely, that smile, on their protracted voyage back to England. Truth be told, he couldn't really make cohesive sense of that journey, for each time he'd thought his fever gone for good it had returned with a vengeance, making it difficult for him to distinguish between his torrid dreams and reality. It sat ill with him, the way he'd been forced to rely on Kate, but in his heart he knew he wouldn't have made it without her. He would not go so far as to say she'd saved his life, but she had probably saved his health.

He had pins and needles in his feet again—a recurring nuisance even though the wounds caused by the manacles had healed months ago.

Heaving himself upright, Daniel wandered over to the little rosewood escritoire which was positioned to look out of one of the two tall windows. It was neat and tidy, with a fully replenished inkstand, a selection of newly sharpened pens, a fresh sheet of paper in the blotter, various letters and papers in the dockets, neatly filed, a stack of blank paper, a seal and wax, all sitting in readiness. There was a single yellow rose in a silver vase, clearly just picked, for the bud was only partially unfurled.

Was there a rose garden at Elmswood? He couldn't recall. It hadn't been the sort of thing to interest him.

There was a comfortable-looking chair positioned in the other window, so he sat down and gazed out at the view. There was the oak tree he'd climbed countless times as a boy, and the lake where he'd taught himself to swim. Over to the left, behind the rose garden—yes, he remembered now that there was one—was his old sanctuary the walled garden. The place where he'd first dreamed his dream of escaping the claustrophobic confines of Elmswood and travelling to far-flung places.

But when he tried to remember the dreams he'd dreamed, tried to recall the experience of climbing, diving, swimming, he could not. It was as if he'd been told the stories by someone else. But then, wasn't that the case with most of his past life—or should that more accurately be *lives*? It was one of his strengths, the ability to put one persona behind him and assume another, never looking over his shoulder, wiping one slate clean before he started to write on another. No memories, no ties, no pain.

Daniel shook his head impatiently. It wasn't like him to be so fanciful. He would rather not be here at Elmswood, but he was, and he'd have to find a way to endure it. Hopefully it wouldn't be for long.

He leaned his forehead on the glass, which had been heated by the gentle English summer sun. There had been trout in the lake back in the day. He wondered if Kate kept it stocked. She would have told him if she had, in one of the letters she'd sent to him regular as clockwork every other month, since they had married, but it was the sort of detail he chose not to remember.

They'd come into his possession sporadically, those carefully penned epistles, usually in bundles of two or three at a time, and as the years had passed, contained less and less detail. She had asked him to approve decisions in the early days, had on occasion asked his opinion on a decision still to be made, but his silence on both counts had led to silence on her part. She'd realised without him having to say so bluntly that he simply didn't care.

But, from the little he'd seen of the house and gardens, it was clear she did. His acceptance of her astonishing proposal all those years ago had been one of the best decisions of his life.

'Sorry I was so long.' Kate set the tray she was carrying down on the table by the fireside. 'Coffee, and there's some spiced biscuits fresh out of the oven.'

Daniel re-joined her, sitting down with a relief that he tried to disguise. Kate made no comment, but that didn't mean she hadn't noticed. Without asking, she poured a small cup of thick black coffee into a familiar-looking cup.

'I brought them back from Cyprus, along with the coffee pot,' she told him, proving his suspicions that she could read his mind too accurately for comfort correct. 'I brought a supply of Turkish coffee too. I acquired a taste for it.'

*'Sketo,'* Daniel said, taking a sip. 'You don't want sugar with it?'

'You mean *metrio*?' she answered. 'No, I like it like this, and I assumed that you—'

'You assumed correctly.' He took another sip. 'This is good.'

*'Efcharistó.'* She smiled, shaking her head. 'Before you ask, that is almost the limit of my Greek. I was fortunate to have Paniotis, my guide, to assist me with shopping and obtaining supplies. Do you remember him? Or Larnaca?'

Larnaca. Cyprus.

It was when he took another sip of the coffee she had poured that he had a sudden flash of memory. The distinctive aroma of it, brewing on a stove, rousing him from the depth of oblivion. A cool cloth gently wiping his brow.

Was it a fevered dream? He didn't know, but he remembered it so clearly.

He'd kept his eyes closed. He'd heard the swirl of water as the cloth was rinsed, the drip as it was wrung out, the soft exhalation she gave as she settled back on the stool or chair she sat on. She—for he had known instinctively that his angel of mercy was female—smelled of English meadows and cool English summer. When she'd leaned over to wash his shoulders her bare arm had brushed against him, and he had sensed the rest of her hovering over him, tantalising inches away. She had washed his chest and his belly, his arms and his hands. Then she had pushed the sheet lower. He had given himself over to the soothing delight of her touch, cast adrift from the struggle to escape and survive, from the endurance test that his life had been for the last year, to float in an alternative world of tender feminine care.

It could only have been Kate. He knew that, and he knew that she had performed heaven knew what other intimate tasks, but he'd managed not to think about any of it. So why think of it now, dammit?

'No,' he said tersely, 'I don't really remember being in Cyprus.'

'I'm not surprised. You were quite gravely ill. It's a lovely island, though, and the people were so friendly. I saw a little of it while I was waiting for you to arrive, but I'd like to have seen more. The ruins of Ancient Kition—'

'Save your rhapsodies, if you please,' Daniel interrupted brusquely. 'I know there are some who enjoy hearing travellers' tales second-hand, but I do not count myself among their number.'

'I had never travelled beyond London before. I would of course have preferred the circumstances to have been different, and I would have liked to have spent a great deal more time at the various stops they prescribed for me,' Kate said, looking as if he had slapped her, 'but I was surprised—extremely surprised, actually—by how much I enjoyed the experience. When I was not worrying about you, that is.'

'Then perhaps you'll take yourself off again once you're rid of me?'

'My life is here, Daniel. It's why you married me—to ensure that Elmswood is fit for its future heir. Though who that is to be now that poor little Diarmuid is no more…'

'The boy died almost ten years ago and neither of us ever met him.' He hadn't meant to sound so harsh, but it was true, and Kate had no reason to look so—so hurt! Daniel drained his coffee. 'The terms or our marriage didn't require you to regard Elmswood as the limit of your world, you know,' he said more mildly. 'You've been away a few months…'

'Nine, actually.'

'Nine! What the devil…?' Far longer than he had imagined. 'Well, the place doesn't look as if it has suffered much during your enforced absence.'

'That is because before my "enforced absence" it was running extremely efficiently, largely thanks to Estelle. Though how you are able to comment at all is beyond me, unless you've been wandering about the estate in the middle of the night.' Kate gave an impatient sigh. 'Sorry, I don't know why I'm so edgy—it's not like me. Would you like a biscuit?'

Daniel took one, because it was easier than refusing and because it was clearly a peace offering—though he wasn't sure he deserved one. Taking a small bite, he discovered to his surprise that it was actually very good.

'One of Phoebe's recipes,' Kate said. 'Phoebe is—'

'Despite what you might think, I *do* note your updates on all my nieces' progress. Phoebe is the youngest, and the one who is currently in Paris, with aspirations to become a chef.'

'Not any longer. She's in London, not Paris, she has opened her own restaurant and she is married.'

'Married! Wasn't the whole point of my eldest niece's marriage…?'

'Eloise, to Alexander.'

'I *am* aware, Kate. I set that match up, if you recall.'

'What I recall is that you almost never replied to my letters.'

'It doesn't mean I wasn't aware of what was going on in your life—or at least what you told me of it.'

'I told you about as much as you were interested to know. Which was not very much.'

'You knew how little I was interested in the estate itself when we met. It was the reason we married.'

Kate set down her cup and folded her hands primly on her lap. 'Yes, it was.'

Daniel refrained with difficulty from rolling his eyes. There was an essay in reprimand in those three words. 'I'm not going to pretend an interest now. I won't be here for long.'

'You won't be properly well for at least a month, more likely three.'

'I am damned if I'll stay marooned in this place for three months.'

'Why not? You could take the time to get to know Elmswood a little. You might even come to appreciate it. It is your home after all, Daniel.'

'Once and for all, this place is not my home and never will be! I hate the very—'

Daniel bit his tongue, taken aback himself by his tone. He needn't panic. No one was going to force him to remain here permanently. It wasn't like him to snap. He was not usually so irrational. It was his illness making him weak, that was all.

'This is more your home than mine,' he said through gritted teeth. 'You are doing an excellent job of filling your father's shoes. I will concentrate on getting fit to return to active service, and it won't take me three months, I assure you.'

'Perhaps not.' She picked up the coffee pot to refresh their cups. 'Though I imagine that Sir Marcus will also have a say in how long you remain here, since it was on his orders that you came in the first place. Do you really think we should expect him imminently?'

He was surprised the man hadn't been waiting on the dock at Portsmouth, but Daniel wasn't about to say that to Kate. His memories of his planned escape were still hazy, but the events leading up to his capture were etched in his mind. That life—the life he'd been leading for the last five years, the life that he'd worked so damned hard to establish—was over. The man he'd been was no more, and yet he couldn't get to grips with that—for he *was* that man, and he was still here, wasn't he?

Kate was eyeing him quizzically. She was waiting for an answer, he realised, though he couldn't remember what the question had been. This woman was his wife. As far as she was concerned he was Daniel Fairfax. She had no idea of the many other men he'd been required to be in his life—so many that right at this moment he wondered if he knew how to be himself. And he was her husband. He'd never played a husband before. He wasn't sure he would relish playing it for any extended period, but for now…? Behind that diminutive, and extremely attractive façade there was a very strong and determined woman. A brave one, whom he suspected would give as good as she got.

Daniel managed a smile. 'Shall we call a

truce? You're right. I'm here now, and there's no point in my constantly lamenting the fact.'

She narrowed her eyes. 'What will you do instead? I don't know you very well, but I do know you're not the type of man to sit about patiently and wait to be told what your next move will be.'

Daniel laughed. 'Don't worry. I meant what I said when I promised I wouldn't interfere or stand on your toes. We've been married ten years, yet we're to all intents and purposes complete strangers. Don't you think it's time we got to know each other?'

'It was eleven years last month, actually—and don't you think it would be a better use of your time to get to know your nieces instead? You're their closest blood relative, Daniel, and you've never met them. Eloise has just had a baby—a little girl—I only found out this morning. We could—'

'No.' Daniel's smile faded. He heaved himself to his feet. 'I can tell by your expression that's not what you want to hear, but I see no point at all in meeting any of them.'

'Why ever not? I know they would very much like to meet you, and will be devastated if you shun them.'

'No! I have not the time to involve myself in their lives…'

'Not even to write them the occasional letter?'

'Even if I had the time I have not the inclination.' His words would hurt her, and he regretted that, but it was better that than give rise to expectations he could never meet.

'Are you seriously saying that you don't want to meet your nieces *at all*?' Kate said now, looking outraged. 'Never?'

He reminded himself that to all intents and purposes they were her children, and just for a moment considered whether he should do as she wanted. Gillian's daughters were no longer girls, but young women with lives of their own. Did they look like his sister? She'd been a beauty. A selfish, utterly self-centred beauty, with no interest in anyone, and especially not her much younger brother.

He'd gleaned enough from Kate's letters to know that her daughters had not inherited her capricious nature. Kate's doing, no doubt. They were Kate's girls, and that was how they must remain. He couldn't risk acquiring any fresh emotional attachment. Recent events had provided a bitter lesson in the folly of displaying that weakness.

'What would be the point?' he said, more gently. 'They won't see me again, and it would be cruel to risk any sort of attachment or raise expectations. Best I remain faceless to them.'

'You mean it's best that they remain faceless to *you*,' she snapped. 'You've never given a damn about them, have you? When we married you told me you had a nephew, but you didn't think to mention that your long-lost sister had already given birth to three girls.'

'I didn't think they were relevant. I certainly did not envisage that within two years they'd be orphaned and homeless, and I don't know what the hell I'd have done about either if you hadn't been here to step into the breach.'

'I'm eternally grateful that I was in a position to do so.'

'I believe you—though at the time I confess I had serious misgivings about burdening you with them.'

'I remember. You said that you'd get your lawyer to find someone to take them on. As if I would dream of doing anything other than taking them in. I've often said if we had not already been married I would have married you for that reason alone. And I have *never*,' Kate said vehemently, 'told the girls that you considered any other outcome.'

'Thus awarding me a great deal more credit than I deserve. I am sorry, Kate, but I won't be swayed.'

'Aren't you even curious to see how the marriage you arranged turned out? You say you know nothing of the girls, but you gleaned enough from my letters to know that Alexander and Eloise would suit very well.'

'I don't respond to emotional blackmail, you know.'

Kate flinched. 'You're right, that was unworthy of me.'

'You care a great deal for them. You think it's in their interests to know me. I'm telling you it's not. You need to trust me to know best.'

Her throat worked as she mulled this over. 'Your work is a great deal more dangerous than you ever led me to believe, isn't it?'

Until the recent debacle, from which he was still recovering, Daniel had never considered his own mortality, but he wasn't a man who needed to be taught anything twice. He had come close to death. The next time—and he was bloody well determined to be given the chance of a next time—he might not be so lucky.

Which reminded him—whatever else he did while he was in England he must sort out the provisions of his last will and testament. Now that he no longer had a nephew to inherit Elmswood, he had no clue as to who would currently be his next of kin. Some distant cousin, no doubt. But he was damned if Elmswood would be taken from Kate if he had anything to do with it.

'Kate...'

'Was it always dangerous? Even when we first married?'

'Kate, I can't—'

'Can't answer that. Except you already have. I wonder that you suggest we get to know one another better. You're not afraid that *I'll* become too attached, I take it? Are you imagining that I'm longing to be a merry widow?'

'I think the last nine months have proved rather conclusively otherwise, don't you?'

She sighed, her shoulders sagging. 'I'm not usually such a shrew, you know. I'm sorry you don't want to meet the girls, for their sake, but I can't force you, and I do understand, though I'm not looking forward to explaining it to them.'

'I'll likely be gone before you see them.'

She got to her feet. 'Then I suggest you utilise the time you have to recuperate. I'm heading over to the Estate Office to make a start on catching up. I'll have Cook send up some soup for you—or is there something else you'd prefer? What do you like to eat?'

'It doesn't matter. I'm not hungry.'

'You should go to bed and rest. No…what I should say is *don't* go to bed, I suppose, and then you will.'

He surprised them both by taking her hand in his. 'This situation is as strange and awkward for me as it is for you.'

'But, as you have pointed out several times, at least I'm on home turf and, unlike you, happy to be here,' she said with a wry smile. 'Your hand is freezing. I really do think you should go back to bed and try to get some rest, Daniel.'

And get out of her way. She was right. There was as little point in him getting to know his wife as his nieces. Yet he was strangely reluctant to let her hand go.

'I'd better not detain you any longer.'

She hesitated, her wide-spaced blue eyes scanning his face as if she was trying to read his mind, before giving him a brief nod, disentangling her hand, and quitting the room.

He listened out for the oddly familiar scrape of the front door on the flagstones—one thing in the house she hadn't remedied—before sinking back into the fireside chair, closing his eyes, and falling into a sudden deep sleep.

## *Chapter Two*

Alone in the Estate Office, Kate found it impossible to settle. Just over eleven years ago she had proposed to Daniel here. She'd been twenty-two years old and the future, as far as she had been concerned then, had stretched a year into the distance, two years at most.

She'd been far more interested in the present, eking out every available moment with dear Papa and, when he'd finally passed away, hurling herself into planning the modernisation of the estates and the renovation of the house and gardens.

Then had come the unexpected arrival of the girls into her already busy life and the years had sped by, leaving her no time to worry about what lay ahead.

But now Elmswood Manor and the grounds

were fully restored, the estate was a model of modern farming, and the girls had flown the nest. Kate was thirty-three years old and the future loomed—a vast, unpopulated space that she had no idea how she was going to fill. Eleven years ago thirty-three had seemed to her the age of an old crone, but now, despite her newly acquired lines, she felt every bit as young and untested as she had done when sitting here watching the clock all those years ago, waiting for Daniel to arrive.

Of course that was nonsense. The girls—young women! She really must stop thinking of them as 'the girls'!—would testify to the passing years, as would Elmswood Manor itself. She allowed herself a mocking smile. Both had blossomed under her care. But while she'd been tending to her husband's nieces, and Elmswood's gardens, she'd neglected herself.

Who was Kate Fairfax?

The last nine months had taught her that she was more intrepid than she'd imagined. Until Daniel's masters had called on her she'd always thought Elmswood the beginning and the end of her world, but having perforce seen a great deal more of the world since then, she would now like to see still more—though under more auspicious circumstances!

She was naïve, she was far from worldly-wise, but years of managing the estates had given her a confidence and a shrewdness that had helped her navigate many potentially daunting aspects of foreign travel. If she was honest, she envied Estelle her freedom now. It wasn't that Elmswood was a burden, exactly, but it was no longer a challenge.

Kate closed the ledger, where the numbers had been dancing about in front of her eyes, and got to her feet to gaze out of the window. Time to put her pragmatic head on again. Why worry about the future when she had the present to deal with?

She had never forgotten that she was married, but her experience of marriage had been husband-free. Until now. She had been too impatient with Daniel. It wasn't like her to be so easily riled, but there was something about him that set her on edge.

It had been different when he was ill—easier, in a sense—for she had known how to care for him, had been clear about her role as his nurse. And while he had not been lucid,—which had been most of the time—she had been able to tend to him without embarrassment, thinking of him simply as a patient in need of care.

Only when he had become conscious had she become *self*-conscious, aware of him as a man.

A very attractive man. There, she could admit that. She'd always found him attractive. Yes, but from afar. Nursing him had brought her into intimate contact with him, and though at the time she'd thought herself detached, later—yes, later—there had been aspects of her nursing that had made her decidedly uncomfortable.

The feel of his skin as she'd washed him, the smoothness of his shoulders, the rough hair on his chest, the ripple of muscle that his illness had not wholly wasted when he moved. His hair was soft, despite years in the sun. He was deeply tanned in places, pale in others. And there were some places where modesty had prevailed, from which she had looked away when she'd washed him, but she'd touched them, all the same. Places which her imagination had lingered on as she'd lain sleepless, listening to his harsh breathing.

Did he remember? She sincerely hoped he did not.

It was bad enough, the effect those memories had on her, arousing all sorts of unwelcome feelings, stirring desires she'd always repressed so easily before. Eleven years of celibate marriage hadn't been endured without vague longings, but now her longings were not vague—they were quite specific.

Was this what Eloise felt when she looked at her husband? And Phoebe? Was her marriage passionate? In the sphere of intimacy they had so much more experience than her, and they always would, for no matter what the future held Kate was married to Daniel very much in name only.

Though if he remained here at Elmswood to recuperate, what then? They were husband and wife—a man and a woman past the first blush of youth and beyond any of the silliness of fluttering hearts and fevered longing. Daniel was a very attractive man, and she wasn't yet an old crone—in fact, she had every reason to believe that he found her attractive, for there had been times when she'd been nursing him… Though of course he'd had no idea who she was.

She was being foolish—very foolish—to be considering an *affaire* with her own husband. A very temporary *affaire*. That no one would know about. An *affaire* that might be her one and only chance to discover what it was she was missing out on.

Though how on earth she thought to propose it to Daniel…

Daniel was an invalid, for goodness' sake! A very cranky invalid. Though the way he'd looked at her earlier, when they had been drinking coffee, hadn't been cranky. If she did suggest they indulged in an *affaire*, then she doubted he'd turn her down. Not that she would dream of doing such a thing.

The sound of a carriage on the driveway made her jump to her feet. Four horses, attached to a very smart, if dusty post-chaise. Surely they had not come for him already? Her stomach sank.

With a start, she realised that was the last thing she wanted. Purely, she told herself as she sped out of the office and across the lawn, which was the quickest route to the house, because Daniel was far from well, and not at all because, despite the fact that he was infuriating, she wanted very much to get to know her husband better.

Mrs Chester, of all people, had emerged from the kitchen to answer the front doorbell herself by the time Kate arrived, breathless.

'We're a bit short-handed,' she explained, 'for I have sent Sylvia off to the village for provisions, and Mary is up to her neck in suds, it being laundry day.'

'And I can see that you are making pies,' Kate said, eyeing the cook's floury hands and apron with amusement. The doorbell clanged again. 'Don't worry. I'll get this.'

'Can't imagine who it will be. Someone for the master, no doubt? Shall I call him?'

'No need.'

Daniel appeared at the top of the staircase. He had changed into country dress of breeches and boots, and was shrugging himself into a coat, looking decidedly heavy-eyed.

'I think we both know who it is, Kate. And it's for the best, don't you think?'

Was it? What purpose could be served by prolonging his stay, if he remained determined to keep his distance from the girls? But what about *her*? Kate thought, panicking. He'd said he wanted to know her better, and she wanted—she didn't know what she wanted.

The doorbell clanged again.

'Isn't there a footman to answer this?' Daniel asked impatiently.

This rather ludicrous question went a long way to restoring her equilibrium. A footman, indeed!

Drawing him a quizzical look, she fixed a smile on her face and hauled open the door. 'Sir Marcus, what a delightful surprise. And Lord Armstrong too. Won't you come in?'

'Lady Elmswood. It is a pleasure to see you again—and none the worse for your travails, I am happy to see. On behalf of His Majesty's Government, allow me to thank you profusely for your sterling efforts. Your gracious co-operation has spared our country a great deal of embarrassment, I don't mind telling you.'

Sir Marcus Denby made a flourishing bow. A tall, elegant man, immaculately turned out in town dress, he stood aside to allow Lord Henry Armstrong to precede him.

'I'm sorry to call without notice, but we thought it best to make sure we all understood the lie of the land, so to speak, in this delicate matter. Fairfax, allow me to tell you that you are looking a great deal better than I expected.'

'Sir Marcus. Lord Armstrong.' Daniel made a very small bow. 'I was, in fact, expecting you. Shall we talk in the—?'

'The drawing room,' Kate said.

'There is no need for you to join us,' Daniel said.

Sir Marcus and Lord Armstrong exchanged a

look at his tone. 'Perhaps your husband is right,' the former said. 'If you will excuse us, Lady Elmswood? The drawing room is this way, I think? I remember it from our previous meeting.'

Sir Marcus claimed to be from the Admiralty. Who Lord Henry Armstrong was, and what interest he had in whatever business Daniel had been involved in Kate had no idea, and was, it seemed, destined not to know, for within the hour she was surprised to hear the grate of the front door opening.

Abandoning her letter to Eloise for the second time that day, she jumped to her feet and rushed out to the hallway, thinking that Daniel was leaving without even saying goodbye, and was just in time to see the two visitors clambering into the waiting coach and her husband, white-faced, slamming the door closed behind them.

'What…?'

'I am to stay, apparently,' he snapped. 'Until the dust settles politically I am to kick my heels here, disporting myself as Lord Elmswood, in the company of my lovely and very faithful little wife, enjoying the fresh country air and my neat and tidy little estate, and be grateful that I am still alive. All to satisfy Sir Marcus's insistence that our carefully constructed cover story be maintained.'

'Daniel...'

'I won't do it! I will not step into my father's shoes.' He turned on her. 'It's your fault! You colluded with them to return me to this blasted place. The hounds of hell wouldn't have dragged me back here if I'd had the strength to resist. But I won't stay. I won't—I can't.'

'Daniel! For heaven's sake, you sound like a three-year-old having a tantrum. Stop throwing accusations and clenching your fists and for goodness' sake calm down. I have no idea what those men said to you...'

'Plenty! I'm apparently a liability at the moment! Me!' He stared at her sightlessly for a moment, his mouth tightening, and then a raking shudder shook his whole body and he deliberately unfurled his hands. 'I need some fresh air.'

He looked, in her opinion, as if he needed to lie down with a cold compress on his forehead, but she suspected if she suggested such a thing he might well explode.

'Then why don't I show you the walled garden?'

It was warmer there, and she'd noticed already how cold he permanently was. There were some convenient and comfortable benches scattered around too. Most importantly it would serve as a convenient distraction.

Daniel let out a juddering sigh. 'I don't suppose there's any point in my saying that I'd rather be alone?'

'Please do say so, if you'd prefer me to follow twenty paces in your wake.'

'I'm not about to collapse, you know.'

'No, you're not,' Kate said, daring to take his arm, 'but if you do I'll be here to catch you.'

He laughed gruffly. 'I'm tempted, just to test you, but I am pretty sure there's a woman of iron inside that dainty front you present to the world. Come on, then, let's see what you've done to the walled garden. I seem to recall some excitement in one of your letters a few years back over some plans you recovered from the attic.'

'Estelle found them—they were your mother's original drawings.'

She nudged him towards the door. The town coach wheels had left big gouges in the carriage-way.

'Sir Marcus and his sidekick must have been anxious to get back to London,' she said, for Daniel was staring at the tracks.

'Lord Henry Armstrong.' Daniel made his

way down the steps and after a brief hesitation took the correct turn to the right. 'He is one of Wellington's most trusted men, if you believe what he says of himself. Personally, I wouldn't trust him as far as I could throw him. He has two daughters married to desert sheikhs in neighbouring Arabian kingdoms, and it's through them that he wields what influence he has in trade.'

'What has that to do with you?'

'As of today, absolutely nothing. My role in that arena has been played out.'

'Daniel, what *was* your role?'

'I'm afraid there's no point in you asking me questions about the specifics of what I was involved in because I won't be able to answer them. So it's better not to ask, and then I won't offend you by my silence.'

'Very well, then, I will curb my curiosity.'

'I'm sorry. For not being able to satisfy your very natural curiosity and for behaving like a spoilt child too,' Daniel said awkwardly. 'It's not like me.'

'We're neither of us behaving like ourselves. The circumstances are rather unusual, to say the least.'

He laughed dryly, running his hand over his

closely shaved head. 'I had been working on an assignment for five years. Let's just say that my assumed identity was compromised and I was captured. I'm not sure exactly how long I languished in prison—it was probably the best part of a year before the British government got me out.'

'So for the last five years you've been pretending to be someone else?'

'I *have* been someone else.'

Semantics, it seemed to her, but she decided not to say so. 'And when this was discovered by the authorities they imprisoned you for it. So what you were doing was illegal?'

'That depends very much upon who is defining the terms.'

'Were you the only one on this—assignment? Were there others captured with you? Did Sir Marcus help anyone else escape along with you?'

'As far as Sir Marcus is concerned,' Daniel said, his lips thinning, 'everyone save his blue-eyed boys are considered collateral damage. It's one of the reasons I'm in his bad books.'

'Because you saved someone?'

'Because I ensured they did not become collateral damage,' he said sardonically. 'And broke with protocol by risking the mission and ultimately compromising it.'

'To save someone!' Kate exclaimed indignantly. 'Are you seriously saying that Sir Marcus is punishing you—?'

'Asserting his authority,' Daniel said grimly. 'He knows damned well that I hate this place, and how little I relish being told what to do.'

'For heaven's sake, you make him sound like a school bully. Surely he cannot be so petty?'

'More like a school prefect. He is a stickler for the rules.'

'But in the circumstances…'

'Kate, I've told you far too much already. If Sir Marcus had overheard this conversation he'd extend my sentence. It's over. Whatever happens next, I won't be going back there. Time to draw a veil over it all—save for my report and the debrief that will follow it when I'm well enough.'

'How long did he sentence you to?'

'Three months. I'm sorry.'

'It's not your fault. And this is your…'

*Home*, she had been about to say, but Daniel had made his thoughts on that extremely clear.

'This is the walled garden,' she said, though that fact was rather obvious. 'I had the door rebuilt, as you can see.'

Daniel visibly relaxed at the change of subject. 'I have only the dimmest of memories of being able to get in this way. I usually climbed over the wall. No one ever came here save me.'

'The girls—I mean Eloise, Estelle and Phoebe—were fascinated by this place when they first came here. Eloise, especially, was a great one for climbing trees. But there's something about a walled garden, I think, that capture's everyone's imagination, isn't there?'

'It's because of the enclosing walls—and even more so when the door doesn't open. It feels like a secret place. It used to be mine.'

'Really?' Kate let go of Daniel's arm to allow him to step through. 'I hope you approve of what I've done, then. What do you think?'

Daniel was standing stock-still, staring around him. 'Would you mind if I took a few moments to myself? I promise I'm in no danger of a relapse, but I'd like to—I'd like to be alone for a bit, that's all.'

'It's fine. I am happy to do the same. Where will I…?'

'I'll come and find you.'

He waited, clearly wanting her to move on, so she did, planning a clockwise circuit.

The air was distinctly warmer within the

walls, perfumed by a complex and distinct bouquet that for the first time made her feel that she had come home. She could hear the industrious drone of honey bees from the hives which were over in the far corner.

She stopped on the path for a moment, closing her eyes, the better to sift through the various scents: grass, new mown, from the central lawn around which each of the other garden 'rooms' were set out; the moist, peaty smell of rich earth from the vegetable and flowerbeds; honeysuckle, always distinctive; the sharp, almost tangy smell of fresh foliage from the trees.

This was home.

This garden that she'd worked so hard to restore and to enhance had always been her own special project, her sanctuary, and dearer to her than anything else at Elmswood, from the restoration of the house to the modernisation of the farms.

Forgetting Daniel for the moment, she gave herself over to the charms of the garden, which had always been able to restore her equilibrium. It was laid out in discrete areas, separated by gravelled paths, with the kitchen garden on her left and the soft fruit trees opposite, peaches espaliered on the south-facing wall. Next came the flowerbeds, and the little pagoda she'd had built beside the succession house for arranging and drying. The beds were a riot of colour, with phlox and sweet peas, larkspur and delphinium, scabious and snapdragons and campanula. Clematis rioted over the trellising, and the borders of alternating mint, lavender and thyme gave off a delicious scent as her skirts brushed against them.

The windows and doors of the succession house were wide open. Oliver, who had first started work here as a young man around the time she had married Daniel, and was now responsible for of all Elmswood's grounds, had left his tankard on the bench outside the tool shed, as he was prone to do.

The nascent vineyard, about which he'd been so sceptical, was starting to take shape, she noted with quiet satisfaction, though it would be a few years yet before it would become productive.

The area the girls called 'the wilderness' occupied the south-west corner of the garden, with the orchard behind it in the north-west corner. Consisting of trees and a flower meadow, it was a lovely cool space, though Kate had often felt it was rather wasted. Now that the girls were no longer here to protest, she might make something of it.

Sinking onto her favourite bench, she let out a long sigh and rolled her shoulders, watching Daniel as he made his way slowly towards her a few moments later.

'I'd currently come second in a foot race with a tortoise,' he said ruefully, lowering himself onto the bench beside her. 'You've totally transformed this garden. I barely recognised it.'

'Restored, really, with a few innovations.'

'The vineyard?'

'Yes, that was my idea. I'm thinking of doing something with this expanse of unkempt wilderness too.'

'I actually like it as it is. I used to climb the trees here, though they've grown a great deal taller since I last saw them.'

'So tree-climbing runs in the family, then? The girls…'

'You mentioned they liked to climb trees. An activity enjoyed by most children, I imagine—hardly an inherited trait.'

Which was perfectly true, Kate supposed, though why he felt the need to point it out quite so harshly! She folded her arms, refusing to be hurt.

'I like this wilderness,' Daniel said, breaking the silence in a more conciliatory tone. 'A little chaos in the midst of order is no bad thing.'

'Somehow I don't think you're referring to gardening.'

'Perhaps not.' He stretched out his legs in front of him. 'When I was a boy I used to imagine this garden was a jungle, full of lions and tigers and even the odd elephant.'

'When I first started working here it was so overgrown that there might well have been all three lurking in the undergrowth. Well, maybe not the elephants. Did you spend a great deal of time here?'

'When I wanted to be alone—which was most of the time.' He took the turquoise from his pocket and began to roll it between his fingers. 'Sometimes it wasn't a jungle but a tropical paradise, with palm trees. At other times that tree over there was the main mast of a sailing ship that I'd climb in the hope of spying land after weeks at sea. At others…' He caught himself, shaking his head. 'What nonsense.'

'I think it's fascinating. Even as a boy your ambition was to explore the world.'

'My ambition was to be anywhere but here.'

'And you fulfilled that ambition rather spectacularly.'

His expression hardened. 'Only to come full circle.'

'Only for three months, Daniel, it's hardly a life sentence,' Kate said. 'You know, if I was the type to take offence, I rather think I would.'

'You know perfectly well that it's not you.'

No, it was Elmswood—the place he'd said the hounds of hell wouldn't have been able to drag him to. Why did Daniel dislike Elmswood so vehemently?

'You don't think that Sir Marcus might relent?' Kate asked.

Daniel was studying his hands, frowning heavily. There was a sheen of sweat on his brow. 'Beneath Sir Marcus's urbane veneer lies a ruthless streak. He left you feeling you had little choice, no doubt, other than to go along with his plan to facilitate my safe return to England.' He lifted his head, smiling at her grimly. 'Tell me, if you don't mind, exactly how they recruited you.'

'Sir Marcus and Lord Henry turned up out of the blue, just as they did today. I had no idea who they were. My first thought, as I've already told you, was that they might have some letters from you. When they announced, in the middle of tea and cake, that they had a grave matter to discuss with me, I thought they were going to tell me you were dead. It was almost a relief to hear that you were in a foreign prison, but it was also a huge shock. I couldn't take it in.'

'And I'm guessing they didn't give you time to ask too many questions?'

'No, they did not. They spent their time very effectively emotionally blackmailing me. I was left with the impression that if I did not co-operate you might well perish. They barely gave me time to pack and to offload Elmswood onto poor Estelle. It was only later that I began to think a little more rationally, and by then I was on my way to Portsmouth, under escort. The escort simply gazed at me blankly, no matter what I asked. I couldn't understand the need for so much subterfuge and secrecy… Daniel, are you a spy?'

He gave a bark of laughter. 'That's a wildly romantic term for it. Not one, I'll wager, that Sir Marcus used?'

'No. He said that you'd got yourself into a *"tricky situation"* while assisting the government with some *"sensitive business"*. He said that they weren't quite sure of your whereabouts, but that they planned to *"extract you"*—I am pretty sure those were his exact words—and they needed me to escort you home. I couldn't make sense of it at first. Why had he used such language? Why couldn't he simply have said that you were in gaol and they were going to get you out? But I reckon Sir Marcus would cut his tongue out rather than talk in such simple terms.'

'Oh, believe me, he can call a spade a spade when required,' Daniel said grimly. 'What else did they hint at?'

'They did say that you would be in a bad way when they brought you to me—though they did not say quite how bad.' Kate shuddered. 'I barely recognised you. You were so thin, and that beard you had…and your hair!'

'To say nothing of the lice that were living in it. Did I look like some sort of cave man? I wonder if I'll ever be able to bring myself to grow my hair again.'

'I like it short. You have excellent bone structure.'

'Thank you kindly, ma'am. Go on—what else?'

'Their biggest worry was that once they had *extracted* you it might trigger some sort of diplomatic incident. In fact they seemed very concerned about that, and about your being recaptured too—because, they said, whatever you'd been involved in was in a very *"warm"* part of the world. I thought at first they meant the weather,' Kate admitted ruefully.

'Ha!' Daniel shook his head. 'Volatile is the word I'd have used, but I'm no diplomat.'

'No, but you must have been very valuable to them for them to have risked so much to extricate you.'

Kate waited, but Daniel, unsurprisingly, had nothing to say to this.

'So they didn't want to lose you again, and they didn't want anyone to know where you were,' she continued. 'It was important to get you home safely unnoticed, which is why they needed me. I mean, they knew you'd need nursing, and they were concerned that you might be indiscreet in your fevered state, so were reluctant to send a regular doctor. But the main point of my being there was to play Lady Elmswood, the dutiful wife, bringing home her sick explorer husband.'

'So I was playing the Earl, was I?' Daniel said, his lip curling. 'I'm glad I was blissfully unaware of *that*.'

'Well, it was a first for me to play the Countess, and though it wasn't a role I thought I'd relish, any more than you, it did ease the journey considerably. I think I became rather good at it.'

Daniel laughed. 'I can just see you, all five foot nothing of you, looking down that very nice little nose of yours and demanding service *now*!'

'Well, that's what I did,' Kate said, willing her cheeks not to flush—because it was a very small compliment, really, and she was thirty-three, and thirty-three-year-old women did not blush. 'I arrived in Cyprus via Paris, Marseilles, Lisbon, Naples and Athens—as I think I've told you, though you might have forgotten.'

'I remember. Lady Elmswood's lightning tour of Europe's ports.'

'They are also, with the exception of Marseilles, very popular with English travellers who would, if required, be able to testify that they'd seen Lady Elmswood on her European tour which was rudely interrupted by her explorer husband having been taken ill while investigating an ancient site on Cyprus. Personally, I thought it a quite unnecessary embellishment.'

'That would have been Sir Marcus's idea—he loves that sort of subterfuge.'

'If I hadn't been so wrought with worry I'd have enjoyed it. When I set sail from Portsmouth, though, I had no idea I'd be away for so long. I thought they would extricate you immediately, but when I arrived in Cyprus in February it was another two weeks before they finally brought you to me. Why did it take so long?'

Daniel shifted uncomfortably on the bench, refusing to meet Kate's steady gaze. 'I imagine they were obliged to bring me out by a circuitous route. But it doesn't matter how I made it out. I made it. And you were waiting. And now I'm here. And I'm to remain here until I accept the error of my ways in disobeying protocol, and until the fuss over my last assignment has died down, and they've decided I'm fit enough to be put to use again.'

Or at least that was what he bloody well hoped. Sir Marcus had, dismayingly, been vague on the subject, committing only to a review. But he'd persuade them when the time came—he knew he would. He was good, one of the best they had, and they knew it.

'I think,' Daniel said, 'we should concentrate on the present and not worry too much about the future. I have no choice but to remain here for now. Sir Marcus, being extremely attached to the cover story he has concocted, insists that I cannot recuperate elsewhere. Though who he imagines will be checking up on me— But there's no point in going over that. I am obliged to stay here, so we're going to have to find a way of brushing along together for the next three months without murdering each other.'

Kate smiled uncertainly. 'I'm sure it won't come to that. Despite what you think, I'm a very easy-going type.'

'Are you? I'm not. I'm used to living on my own, on having everything my way and, more importantly, not allowing anyone else a say.'

'Good grief—and you call me a despot!'

Daniel grinned. 'I prefer to think of myself as self-sufficient.'

'I prefer to think of myself as practical and pragmatic.'

'Now, that I know to be true, for I've seen you in action. You managed to keep me fed and watered and washed on ships where I'm pretty sure the crew were living off ship's biscuit and had not seen a change of clothes, let alone a change of bedsheet, in weeks.'

'That's because Lady Elmswood was very adept at looking down her nose disdainfully and barking orders,' Kate said.

'Ah, but when it came to tending her husband she was a tender ministering angel.'

'I can't imagine how you remember anything of my ministering,' Kate retorted. 'You were delirious much of the time, and asleep the rest.'

'Just because I kept my eyes closed it didn't necessarily mean I was asleep.'

Kate was blushing. She blushed charmingly. It was unfair of him to tease her, but she was a very pleasant distraction, and after the grilling he'd just endured he was in dire need of one.

'You have a very gentle touch with a flannel.'

'If I'd known you were awake I would have happily let you wash yourself.'

'Precisely the reason I pretended to be asleep.'

She slanted him a look, her mouth quivering on the edge of a smile. 'I did only what any wife would do for her husband.'

'I'm not complaining, believe me.'

She turned towards him. 'Far from complaining, I seem to recollect you enjoying it rather too obviously.'

Her eyes were almost the same colour as his turquoise talisman. Colour tinged her cheeks, but the look she gave him was not in the least bashful.

'Perhaps it would have been better if I'd forced you up on deck and sluiced you down with a bucket of cold salt water each day?'

'If you continue to look at me like that, a bucket of cold water is exactly what I'll need.'

'There's a pump over by the succession house,' she said tartly. 'Shall I fetch one?'

Daniel laughed, amused and aroused in equal measure. 'I already know you well enough not to call your bluff.'

He leaned towards her, abandoning himself to the moment, surrendering to the urge to touch her, to test the challenge in her eyes, trailing his fingers from her shoulder down the bare flesh of her arm, lifting her hand to his mouth, kissing it lightly.

She caught her breath. 'What was that for?'

'We've been married eleven years and I don't believe I've ever kissed you.'

She leaned towards him. 'You still haven't.'

This time it was he who caught his breath. Did she mean it? Shocked, he realised he had no idea. This woman was his wife of eleven years and he didn't know her at all. He did know, quite unequivocally, though, that he wanted to kiss her—and that shocked him too, for it had been a very, very long time since he'd felt any form of physical desire.

Eyes locked on hers, he turned her hand over, and kissed her palm, allowing his lips to linger, and felt his heart picking up a beat as she inhaled sharply. He kissed her again, softly on her palm, his tongue tasting her skin. She gave a little sigh and he pulled her closer.

'Kate— Oh, I beg your pardon!'

Daniel started.

Kate yanked her hand free, jumping to her feet. 'Oliver! How lovely to see you. You have the garden looking absolutely wonderful.'

Oliver, whoever the devil *he* was, was staring at Daniel. Tall, tanned, with bright gold hair and blue eyes, he looked to be about Kate's age, perhaps a little younger. His clothing—flannel shirt, breeches and brogues—was rustic, but his voice was educated.

'Daniel,' Kate said, as he got to his feet, 'this is Oliver St James, my—our head gardener. Oliver, this is my husband.'

'Lord Elmswood. It is a pleasure to meet you.' The man made a low bow. 'You must excuse me. I had no idea that Kate—Lady Elmswood—was otherwise engaged. I thought she'd want to know how the garden— But of course it can wait.'

'No, don't go on my account.' Daniel turned to Kate. 'I have taken up far too much of your time already.'

'But we haven't...'

'I'm not going anywhere,' Daniel said wryly, 'except perhaps my bedchamber. I confess I am a little weary.'

'Are you feeling ill? Has the fever…?'

'No! Don't fuss. I simply need a little time to myself, and I am sure you have a hundred things to do. I'll see you later. Good day to you, St James.'

# *Chapter Three*

It was another beautiful day. Kate set her breakfast tray down on the table and pulled up her usual chair. It felt so strange, being alone in the dining room. It wasn't the silence, for until the second pot of tea was brewed she and the girls had always preferred to be left to their own devices, it was the lack of physical company.

There was no one to challenge her for the last cup in the pot; no Phoebe to bustle about, seeing to each of their various preferences for food; no Eloise tapping her pencil on the table as she planned her tasks for the day; no Estelle, the only one who would have preferred to talk, biting her tongue until the unofficial silence was over.

Of course it had been a long time since all of them had sat down to breakfast together, for Eloise had been married for four years, but while Estelle had still been here the absence of the other two hadn't felt so pronounced.

It might be strange, but it was also strangely liberating. Now, Kate thought, as she poured herself the first and best cup of tea, she could enjoy her breakfast in blissful silence, plan her tasks for the day in her head, as she had always done, and work through them at her own pace without interference—something she had never had the luxury of doing.

'There you are!'

It seemed it was a luxury that was going to continue to be denied to her.

Kate set her untasted tea down as Daniel, dressed in a loose white silk tunic and trousers, wearing his slippers but this time without the gorgeous matching dressing gown, came into the room.

'I didn't think you'd be up and about so early,' she said.

'I'm always up and about early,' he answered testily. 'Did you put a sleeping potion in that soup you sent up last night? My head feels like it is stuffed with wool.'

'Sit down. I'll pour you some tea.'

'Dear God, no. I need coffee. I'll ring for some.'

Kate pushed her chair back, getting hastily to her feet. 'I'll fetch it. Sit down.'

'You haven't had your breakfast yet,' Daniel said.

'Sit down, Daniel,' Kate said tartly. 'There's no point in ringing the bell. It's half past six in the morning. There is no one to answer it. I will fetch your coffee.'

'I'll get it myself.'

'But...'

'I'll find it,' he said. 'The kitchen, the hot water, the coffee—whichever one of those you were going to tell me I wouldn't be able to find.'

'All of them. Are you sure?'

'I don't want or need you to run after me. I'm perfectly capable of looking after myself. I've been doing it most of my life. And your tea is getting cold.'

Nonplussed, Kate sat back down at the table and took a sip of her tea. So much for her breakfast of contemplation. She was destined for a breakfast of confrontation. She smiled to herself, helping herself to a slice of bread and butter, because there was no point in her pretending that she wasn't looking forward to it.

She had never in her life taken breakfast with any man other than her father, and Papa had always hidden himself behind yesterday's newspaper, which old Lord Elmswood had sent down from the house at the end of each day. Sitting at the table with Daniel was a very different prospect.

She had tried not to think of her behaviour in the walled garden yesterday, tried not to imagine what would have happened if Oliver hadn't appeared. Daniel had kissed her hand—that was all he'd done. Just kissed her hand, for goodness' sake! But even now she could feel the warmth of his lips on her skin, the visceral kick of her response, the urgency of her desire for more.

The way he'd looked at her too, had left her in no doubt that he was as attracted to her as she was to him. She couldn't say how she knew, but there had been a—a heat in his eyes, and the way her skin had tingled, the way she had been so keenly aware of him sitting inches away from her—she knew he'd felt it too. If only Oliver hadn't turned up.

It was just as well he had, for poor Daniel had clearly been exhausted by the events of the day, and she'd been racked with guilt afterwards.

She ought to have ordered him to his bed after Sir Marcus and Lord Henry left. Yes, she could just imagine the effect that would have had...

'What are you finding so amusing?' Daniel sat down next to her at the oval table, placing a tray with the Turkish coffee pot and cup down in front of him.

'That was quick.'

'Would you rather I'd been longer? Are you one of those people who prefers silence at breakfast?'

'Are you?'

'I don't often have any choice, unless I talk to myself.' He poured the first cup of his coffee and took a sip, closing his eyes. 'That's better. *Did* you put laudanum in my soup?'

'Of course not. You slept well, then?'

'I'm not sure if it was sleep—more like black unconsciousness. Is that all you eat for breakfast, bread and butter?'

'Would you like some? Or I can make you some ham and eggs, if you prefer.'

Daniel shuddered. 'Nothing, thank you. Do you always get your own breakfast? I'm sure I saw a cook yesterday, answering the door. Grey-haired woman, shaped like an apple, covered in flour.'

Kate giggled. 'Mrs Chester. She is married to one of your tenant farmers who likes a much more substantial breakfast to set him up for the day than bread and butter. So she comes in afterwards, about eight each morning, and goes back to the farm in time to serve her husband's dinner.'

'What about *your* dinner?'

'She leaves it already prepared with cooking instructions. Don't worry, I won't poison you.'

Daniel set his cup down, turning towards her. 'Have you taken some sort of vow of poverty or have you recently taken up gambling? Because the last time I saw a statement from my bank—admittedly, it was over a year ago—there were funds aplenty.'

'There still are. Elmswood is a very profitable estate.'

'Thanks to you. So why do you live so frugally?'

'I live contentedly and comfortably. Do you want a slice of bread and butter?' The look of horror he gave her made her giggle again. 'Don't you ever eat anything at breakfast?'

'I'm partial to something called *ful medames*, which is beans cooked in oil with salt and served with flat bread, but I doubt even you, resourceful as you are, could conjure that up.'

'No, but I bet Phoebe could. She is always wanting new receipts—especially for what she calls "real people's food". I have a whole sheaf of notes from my limited travels to send her. If only she were here I'm sure she would make it for you, she's so clever at working out ingredients. And she'd be delighted to…'

'No, Kate. Let's not go over that again.'

'But if you're going to be here for three months, surely…?'

'At the most. It will likely be less, if something urgent comes up. And something always crops up unexpectedly.'

'You said that they want us to be seen out and about together,' Kate pointed out.

'They can force me to remain here, but what I choose to do with my time is my own business.'

'But you can't hide yourself away, Daniel. What is wrong with Elmswood that you don't want to see more of it? Surely you must have some happy memories? Your sister…'

'My sister didn't give a damn about me. She eloped with that fly-by-night character without a thought for the consequences, and as far as I'm aware she forgot I ever existed.'

'I'm sorry. I didn't mean to touch a raw nerve. I had no idea.'

'Why should you? We barely know each

other,' he retorted testily. 'And it's hardly raw—it happened decades ago.'

And yet he remained hurt and angry, Kate noted.

Daniel seemed to be regretting his outburst. 'As you know, I didn't even know I had one niece, never mind three, and a nephew into the bargain, until my father died. You've been a much better mother to them than Gillian ever would have been.'

'What was she like, Daniel? I mean, I know what she looks like from the portrait…'

'What portrait?'

'I forgot—I'm so sorry. I found it in the attics. I had no idea who it was until the girls came to Elmswood. If you want to look at it, you'll find it on the wall in my bedchamber. Phoebe had some fanciful notion of reuniting them. Of all three, she is the most attached to her mother's memory, but none of them say very much about her. So tell me, Daniel, what was she like?'

'Utterly selfish. Extremely beautiful. Heedless. Charming, provided she got her own way. Petulant when she didn't—which admittedly wasn't very often. She was the apple of my father's eye.'

'Really?'

'Oh, yes, she had him wrapped around her little finger. He indulged her every whim.'

'He must have been quite devastated when she ran off, then.'

'More furious than anything. The one thing my father would not tolerate was insubordination.'

'He did like to have his own way, but I don't remember him as a martinet.'

'Frankly, Kate—and don't be offended by this—that was most likely because you were not of any particular relevance to him. At least not that he knew of.'

'You did say all those years ago that he'd never have tolerated a female estate manager.' Kate wrinkled her nose. 'Papa was very easy-going and very loyal, which probably explains why he and old Lord Elmswood got on well enough. But I'm still very surprised that his estrangement from your sister was so permanent. If she really was the apple of his eye, surely he'd eventually have forgiven her?'

'His word,' Daniel said with a marked sneer, 'was law. You may not have seen that side of him, but trust me—I know. He would not bend, not even for Gillian—even if she asked him to, and I'm not at all convinced that she would have.'

'It sounds to me like a dreadful case of reaping what you sow. To indulge a child's every whim inevitably produces an adult who thinks they can do as they please and damn the consequences,' Kate said dryly. 'I would never go so far as to say *poor Gillian*, but it does sound as if your father made excellent work of making the worst rather than the best of her.'

'That's certainly a charitable way of looking at it.'

'The girls aren't the least bit like her, if that's what you're worried about.'

'I'm not. I'm sure they are fine young women whom I would like very much. But unfortunately that is a pleasure that must be denied me, given my line of business. I can't afford ties or distractions. I can't be Uncle Daniel when I am—well, whoever I happen to be next.'

She swallowed her disappointment, telling herself that he wasn't being cold, only practical. 'For the next three months you are to be my husband. How will you like that?'

'It will certainly be novel, but I am sure of one thing.' He reached across to press her hand.

'Marrying you was the best decision I've ever made. I mean it.'

'Why, thank you, Daniel. I think it was my best decision too.'

'I don't know what I'd have done if you hadn't proposed to me. I remember sitting opposite you on that cut-down chair—yes, I did know it was cut down—and wondering what the devil this very surprising and very determined chit of a girl was going to suggest. But even if you'd give me a hundred guesses I wouldn't have come up with the answer.'

'Were you truly so shocked? You covered it up extremely well!'

'I was astounded, not shocked, but within five minutes I realised that it was an inspired idea, and what I remember more than anything was feeling profound relief. And gratitude.'

'You played your part very well. Papa never guessed that it was my idea, you know.'

'Oh, one thing I *can* do is play whatever part is asked of me. I'm glad, though, that it ensured he could be comfortable in his last year.'

'He took a lot of persuading to move out of our cottage and into the manor. I couldn't understand it at first. I thought he was concerned about what people would say—you know, the estate manager moving into his former employer's home and getting ideas above his station. But it wasn't that at all. He simply didn't want to leave the cottage where he and Mama had been so happy and contented. I barely remember her, and Papa rarely talked about her, but it was clear he loved her very much. So in the end I moved the entire contents of the cottage here and Papa was able to enjoy his last year on this earth. Sorry.' Kate blinked. 'Tears at breakfast. I promise you that won't be a regular occurrence.'

'He died ten years ago,' Daniel said, frowning. 'I'd have thought after all this time… But I know you were close.'

'We were—of course we were. And in a way, the estate is his legacy, so I'm reminded every day—' Kate broke off, mortified. 'Sorry, that was thoughtless of me.'

'In what way?'

'Well, Elmswood Manor must be full of memories for you too. I know it's been more than eleven years since Lord Elmswood died, but you've been abroad for all that time, and being here now—well, as I said, it must reawaken long forgotten memories.'

She waited, but Daniel said nothing, staring off over her shoulder out of the window.

'Why do you hate this place?' she asked.

'That's at least the second time you've asked me that.'

Silly of her to imagine he would answer a direct question, but his irritation made her even more determined to find out.

'How tedious of me,' Kate said. 'I do beg your pardon.'

Daniel got to his feet. 'It's a lovely day. I think I'll get some fresh air.'

'Would you like me to come with you? We could take a walk around the grounds.'

'Don't you have better things to do?'

'I have a hundred *other* things I could do, though nothing I'd *rather* do, if you would care for my company. Though if you wouldn't, then please just say so. I think it's better for both of us that we be frank with each other, don't you?'

His brow lightened and he smiled faintly. 'Then I'll confess that I'm like a bear with a sore head in the morning until I have had my coffee.'

'On top of which, you really did have a sore head this morning, and I added tears and recriminations into the mix. Would you prefer to be alone? I really don't mind.'

He held out his hand, helping her to her feet

when she took it. 'I would very much like my wife's company, if I'm not keeping her from more pressing concerns.'

'You are, actually,' Kate said, smiling up at him, 'but, strangely, I find the prospect of spending the morning in your company a far more beguiling prospect than going through the accounts and paying bills.'

'What about your precious garden? Won't your horticultural Adonis be keen to show off the results of all his hard work?'

Kate chuckled. 'Estelle used to whistle and say "Good golly, it's Ollie!" whenever he appeared. It became one of our silly family jokes. He *is* ridiculously handsome though, isn't he?'

'Have you an ambition to play his Aphrodite?'

'Wasn't she the goddess of love?'

'Love and desire—the female equivalent of Adonis. The story goes that she fell in love with him, and then for reasons known only to herself handed him over to another goddess, Per sephone, who was to act as his protectress. When Persephone refused to give Adonis back the two agreed to share him, though Aphrodite claimed two-thirds of the prize specimen's time, leaving the unlucky Persephone with only a third. Poor Adonis died when he was attacked by a wild boar which had been sent by another god, who was either envious of his hunting skills or jealous of Aphrodite's passion for him.'

'Good grief! I had no idea that mythology was so salacious.'

'Oh, that's tame for the Greeks.'

'I'm afraid I'm woefully ignorant when it comes to the Classics. It's not a subject taught at the village school.'

'It was ranked second only to sport in terms of importance at the school I attended.'

'I'll wager you favoured sport rather than Latin and Greek?'

'You're quite wrong. In fact there was a time—' He broke off, shaking his head ruefully. 'I don't know how we came to be discussing the Classics.'

'The notion of Oliver being Adonis to my Aphrodite.'

Daniel's expression cleared. 'And is he?'

'I thought I'd made it perfectly clear yesterday where my preferences lie.'

He smiled at that, just exactly as he'd done yesterday. 'As did I, I believe.'

It was a wicked little smile, and it was having exactly the same effect on her as yesterday. She felt quite unlike herself, reckless and bold.

'You kissed my hand,' Kate said, affecting a dismissive tone. 'I don't consider that definitive proof one way or the other.'

'Are you throwing down the gauntlet? Because I should warn you I never refuse a challenge.'

Her heart began to beat very fast. 'I don't want you to.'

He put his arm around her waist, pulling her tight against him. 'Be careful what you wish for, Kate,' he said, and then his lips met hers.

Be careful what you wish for, indeed.

She closed her eyes and tried to purse her lips against his.

He laughed.

Her eyes flew open.

Mortified, she tried to escape his hold, but he tightened his arm around her.

'I'm sorry—but how was I to know you'd never been kissed before?'

'Perhaps because I'm your wife and you know perfectly well that you've never kissed me.'

His smile faded. 'Good grief, do you really mean that you have never...?'

'Never.'

'Kate, I am very far from being any sort of rake, but I must warn you that I have—'

'Daniel, I'm not in the least bit interested in what you have or haven't done in the past.'

'Nor am I.'

He smiled again, sliding one hand up her back, his fingers feathering the skin at her nape. 'Did you know that your mouth is the perfect shape for kissing?'

'Is it?'

'A cupid's bow, curling up at the corners so that you look as if you're smiling even when you're not. Here.' He bent his head, pressing a kiss to one corner. 'And here.' Another kiss. 'And then there's this tempting little dent in your top lip.' Another kiss.

His fingers slid into her hair, angling her head towards him, and he covered her mouth with his. His lips were soft on hers. She stayed motionless until his tongue gently urged her mouth open, and then her senses jolted to life.

He kissed her slowly, his mouth moving carefully over hers, and she could have swooned with delight. Closing her eyes, she put a hand on his shoulder and stepped into a whole new world of sensation, following his lead, shaping her mouth to his, and kissing him. Slow, soft kisses, that heated her blood, that made her feel as if she were melting.

Her heart was hammering as their mouths moved and their tongues touched, and if it hadn't been for his hand around her waist and her hand on his shoulder she was pretty sure her knees would have given way.

And then the kisses stopped, and he lifted his head, and she opened her eyes, dazed, and touched his cheek, as if to reassure herself that he was real, and he smiled at her, and she smiled back, and he let her go.

'Well,' Kate said, 'now I know.'

'Was it worth the wait?'

She laughed, feeling skittish and girlish and quite unlike herself. 'I haven't decided yet. Perhaps one more?'

Daniel gave up pretending to eat the plate of cold meat and pushed it aside.

'Aren't you hungry? Are you feeling feverish? The sun is hot and we walked for more than two hours in the gardens—and you had only those strange clothes on, with those odd shoes and no hat, so perhaps…' Kate trailed off, grimacing. 'Sorry.'

He was tired, and he was unsettled, but he wasn't about to admit to either. 'The fact is that I am not particularly fond of ham.'

'Why didn't you say? I could get you…'

'Kate, sit down. I don't want anything more, and if I did want anything I am perfectly capable of asking for it myself. As to my unconventional attire—those clothes were designed to cope with the heat and humidity of India, but if you don't like them…'

'You've been to India!'

It had been a silly slip, but too late to deny, and what the devil? It was hardly treasonous. 'A country which taught me a good deal,' Daniel said, 'including how to dress sartorially.'

'Do you speak the language?' Kate asked, agog. 'What *is* the language?'

'There are a great many dialects. I learned enough for my purposes.'

'I don't suppose there's any point in my asking what those purposes were?'

'I'm sorry, but you know the answer to that.'

'What other languages do you speak?'

'English is the only one that need concern you. I'm sorry,' Daniel added when she scowled, 'but I did warn you that asking questions was pointless.'

'Including any question about what you like to eat? If you would at least answer that question

I can inform Mrs Chester, and then she won't be offended by your sending back a full plate.'

'I ate every bit of that vegetable concoction, whatever it was.' Daniel tilted his side dish towards her 'See—empty plate, Nurse.'

She bit her lip, but he could see the laughter in her eyes.

'It was garden peas, runner beans and lettuce, cooked in chicken stock with mint,' she said.

'Let me guess. Another one of Phoebe's recipes?'

'If I said it was, would you refuse to eat it?' Kate snapped. 'It would be easier if you could tell me what kind of things you like to eat, Daniel. It doesn't commit you to anything more profound than eating dinner.'

Her insight took him aback. All morning as he'd wandered around Kate's precious gardens, content to be in her company and be able to smile, asking enough pertinent questions to mask his indifference to it all, he'd felt the weight of the sentence Sir Marcus had imposed weighing on him.

Three months, with no guarantee of release at the end of it. What was he to do here for three months? And how the devil was he to avoid becoming part of the furniture? How his father would have loved that! He was determined to do all he could to avoid it, but Kate was right. He had to eat.

'Fish,' he said. 'lots of vegetables and pulses. I like chicken, pigeon and rabbit. I don't like beef or pork or ham, and I loathe the English way of loading a plate with slabs of roast meat or wedges of the stuff. Peasant food, I suppose is what I really like. Does that help?'

Kate smiled warmly. 'Thank you. Now, that wasn't too difficult, was it.'

He got to his feet, holding out his hand. 'Fair point. Perhaps we should discuss how we're going to get through this interlude in both our lives. I think I saw a bench on the terrace facing the south lawn—shall we sit there?'

'It's very hot today.'

Daniel laughed. 'You've obviously never been to Arabia.'

'Meaning you have, I presume? Or is that yet another question you're not permitted to answer?'

'Oh, what the devil? I'm not supposed to say anything at all, but provided you swear never to tell Sir Marcus then I will admit that I have been to Arabia, and that I speak reasonable Arabic, as well as a smattering of French, German, Italian, Spanish and Greek.'

'Good heavens, that is impressive.'

'Not really. I have an ear for language, that's all.'

It was on the tip of her tongue to make a comparison with Estelle, and her ear for music, but he would only brush it aside as irrelevant or a coincidence.

'It's impressive all the same,' she said, making for the bench.

'No, don't sit down yet. Let me move it so that you're in the shade.'

'Daniel, be careful.'

'It's a wooden bench, Kate, not a marble plinth.' He moved it, pleased to find that it was not as heavy as it looked, and sat down beside her.

'Did you live in the desert when you were in Arabia?' she asked. 'Did you ride a camel and sleep in a tent?'

'Yes, to all three. And I can tell you that the tent was made of goatskins.'

Kate sighed. 'I wish you could tell me more. I am imagining you with white robes and a headdress…'

'Don't forget my harem.'

Her eyes widened. 'Do they really have such things?'

'A harem is simply the women's quarters in a household, occupied by a wife, her daughters, servants, cousins—her mother sometimes.'

'Like Elmswood, then, when the girls were here.'

'A little more restricted,' Daniel said dryly. 'You'd have had to give your gardener instructions through a metal grille, and he certainly wouldn't have been able to roam about half-naked if any of you were in the garden.'

'Oliver was digging, and he put his shirt back on the moment he realised he wasn't alone. Are the women there really so restricted?'

'It varies from kingdom to kingdom.'

Lord Armstrong's eldest daughter had made enormous changes in Q'adiz, he remembered. Celia, that was her name. A formidable woman. Though, like Kate, she hid her strength behind a pretty façade, there was steel in those eyes of hers. She wasn't much older than Kate either.

For a moment he was tempted to tell his wife about his encounter with her—such a contrast to her father, who was a slippery customer if ever there was one. But he'd already broken the rules.

'We didn't come out here to talk about Arabia.'

Kate sighed. 'No, but I wish we could. You have led such a fascinating life, and I would love to hear about some of the places you've been.'

'I was working, not taking in the sights.'

'Yes, but you must have seen so many wonderful things, even when you were working.' She wrinkled her nose. 'Whatever you mean by "working", which I can't imagine…'

'No, you can't.'

She was silent for a moment, staring down at her hand. 'I'm not sure how I'll cope when you go back, now I know how dangerous it can be. What if you're captured again?'

'I won't be. Once bitten twice shy.'

His ankles still throbbed where the manacles had been. And the heat had been overpowering. But it was the smell that had been the worst of it. And the vermin. And the dark. Yes, the dark had been the worst. Those long days and nights he'd lost count of, that rush of terror, panic, as he despaired of ever being free. Clawing at the walls. Hammering on the cell door. The humiliation he'd felt when they'd let him out and he'd realised it had been a game for them.

He hadn't let them win, but he didn't think he'd be able to go through it again.

'Daniel? I'm sorry, I didn't mean to bring it all back.'

He was crushing Kate's hand between his. He uncurled his fingers, releasing her. It was over. One more life lived and done with. The man in the cell hadn't been him. What he had to do was concentrate on this version of himself.

'There's one thing I can usefully do while I'm here. My will,' he clarified, when Kate looked at him blankly. 'Shall I make Elmswood over to you?'

'You can't do that!'

'Why not? It couldn't be in more capable and caring hands.'

'That's not the point. The estate should go with the title.'

'I have no idea who will inherit that, and I don't give a damn, but I do care about the possibility of you being unceremoniously turfed out by him. This is your home, you've looked after it for the last eleven years, you deserve to keep it.'

'It's your home too.'

'No! Never!'

He hadn't meant to shout. Kate was staring at him, shocked. He'd shocked himself with the strength of his feelings. He didn't give a damn about Elmswood, so why get upset about it?

Three months at the most he had to sit it out here—it didn't mean he was filling his father's shoes, and he wasn't even here at his father's behest. What he had to do was see this as just one more assignment, one more role. Not Lord of the Manor—that part was being played by Kate, who had not a drop of Fairfax blood in her, and was moreover a woman. And that, he thought, tickled by the notion, would have made his father furious.

His wife was eyeing him as if he were a pot about to boil over. 'Please excuse my temper. I think perhaps I have overdone it a little after all,' he said.

'It's my fault. I was so caught up in seeing all the changes in the gardens I forgot that you've only just risen from your sickbed. And you indulged me,' she added wryly. 'Don't think I didn't notice how tedious you found it.'

'I found the botany boring, but not the botanist.'

She laughed. 'And you said you weren't a diplomat!'

'Oh, I'm not—not at all.'

She was blushing. It fascinated him, the way the colour stole up her throat to her cheeks, and yet there was not a trace of false modesty in the way she reacted, eyeing him frankly, weighing up her response, trying to decide whether to put him down or respond in kind.

'Daniel, delightful as this is, we can't flirt away the next three months.'

'Why not? I'm thoroughly enjoying it and it seems to me that you are too.'

'Oh, you know perfectly well that I am. As you are well aware from this morning, I'm as much a novice when it comes to flirting as kissing, but I think I might prove to be rather good at both.'

'What a bold piece you are!'

'Of course I am. I wouldn't have proposed to you elsewise.'

'Have I told you that I'm very glad you did?'

'Yes.' Her smile faded. 'But seriously, Daniel, what are we going to do? What are we going to tell people?'

His heart sank. 'Do we have to tell people anything?'

'Think about it! Elmswood has been without an earl for a very long time—long before you inherited, remember, for your father was rarely seen in his later years. And you are the Earl, whether you wish to use the title or not. The elusive and completely unknown Earl. But word will already be out that you're here. People will be desperate to meet you.'

'I'm ill. Far too ill to receive anyone.'

'Actually, I agree with you on that point, but for how long do you think that story will hold up to scrutiny? The few servants that we have all live out, and they have family, friends. People will talk and they will speculate. It's inevitable. One of the reasons you married me is because I am a practical, pragmatic person. I'm being both right now. We need a story and we need a plan.'

'I'm an explorer. I've been very ill. I'm home to recuperate. I'll be off again to darkest Africa just as soon as I'm able. There—that's the beginning, the middle and the end of the story.

'But Sir Marcus said we should—'

'I don't give a damn what Sir Marcus thinks we should do. I'm here, and I'll stay here until they realise that they need me, which will be sooner rather than later. So there's no point in me getting to know our neighbours or paying house calls or involving myself in estate business or—before you suggest it again—in my meeting my nieces.'

'You can't meet Estelle anyway. She's off traipsing around Europe.'

'Don't be waspish, Kate, it doesn't suit you.'

'I'm not usually waspish. It's your fault. Oh, dammit. I sound like a petulant child and I'm not.'

'No, you're not. You're a very sorely tried woman who has been to hell and back for an ungrateful, curmudgeonly husband.'

Shifting on the bench, he put his arm around her, pulling her up against him. With a sigh, she let her head rest on his shoulder. She smelled of something floral and peculiarly English. Daniel let his chin rest on her hair.

'Do you like lemon with your tea, or cream?' he asked.

'What an odd question. Neither. I like milk. Why?'

'And do you like to put it in your cup before the tea or after?'

'Before. Doesn't everyone? Why…?'

'So that I can prepare your tray properly in the morning if I'm up before you. It was obvious to me this morning how important your first cup of tea of the day is.'

She gave a little huff of laughter. 'As important as your coffee is to you. Although I thought I'd disguised it better than that. Are we to take breakfast together, then?'

'I'd like to if you would.'

'I rather think I would. What about dinner?'

'Oh, we'll definitely dine together. I have consumed my last bowl of nourishing broth in bed.'

'And for the rest of the day, Daniel?'

He let her go, getting to his feet. 'Let's take it a step at a time, shall we?'

## *Chapter Four*

'What are you looking for?'

'My garden diary,' Kate said, staring at the side-table where she always kept it, as if it might magically materialise. 'It's a green leather note-book...'

'Oh, that one. I put it on your desk,' Daniel said.

'My desk! But I don't keep it on my desk. I keep it here, on this table.'

'Where *I* was sitting, having a cup of coffee and reading my book. So I moved it.' Daniel re-trieved the notebook from the desk. 'Here.'

'I didn't realise you liked to sit there.'

'Only when I'm alone. I know it's your chair, normally.'

'No, this is your house—please, I want you to feel at home.' Kate looked around her helplessly. 'I'll take Estelle's chair, and I'll find somewhere else to keep my diary. There's a footstool with a lid. Eloise used to keep some of her embroidery silks in it. It sits— Oh.' She looked in consternation at the empty space against the wall.

'It's in the library,' Daniel said with a rueful smile. 'Me again, I'm afraid. I wanted to get a book from one of the top shelves and I couldn't find the library steps.'

'That's because they are kept here, in the cupboard.'

'Why aren't they kept in the library?'

'They were the perfect height for us to stand on when we allowed Eloise to adjust the hems on our gowns. She used to make all our clothes, you know. She is so clever. This one I'm wearing is one of her creations.'

Kate gave a little twirl, holding out the skirt of her powder-blue morning gown.

But Daniel frowned. 'She's been married to Alex for—what?—four years? Please don't tell me that it's been four years since you had a new gown?'

'I don't need any new gowns. I don't go anywhere. Before she married, Eloise—' She broke off, seeing Daniel rolling his eyes. 'What?'

'Nothing.'

The way he smiled so blandly riled her. She

set her diary back down on the desk. 'I don't mention the girls in order to make you feel guilty, you know.'

'I've been here two weeks. You mention one or other of my nieces at least once in every conversation we have, and it has nothing to do with my feelings—or lack of feelings—for them, and everything to do with your own. You have built your life around those three, and I laud you for it. In fact I'm extremely grateful for it. But they have their own lives to live now, and it's time, don't you think, that you started living yours?'

Her temper flickered. She tamped it down. 'I *am* living my own life,' Kate said through gritted teeth. 'It may seem very mundane to you, but, as you've pointed out several times, it is *my* life, and none of your concern. However, since you feel able to comment on my behaviour, let me offer an observation on yours. In two weeks you've barely been over the door. You do nothing, as far as I can make out, save read and brood. You don't even go into the walled garden. I thought that was your sanctuary?'

'It's your sanctuary now. I have been endeavouring to keep out of your way.'

'Oh, for heaven's sake! Admit it! You've been hiding—not only from anyone who might come calling, but also from this house. Do you think it has escaped my notice that you haven't gone anywhere near the rooms where your father spent his last years? Or that you're sleeping in one of the guest rooms, not your old room or the master suite? Why is that?'

'Why are you getting agitated about my sleeping arrangements?'

'I'm not getting agitated! I have an excellent and very even temper. Not even in the early years, when I was dealing with three girls—there, I've mentioned them again—who could throw tantrums on a spectacular scale, did I once lose my temper. Though, to be fair to her, Eloise never threw a tantrum. I'm talking about the Twinnies.'

'The Twinnies? Oh, you mean Estelle and Phoebe. But they weren't young children. Surely they were beyond the tantrum stage?'

'They were fifteen, and they had just lost both their parents and their brother.'

'I'd have thought they'd be glad to have you, then.'

'Daniel, for heaven's sake! They didn't want *me*—they wanted their mother!' Kate exclaimed, losing her hold on her temper. 'Children tend to love their parents unreservedly. I certainly did. It is you who are the exception to the rule.'

'We were talking of you, not me. And I have no idea why you are so angry with me.'

'I'm not angry with you. I'm— You are driving me mad, Daniel, to be honest. You lurk about the place, shifting things so I can't find them…'

'Putting them in more sensible places, is how I'd put it.'

'Moving things from where they've always been. The coffee beans, for example. It took me almost half an hour to find them this morning. Why on earth did you put them in the cold store?'

'Because it keeps them fresher. And why on earth you felt obliged to get up at the crack of dawn in order to make my coffee for me when I'm perfectly capable of making it myself…'

'Well, I won't do it again. You can get your own in future.' Kate folded her arms across her chest and glowered.

'That will teach me.'

'Don't mock me.' She gave a shuddering sigh. 'Even though I deserve it.'

'Ah, but you don't.' Daniel held out his hand. 'Truce?'

She shook it, smiling weakly. 'Truce,' she said,

before dropping wearily onto the sofa. 'I know you're not interested in the girls, but they've been my life for the last nine years, and in the months I was abroad I missed out on so much. Eloise and Alexander have become parents. Phoebe has become a wife and the chef patron of her own restaurant. I had a letter from her this morning telling me that her husband of less than a year has gone abroad for some indeterminate time. And poor Estelle—having to kick her heels here alone, then being obliged to leave—I feel so guilty about that.'

Daniel sat down beside her. 'It sounds to me as if they are all very happy, quite independent of you, and getting on with their own lives. And as for Estelle, it was high time she left and made something of herself. She owed it to you to look after Elmswood while you were elsewhere, but by the sound of it she was more than happy to leave.'

'She was.' Kate stared down at her hands. 'Doesn't it occur to you that I might miss them? That their leaving to live their own lives—something I assure you I'm delighted about—has left a huge gap in mine?'

'But that's precisely what I've been saying. You're not exactly an old maid—why do you keep harping on about the past when you could be looking to the future?'

'I don't *harp on*,' Kate snapped. 'Just because you like to pretend you have no past of any sort…'

'I am not permitted to talk about it. That's a very different thing.'

'Is it?'

She lifted her head to meet his gaze. Slate-grey eyes, staring coolly into hers. It irked her, the way he'd so completely and quickly recovered his composure.

'There's no embargo on your talking about your past before you left Elmswood, and yet—'

'I was barely sixteen. There's nothing to tell.'

Save how he came to loathe his family home and why he was so determinedly indifferent at best to his father.

'I'll move the steps to the library,' Kate said. 'You're right—it's silly of me to keep them here.'

'And I'll put the footstool back in its rightful place. And stop using your chair. I'm sorry if you're finding my presence here a trial.'

'Don't be ridiculous, Daniel. As you pointed out, I'm not an old maid yet, so set in my ways I can't cope with change. It's not that. But I'm finding your trying to pretend you're not here a trial.'

'I feel like a house guest who has overstayed his welcome. I am extremely conscious of the fact that you've been away for nine months on my account, and I don't want to take up any of your time, or interrupt your routine, any more than I have to.'

'It wasn't your fault I was away from home for nine months. I think one of the reasons I'm so out of kilter is that it's made me realise how limited my life has become.' Kate wrinkled her nose. 'The girls don't need me any more, and Elmswood—well, it doesn't exactly run itself, but it could easily be run by someone else. Especially now, since there's little in the way of improvement left undone. The fact is I have too much time on my hands and I'd like to spend some of it with you. I rather thought that was what we agreed when we talked two weeks ago.'

'Have you had enough of looking after Elmswood, Kate? Has our arrangement become a bind?'

'No, that's not what I meant at all, but— Oh, I don't know, we didn't really think too far into the future when we married, did we? The last eleven years have passed in the blink of an eye and I'm not sure I know who I am now, if not aunt to the girls and chatelaine of Elmswood. I no longer have a purpose. It's odd.'

'Now you know how I feel.'

'I suppose...but in your case the situation is only temporary.'

'Until Sir Marcus thinks I've learnt my lesson. As it happens,' Daniel said tightly, getting out of his chair and making for the window, 'I received a letter from that august gentleman this very morning. It seems he is keeping a closer eye on me than I thought. He writes that he is concerned that I have had a relapse, for he can think of no other reason for my having failed to carry out his wishes.'

'What wishes?'

'Orders, to be more accurate. That Lord and Lady Elmswood disport themselves for the delectation of the county set.'

'Oh, *that* is why you are in such a—' Kate broke off, grimacing.

'Foul mood?' Daniel sighed, sinking down onto the window seat. 'What good it will do, I have absolutely no idea, save to back up the preposterous and quite unnecessary cover story he has concocted to explain my unexpected return. And the three months, incidentally, are non-negotiable. I'm here under your feet for the duration.'

'I see.'

'No, you don't—not really. You will be required to play my Countess, which means your time is not going to be so much your own as you would like.'

'I've already told you I have plenty of time on my hands,' Kate said. 'I am happy to accompany you on your jaunts out and about.'

'I don't think driving about the countryside is exactly what Sir Marcus has in mind, Kate.'

'What, then? Calling on tenants? Going to church? That is the extent of my social life. Our nearest neighbour until recently was Squire Mytton, who is known locally as Mad Jack. Amongst his many other exploits he rode one of his horses up the grand staircase in a hotel in Leamington Spa and then jumped it out of the window. He also kept a bear in his house which he let loose at night, much to the alarm of his guests—in fact I heard that he sometimes rode it round his drawing room. Oliver has told me that he's put himself forward to stand for Parliament again this year, but his debts have finally caught up with him and he's now living in exile in France. I believe the estate is up for sale. So, for obvious reasons, I don't socialise much with my neighbour.'

'Squire Mytton isn't your only neighbour.'

'Daniel, when it comes down to it, as far as the local gentry are concerned I'm Kate Wilson, the old Lord Elmswood's estate manager's daughter. You left England almost before the ink was dry on our wedding certificate, and my priorities at the time were my father and the estate. Then came the girls, and then— Well, I suppose it's simply always been accepted that I prefer to be left to my own devices—which is the truth.'

'You mean you've been shunned because of your humble background?'

'I mean that I've never cared for that sort of socialising—parties, taking tea, country dances. Are you saying that Sir Marcus expects us to embrace it now? What happens when you have returned to your duties and I am left with a stack of invitations to fulfil alone? Assuming that people accept me in the first place, which I'm not at all convinced they will. I find that unacceptable. He asks too much.'

'My thoughts exactly, But unfortunately I don't see that I have any option if I am to have any chance of returning to active service.'

'And that is what you want more than anything?'

'It's my life…the only one I know or want. I'm very good at what I do, and I want to continue doing it.'

'Have you never once considered retiring, coming back here and taking up—?'

'Do *not* say this is my rightful place.'

'But it's what most people will think, Daniel, if we do as Sir Marcus wishes and start showing ourselves off to the great and the good of the county. They'll be delighted to have a proper blue-blooded earl, and not just his low-born wife, grace their homes and their parties.'

'You're not serious? That's surely not how they view you?'

Kate shrugged uncomfortably. 'To be honest, I have never had any desire to put it to the test. Now it looks like I have no option, for if your career depends upon it, there's no question of us not doing as Sir Marcus bids us.'

Daniel swore softly. 'You've done more than enough already. I'm sorry to put you in such an invidious position. You've helped mitigate the damage caused by my lapse of judgement, and now, instead of being permitted to return to your comfortable, peaceful life, you are being punished too.'

'What lapse of judgement?' Kate asked, joining him at the window seat. 'Do you mean the man you saved—assuming it *was* a man? Or shouldn't I ask?'

'Dammit, I don't see why you shouldn't ask! It's not fair to expect you to fall into line without any understanding of how this blasted situation arose. He was a local man, with a wife and four children. He had been my associate—by which I mean he'd been working with me on behalf of our government—for two years. He was loyal, hard-working, and he trusted me. He'd welcomed me into his home. I had bought presents for his children. I was not prepared to throw him to the wolves when the net closed in on him.'

'So you ended up ensnared instead?'

'I didn't intent to get caught.'

'But if you hadn't acted—'

'Don't make a hero of me, Kate. I cultivated him because I needed him. I bought presents for his children because it made him happy, not because I gave a damn about the children.'

'You sound so—so cold and calculating.'

'It's called detachment, and it is vital both for self-preservation and the integrity of the mission.

Unfortunately I broke that golden rule and now I am paying the price for it.'

'For better or for worse… That is what we promised all those years ago,' Kate said, after a moment of thinking this over. 'We're in this together. I'll help not because Sir Marcus orders me to, but because I want to. And, yes,' she added, 'before you ask, I *am* sure.'

'Thank you.'

'What must we do?'

'On that topic, the man is vague.'

'Well, then,' Kate said, 'that leaves us room for manoeuvre, don't you think? One thing I *do* know, though, stepping into your father's shoes won't work. He was a recluse, remember, and he was a widower. So unless you're going to kill me off and barricade yourself in here…'

To her relief, Daniel laughed. 'Don't tempt me. Not into killing you, but into locking the pair of us up here.'

'We'd drive each other mad.'

'Do you think so? Now that I know where the library steps live, and Eloise's precious footstool…'

'And I know where to keep the coffee.'

'And you know where to keep the coffee.' Daniel reached for her hand. 'I think we might get along surprisingly well, locked away here with no one to disturb us.'

He was making circles on her wrist with his thumb. The rhythmic movement was soothing and at the same time arousing.

'Sir Marcus told me that I should keep company with my lovely, loyal little wife. I'd say that locking ourselves away here, just the two of us, fulfils that requirement, don't you? Aren't you in the least tempted?'

'If you continue to do that I'll show you just how tempted I am.' Reluctantly, Kate pulled her hand free. 'I think we ought to be practical.'

'You're right, of course, but— Do you know? I think I might have an idea.'

'You have a gleam in your eye that worries me. Have you decided to kill me after all?'

Daniel laughed. 'No, this plan requires you to be alive and kicking. We've been married eleven years. That's a long time for a man and wife to be apart. Now that we are finally reunited we have a lot of catching up to do, don't you think?'

'We hardly know each other.'

'Precisely, and with only three months before I go off to darkest Africa again our time together is precious.'

'I thought we had decided against locking ourselves away here. Sir Marcus said...'

'I know, I know—that we must show ourselves off. And we will, sufficient to comply with his instructions, but I see no reason why we should encourage invitations that I won't be here to fulfil and you're not interested in once I'm gone. So we'll tell people that we intend to take a belated honeymoon.'

'A honeymoon! Daniel...'

'It's a story we'll put about, that's all—a story that allows us to obey Sir Marcus's orders on our own terms, without forcing us to play the Earl and his wife. We'll have to act out a few set pieces—attending church services, is an obvious one—and we can throw some sort of party—a garden party, to show off your restoration work—but aside from that we can suit ourselves. No callers, no obligation to make calls, or receive calls, or attend other people's parties, but every excuse to get out and about into the countryside together. And when we are here in the house—behind closed doors, so to speak—we can suit ourselves. I will endeavour not to get under your feet, and you can continue as usual—or not, as you choose. What do you think?'

'It would look odd if I carried on with my estate duties and didn't involve you.'

'Can't you delegate to St James? Didn't you say he assisted Estelle while you were away?'

'From what I've gathered this last week he proved invaluable. He has an excellent grasp of what needs to be done, and a good head for figures. He was privately tutored when he was younger, you know.'

'I did wonder… He doesn't have a local accent.'

'No. His father was head gardener at a large estate—I think it was in Gloucestershire—and Oliver was the same age as the young gentleman of the house. They grew up almost as brothers, despite the difference in their stations in life, and Oliver was permitted to attend lessons.' Kate frowned. 'I'm not sure of the details—he doesn't talk much of his past—but I believe the boy's parents were much absent.'

'In such cases I'd have thought the boy would have been sent off to school.'

'He was, though at an older age than you, for I am sure Oliver told me he was fifteen when he left Gloucestershire to take up his first post as a gardener.'

'It seems like a waste of a good education.'

'Oh, no, Oliver doesn't think so at all. His heart is first and foremost in the garden. He can make anything grow, and he has such an eye for design...'

'Capability Brown in the guise of a Greek god, with a private education to boot. It's just as well we're not really married or I'd be jealous.'

'Of Oliver? He's five years younger than me—and we *are* "really married".'

'We're not in the true sense of it, Kate. I've never expected you to honour all the vows we made.'

Her jaw dropped in astonishment. 'You cannot possibly have imagined I'd take a lover! Can you imagine the scandal—to say nothing of the kind of example I'd be setting the girls?'

'Discreet liaisons conducted outside the marital bed are hardly unheard of in polite society.'

'Well, it didn't occur to me to indulge in such behaviour, discreetly or elsewise,' Kate said tartly. 'And now, no doubt, you're thinking I'm a gauche prude.'

'Oh, no, you're very far from the mark there. You are opinionated and fiercely independent, you're incredibly loyal and brave, you've been a better mother to those three girls than their real mother could ever have been, and a better nurse to me than any qualified medical man or woman. And you are distractingly, delightfully, adorable. That is what I think of you. One minute I'm stamping my feet and throwing my rattle onto the floor, and the next it's all I can do to stop myself from kissing you.'

The way he looked at her made her mouth go dry and set off a fluttering inside her. Daniel didn't see her as Aunt Kate or as Lady Elmswood. She wasn't even sure that he saw her as his wife. But he was *interested* in her, and she was in no doubt that he was attracted to her, and that was both a powerful and, as far as she was concerned, unique combination. One that made her reckless.

'If we did pretend to be taking a belated honeymoon wouldn't we be required to kiss—for the sake of appearances?'

She leaned towards him and he slid his arm around her waist, his eyes sparkling with amusement. 'Sir Marcus has practically commanded us to do so. It would be positively treasonous to ignore a direct order from such a senior member of His Majesty's government. In fact, I think a little light rehearsal might be in order, don't you agree?'

Kate reached up to curl her fingers into the silky short hair at the back of his head. 'Definitely.'

Lavender, that was what she smelled of, Daniel thought hazily as their lips met. There was nothing hesitant about her this time. She opened her mouth to him and the taste of her, the flick of her tongue, the little sigh she gave, had an instant effect on him.

It was just a kiss, but his body thought differently. Heart hammering, blood rushing, his hands cupped the soft, round flesh of her rear, pulling her up against him. He was already hard. She tasted so good. She felt so good. And her kisses. Dear heaven, her kisses.

He dragged his mouth from hers, but only because he wanted to taste more of her. Her neck. The hollow of her throat. Definitely lavender. He kissed the swell of her breasts, let go his hold on her very delightful rump to cup them, revelling in the way it made her gasp, the way her eyes flew open, the way she watched him, fascinated, making no attempt to disguise her arousal as he stroked her nipples to hard peaks through the material of her dress.

And then their mouths met again, and their

kisses deepened, and her hands clutched at him, at his shoulders, his back, as she pressed herself against him with such utter abandon that it would have been easy, so very easy, to give himself over to the wild rush of wanting that ripped through him.

He'd never felt like that.

Struggling for breath, Daniel forced himself to slow, to ease her away from him and to stop.

'Are you all right?' he asked inanely.

Kate stared at him for a moment, as dazed as he was by what had happened, then she smiled. 'I don't know, was I?'

He was surprised into a crack of laughter. 'I think we might have to tone down our performance just a little for public consumption.'

'Well, you know what they say.' She put her hands on his shoulders, standing on her tiptoes. 'Practice,' she whispered, 'makes perfect.' And then she kissed him again.

Daniel awoke with a start. The sun was slanting through his bedroom window but, groping for his pocket watch under his pillow, he saw that it was only just after five. He was wide awake, and for once he couldn't recall enduring any of the nightmares which had haunted him since his escape from prison.

Stretching his limbs, he was conscious of the usual tension in his feet, which he still braced in his sleep even though it had been months since he had been chained by manacles, but his neck and shoulders were free of the usual aches.

Pushing back the bedcovers, he got slowly to his feet and began the series of stretches that had formed his morning routine ever since he had first been shown them all those years ago in India. Even with the manacles on he'd managed to complete a rudimentary exercise regime in his lucid intervals, before the fever had taken hold, determined to preserve his strength, relishing the small oasis of calm that the associated breathing exercises provided.

His protracted illness had put an end to that practice, and it would have been tricky, to say the least, to find sufficient space on the endurance test of his journey back to England on board various ships, even if he had been well enough. But for the last two weeks he had been working himself hard, three times a day, and as he adopted the asana yoga position he'd been taught to call the plough, he could feel a noticeable tautening in the muscles of his back and his belly.

Refreshed and invigorated, Daniel inspected himself critically in the mirror. Thank the stars that he had been unable to do so when he had been at his most physically frail. He'd never thought of himself as vain, but he had always been proud of the physique he'd worked hard to maintain, even in youth, when his prowess on the athletics field had been his one saving grace at that great barrack of a school his father had exiled him to.

*Fairfax, whose only talent is to run away very fast.*

His lip curled at the memory. It had never failed to astonish him, both then and now, how easily a boy or a man could be forced into becoming one of the crowd or risk alienation.

*Fidelitas, veritas, integritas.*

Fidelity, truth and integrity.

The irony of the meaning of the school motto still amused him, for he'd been true to himself always in eschewing the two things which would have brought him into the fold. He would not fight. He would not be part of a team. It had cost him several miserable years and an execrable annual report being sent back to his father, but he'd refused to buckle and swim with the tide. No one could teach him anything about integrity.

Daniel gave himself a shake, turning away from the mirror. He never permitted the past to intrude on his thoughts. Being in this damned place was to blame. He had never been happy here, had always dreamt of escape, and he had achieved his dream. It was because he was determined to hold on to that dream that he was back.

It was three months, not a life sentence, just as Kate had said, so why did he feel so unsettled? His father was dead, Gillian was dead, there was nothing here that could hurt him or alter his resolve, and yet he couldn't shake off the feeling that there was something lurking here…an evil spirit waiting to pounce.

Now he really *was* being fanciful! Bad memories, an unhappy childhood and a lonely one too—that was more than enough to explain his jaundiced view.

Pushing open the window, he gazed out. The sun was climbing in a very pale blue summer sky. The south lawn was damp with dew, softly green, and the huge oak filtered light through to the lake so that it danced, dappled and golden, on the still waters where a pair of swans were gliding.

The English countryside at its most idyllic, pastel-coloured and gently warmed—so very different from the bold, bright palette and harsh heat he was used to. Yet it did have an allure. And he was looking forward to enjoying more of it with Kate, now that their little fantasy of a honeymoon would keep the world—*her* world—at bay.

Kate!

Kate's kisses.

Despite the fact they'd been married for eleven years, he'd never thought of her as his wife. His willing wife. Dear Lord, yesterday all too willing. Her kisses were no longer innocent, but the manner in which she gave herself so entirely over to them, without thought of the consequences, betrayed her. Not that she pretended experience. She was refreshingly, enchantingly honest.

He'd never met anyone like her.

Hardly surprising, mind you.

Would their faux honeymoon be infused with real passion? There was no question of what he wanted, or what Kate thought she wanted, but would it be right? In the eyes of the law it was not only expected but required—but, using his own strict code of conduct, would it be appropriate for him to make love to his wife?

Not a question he'd ever thought to ask of

himself, and not one he was prepared to answer at this moment. He was regaining his strength, but he'd rather Kate didn't see him naked until he'd put some more work in. Though she had, of course, seen him naked at his lowest ebb.

The trundling of a wheelbarrow caught his attention. Oliver St James, making an early start. The gardener looked up, saw Daniel, smiled and saluted.

Something resonated in the depths of his memory. Another summer's morning, similar to this one, leaning out of the window just like this. And Leo waving. But as soon as he tried to pull the memory into focus his mind went quite blank. If Leo had been there it had been that last summer.

Daniel cursed under his breath. Damn this place.

Outside, St James was now entering the kitchen garden. At least he had his shirt on, doubtless aware that it was too early for Kate to be up and about. Not that she seemed in the least bit interested in the show of muscles and tanned skin that *Oliver* seemed determined to put on for her. Kate's taste was more discerning.

Grinning to himself, Daniel left the window open and pulled on his dressing gown. If his clever, witty, annoyingly observant, distractingly attractive wife was going to see him naked during their honeymoon, then he was going to do his damnedest to make sure he looked his best.

There were few things about Elmswood that he remembered with pleasure, but the lake had always been one of his favourite places. On impulse, he decided he was going for a swim.

Kate pulled back the curtains and leaned out of her bedroom window to drink in the fresh, verdant smell of the early morning. There was only a tiny wisp of cloud in the sky. It was going to be another perfect summer's day.

A loud splash drew her attention to the lake. She thought at first it was one of the swans, flapping its huge wings as it disappeared into the shadow cast by the oak. It was not a swan which emerged from the shadow, however, but her husband, who had just dived into the water and was now scything through it at speed.

She shaded her eyes, squinting against the glare of the sun. Daniel had reached the far end of the lake and turned. He swam effortlessly, his arms powering over his head in a regular, hypnotising rhythm, his feet hardly breaking the surface. His head looked as if it were facing down into the water. How did he breathe?

She had never seen anyone swim like that, moving like an arrow in a straight line through the water, barely slowing to turn at the end of each lap. She started to count but lost track, distracted by the occasional tantalising glimpse of thigh and buttock, by the arc of water from his cropped hair as he stopped in the middle of the lake to tread water before resuming his marathon.

The sides of the lake had been cut steeply into the slight incline of the lawn. Though it looked as if it had always been there, she knew it had been excavated about a hundred years ago, and was no shallower than ten feet—in the middle almost twenty feet deep. For that reason she had never allowed the girls anywhere near it, since none of them could swim.

How would Daniel manage to clamber back out? He was lying on his back now, drifting towards the centre of the expanse of water. She wasn't close enough to see if his eyes were open or closed, but she could see his chest heaving, could clearly see that he had put on weight.

When he rolled over and swam lazily for the bank by the oak tree she knew she ought to look away, but she could not bring herself to. To ensure that he got out safely—that was what she told herself. He placed his hands on the bank and hauled himself from the water in one fluid movement that astounded her, bending to retrieve the red silk dressing gown, allowing her only the most fleeting glance of a lithe, toned body that she barely recognised before he covered himself.

Something distracted him, making him turn towards the house. Belatedly realising that if she could see Daniel he could see her, Kate hid behind the curtain. Peeking out, she saw that it had been Oliver, making his way from the succession house or the kitchen garden along the border of the lawn with his wheelbarrow.

Daniel didn't wait to bid him good morning, but strode barefoot across the lawn to the terrace. Kate smiled to herself. It was preposterous for her husband to be jealous of Oliver, and it was even more ludicrous of her to be flattered. But she was, nonetheless.

# *Chapter Five*

Two days later, Kate and Daniel elected to put themselves on public display for the first time at church, marking their debut as Lord and Lady Elmswood.

Kate wore a morning gown of salmon-pink. It was silk, the short puffed sleeves and the décolleté trimmed with cotton lace and, although simple, she thought it far too pretty for daily wear. As a consequence she had rarely worn it. With the straw bonnet she planned to wear, along with a lace shawl which had been a gift from Eloise, and a pair of new gloves—another gift from Eloise that she had never worn—she felt she would do her adopted character of Lady Elmswood justice.

'Good morning, dear wife,' Daniel said when she appeared for breakfast in the dining room. 'May I say that you look absolutely charming?

The gown is perfect. Not too elaborate, but a little bit more sophisticated than your usual attire.'

'I feel overdressed. People will notice.'

'You look delightful, and the whole point of the exercise is to ensure people take notice of us. Are you nervous? You've no need to be—we are simply going to church.'

'I hate to be the centre of attention.'

'Then I will nobly ensure that *I* am the focus of their attention. All you have to do is follow my lead.'

'What are you planning?'

'Stop looking so fearful. I'm not planning anything outrageous, save feeding some interesting snippets of our story to an eager audience.'

Daniel, his hair still damp from his morning dip, was also dressed formally for the occasion, in a beautifully cut olive-green coat and tight-fitting trousers that he wore with shoes, instead of his usual flowing tunic, loose trousers and slippers. As ever, he was freshly shaved, and, as had become their custom, he had her tea, bread and butter waiting for her.

With every passing day she noticed an improvement in him. Though he was still lean, there was now a litheness to his movements, an energy that had been lacking, as he jumped to his feet to greet her.

'No need to ask if you slept well—you look radiant,' he said, ushering her into her chair, pressing a kiss to the nape of her neck. 'And you smell fragrant. Lavender, I believe. Is it the scent of your soap I can detect?'

'Yes.'

'Do you make it yourself, using lavender from the garden?'

'No, the rather prosaic truth is that I buy it from a woman in the village.'

Kate poured her tea and Daniel pushed the bread and butter towards her with a smile. 'Don't worry, I'll be quiet until you've had your first cup.'

'You look as if you've already drunk a full pot of coffee.'

'I have, and I will confess to having a slice of your bread and butter too. I hope you don't mind.'

'Please, help yourself to another. It's not *my* bread and butter. I'm not surprised you're hungry after your morning swim.'

'You saw me?'

'I see you every day.'

'*All* of me?'

He was teasing her, daring her, and that gleam in his eyes made her determined to surprise him. 'Enough,' Kate said, 'to note that your physical condition has improved a great deal since the first time I saw you naked.'

He laughed. 'That wouldn't be difficult. I hope that next time you'll be impressed by the massive—'

'Daniel!' Kate spluttered her tea.

'Improvement in my stamina, I was going to say,' he finished, grinning. 'Are you ready for your second cup?'

'Thank you. You are full of the joys this morning.'

'I am looking forward to our first performance, my dear.'

'That's the second time you've called me that.'

'Do you prefer darling? I did consider that, but it seemed rather presumptuous, considering that we are only just getting to know one another.'

'I much prefer Kate. Do you mean that you are acting right now, even though we are alone?'

'I find that when assuming a role it is always more credible when I immerse myself in it—it makes it less likely that I will slip up. What kind of couple do you think we should be? Not too tactile, I don't think—we are an earl and a countess, after all, and of a certain age too,' Daniel said, with a droll look.

'I can't imagine what you mean by slipping up. I am not likely to forget your name. I must say you're taking this very seriously.'

'I take every role I play seriously.'

Kate buttered another slice of bread, considering the implications of this remark. 'Are you always playing someone else when you are working? Are you never yourself?'

He shrugged. 'There are always elements of me in whoever I am required to be—that is what makes my roles believable, and that's why I asked you what kind of couple we should be. I said we shouldn't be too tactile, but if you are known as a demonstrative woman…'

'I hug the girls, the girls hug me, but that's about as far as it goes.'

'That is helpful. So I did right, then, not to throw my arms around you when you came to breakfast?'

She eyed him askance. 'Are you teasing me again?'

'And although I will likely wish to embrace you more in public,' he continued, ignoring her question, or so intent on his own train of thought that he hadn't noticed, 'I'll make it obvious that

I am restraining myself. I shall start to put my arm around you and then suddenly remember we are in company. Or I shall take your hand, just for a few moments. Or you can take mine. You know the kind of thing?' Daniel smiled at her expectantly.

'No, I don't. I have no experience of that kind of intimacy.'

'Oh, it's all new to me too.' He studied her for a moment, his lips pursed. 'Not intimacy—that would be a lie—but it's never been associated with the emotional ties you and I must feign. To be blunt, I have restricted myself to enjoying mutually convenient arrangements shared between consenting adults.'

'That *is* blunt and, if you will forgive me for saying so, a rather cold way of describing affairs of the heart.'

'Ah, but my heart was never engaged.'

Kate pushed her empty cup away. 'I'm not sure that we need to discuss our roles in such candid detail. Can't we simply be ourselves?'

'But we're not being ourselves, are we? We're being Lord and Lady Elmswood. There's still another half-cup in the pot—don't you want it? Here, I'll pour it for you.'

'I hadn't imagined we'd have to pretend even when we are alone.'

'It's not pretending. If you think of it as pretending you'll fall out of character. What you have to do, dear wife—I beg your pardon, dear Kate—is embrace the situation.'

'Though I must not embrace you?'

'In company, no. But while we are alone—please feel free!'

She was obliged to laugh. 'But seriously, Daniel...'

'I'm being very serious. I am determined to carry out Sir Marcus's orders in my own way, but I'm under no illusions. What Sir Marcus *didn't* say in his letter—and what he does not say is always more important, in my experience, than what he alludes to—is that my future career depends upon my toeing the line, and he will have his beady eye on me to ensure that I do.'

'Is your acquaintance of long standing?'

'I've known him since I was sixteen and first went to work at the Admiralty.'

'So when you went off to London, was it with the ambition to enter into—is it permissible to call it foreign service?'

Daniel frowned. 'I'm an explorer, remember?'

'Yes, yes, as far as the world is concerned you

are an explorer—but I know you are not, and I cannot erase the knowledge from my mind.'

'But that's exactly what you must do, don't you see? If we are to continue to live as we have done, you must do exactly that.'

'I can't. That's ridiculous.'

'Listen to me, Kate—and this is me speaking… I'm not acting. We've lived with the convenient myth of my being an explorer for eleven years and our marriage has been a success, hasn't it? You've been happy?'

'Yes, but—'

'I've been serving my country and making a damned good job of it. You've been restoring Elmswood and raising your girls and making an excellent fist of both. We both wish to restore that status quo, don't we?'

'Yes, but—'

'And in order to do so we must get through this hiatus lasting three months, playing out the charade that Sir Marcus has specified, showing ourselves to the world, acting the happy couple reunited until we are once again parted.'

'I've been wondering about that, Daniel. If we are supposedly so happy to be together after all this time—'

'Then why don't we remain together? I've

been thinking of that too. We need a story, and it needs to explain not only why we've remained apart for eleven years, but why we're intent on spending the next eleven or twenty apart too. It needs to be a believable story, one you can recount with confidence, for you are going to have to be the one to field the questions when I am gone.'

'Oh.' Kate drank her cold last half-cup of tea in one gulp. 'I hadn't thought of that.'

'I always approach the process of creating a new history for myself as if I was writing a novel. We know the beginning, and we know how it must end, but how we get from one to the other will depend very much on the kind of people we are, and what kind of story suits our characters. Which is why we should remain in character as much as we can—do you see?'

'I see that you have given it a lot of thought.'

'It's my job, Kate.'

'Is it permissible to ask how that job came about?'

'Through the Admiralty, in a roundabout way.'

She pursed her lips. 'By which you mean it's *not* permissible to ask. I remember the last summer you spent at Elmswood, before you went off to the Admiralty well, because it was so hot. I was envious of you and the young man you had staying being able to swim in the lake to cool down, though of course I was far too young—What is it? What have I said?' Kate asked, for he had gone quite pale. He was staring at her blankly, his eyes unfocused. 'Daniel? Are you feeling unwell?'

He started, reaching for his coffee cup, setting it back down when he saw it was empty. 'So watching me swim is an established habit with you, is it?'

His smile was singularly unconvincing.

'We could hear you both from the Estate Office, laughing and splashing about in the water. I tried to see from the window, but Papa pulled me back and said what was going on was indecent and no sight for a young girl to witness.'

'What do you mean?' Daniel snapped.

'Presumably you were not swimming fully clothed. What else would he have meant?'

'Nothing. I don't know. My own father did not approve of Leo.'

'Leo?'

'Leo Bainbridge. He was my Classics tutor, but he was only five years older than me, so…'

Daniel drifted off again, staring vacantly over her shoulder.

'Are you sure you're up to going to church? We can postpone it till next Sunday,' Kate said after a moment.

Once again he started. 'I'm perfectly well. It's time we set off,' he added, consulting his watch. 'I took the precaution of informing Mrs Chester of our plans yesterday, so if you're right about how quickly word spreads we will be expected. Are you ready to face your audience?'

'I'm not sure that I am.'

Now quite recovered, he pulled her to her feet, wrapping his arms around her. 'There really is no need to be nervous. All you have to do is be a slightly different version yourself—a Kate who is delighted that her long-lost husband has recovered his health.'

'That's easy, because it's the truth.'

'Is it such a big step, then, to imagine yourself as a Kate who is also delighted to get to know her long-lost husband a little better?'

'That's also easy, because it's also the truth.'

'And a Kate who is eager to show him off to the county?'

'Like some artefact I collected while I was travelling abroad, you mean?'

Daniel chuckled. 'If you like. And I shall at first be delighted to be paraded about, entertaining everyone with tales of the sources of rivers I have traced, and the strange and wonderful beasts I have encountered along the way.'

'They will wonder that you have not shot any of those strange and wonderful beasts and had them sent home to adorn our walls.'

'Then I will tell them that I believe those strange and wonderful beasts should be left free to enjoy their natural habitat.'

'Is that what you truly think?'

'Of course it is—don't you?'

'I must confess I've never given it much consideration, though I've never been an admirer of stags' heads or those tiger skins that were so popular for a while. Have you never hunted?'

Daniel shuddered. 'I've been obliged, a couple of times, to take part in a big game hunt, but I contrived to ensure that the game being hunted escaped unscathed. There are times when, even for the sake of being true to my role, I won't compromise my principles. Which is why,' he added wryly, 'I've never before played a husband.'

'So this really is new territory for us both?

Are we destined to quarrel when the time comes for you to leave?'

'We are both so accustomed to arranging our own lives I suspect we are destined to quarrel on a regular basis. One reason why our honeymoon is such an excellent idea, since it ensures we can have the time we need to be alone. While the world thinks us locked away in our love nest, I will be hiding in the library and you will be lurking in the walled garden.'

'You never know—we might find that we enjoy each other's company.'

'As we do already in real life?'

Kate smiled up at him, putting her arms around his neck, tiling her face invitingly. 'I think so.'

He kissed her, softly but swiftly. 'I think so too.' Then he put her from him. 'But I think we need to be careful not to enjoy it too much. Are you ready to face your audience now, Lady Elmswood?'

'Let me don the rest of my costume. I can't possibly attend church without gloves and a bonnet. Give me five minutes and I will be ready to make my debut.'

The church was packed to the rafters when they arrived, with standing room only. Mrs Chester had obviously done her work well. A number of the pews reserved for the local gentry, usually sparsely populated, were crowded this morning.

Kate fixed a smile on her face and kept her eyes down as they made their way to the Elmswood family pew at the very front, conscious that all eyes were on her—or rather on Lord and Lady Elmswood. Daniel, on the other hand, made a show of nodding and smiling, even making a small, apologetic bow to the waiting vicar before they both sat down.

Despite the fact that she'd been sitting in this pew for eleven years, Kate always felt uncomfortable at the front of the church. She and Daniel had been married in the drawing room at Elmswood Manor, so this was the first time that they had attended church together.

The service opened with a prayer, and Daniel slipped his hand into hers, slanting her a complicit smile. Their legs brushed against each other inside the narrow pew. Though Kate kept her head bowed, she was aware that Daniel was looking around him, making no pretence of praying.

Was he a regular churchgoer? She doubted it. Was it even possible to attend church services in darkest Africa? Had he ever actually visited darkest Africa?

She could probably write the facts she knew of him down on a visiting card, and as for the essence of him—he was a paradox. Every time she tried to ask him about his past he avoided the issue. He fed her tantalising snippets, then retreated into silence. He hated Elmswood and he loathed his father. He claimed to be indifferent to his sister, but his occasional outbursts gave lie to that. And as for his nieces—why was he so utterly determined not to meet them? He had given her a very reasonable and logical explanation, but somehow she was sure there was more to it.

He had been so odd too, talking about the man whose life he had saved. He'd bought presents for those children, had dinner in the man's house, yet he refused to admit to caring about him. It was almost as if he was afraid.

And then there was another Daniel—the Daniel who joked and teased and flirted and kissed, playing the part of her long-lost husband. And yet it seemed to her that was the only time he wasn't acting. She liked him then, quite unreservedly. At other times—oh, he was infuriating and perplexing and intriguing. But he was never boring, and she had never felt so—not alive, exactly, but on edge, excited, anticipating the day, looking forward to his company.

Guiltily, she realised that she wasn't missing the girls anything like as much as she had imagined she would. It wasn't that she'd stopped thinking about them, but they were no longer at the forefront of her mind. That position was occupied by the man sitting by her side. Though he wouldn't be there for ever. In two and a half months he would be gone and she would be a free woman.

If only she had the smallest clue as to what to do with herself. Perhaps she'd travel to a far corner of the globe and hunt out some rare species of plants. There was a book in the library at Elmswood by some Cornish botanist who had done just that, full of the most beautiful illustrations. The desert plants in particular had struck her, so oddly lush and such vivid colours.

Trevelyan—that had been the author. Daniel Trevelyan. Another Daniel. The illustrations had such a delicate, feminine touch she had been surprised, the first time she had opened the book, to discover that they had been painted by a man.

Whether the Admiralty had made him or not, *her* Daniel was his own man. So much his own man that he struggled to follow Sir Marcus's orders, and felt obliged to redefine them to suit himself.

As the vicar embarked on his sermon Kate caught her husband's eye and smiled. Sir Marcus, albeit unwittingly, had defined a role for her to play, and she intended to enjoy it while it lasted.

'Yes, I was very fortunate indeed that my wife was able to come to my rescue,' Daniel said for what he reckoned must be the tenth time.

He and Kate had been standing surrounded by avidly listening faces just outside the church door for the last hour, answering a battery of questions and fielding an onslaught of invitations.

'Yes,' he said, continuing to smile, 'I was taken ill on the little island of Cyprus. Do you know it? It is in the eastern Mediterranean. A charming place, with some very ancient sites. Kate was able to explore some of them when she was not nursing me. She is an excellent nurse.'

The 'excellent nurse' was looking decidedly dejected.

'It was nothing—any wife would have done the same,' she said, but the woman who had asked the question ignored Kate's reply and continued addressing Daniel.

He tamped down the prickle of irritation. Despite being warned, he had not been prepared for the level of interest shown in him, and despite what Kate had said about being 'only' the estate manager's daughter, he had not been prepared to witness her being sidelined and ignored. The so-called elite of Shropshire weren't remotely interested in Lady Elmswood, who had lived among them for the last eleven years. But in stark contrast they were quite consumed with interest in her absent husband, in the reasons for his sudden and surprising marriage to an employee's daughter, of all people, and in the explanation for his immediate abandonment of both his bride and his newly inherited estate.

Ignoring yet another pointed remark about the secrecy of his nuptials—which, he had been informed with a titter, would have given rise to a very different kind of speculation had Lady Elmswood produced an early heir—Daniel put his arm around Kate's waist, pulling her closer.

'It is no exaggeration to say that my wife saved my life,' he said. 'And that despite having to survive in a foreign land, often with only the most basic of facilities.'

'Facilities?' the woman—Wycham? Was that her name? He vaguely remembered her—smiled blankly.

'The personal facilities,' Daniel said, casting Kate a mischievous smile. 'They were exactly what one comes to expect when one is exploring antiquity, madam, but not what my lovely wife is accustomed to. To be blunt, they involved a shovel and a bucket of sand. If you understand my meaning.'

He felt Kate's shoulders shake, and threw her a conspiratorial smile.

'Lord Elmswood! But I suppose I must forgive you being indelicate, for you are not accustomed to polite society…'

'Oh, on the contrary, madam. I am used to consorting with royalty. I was once the guest of an Arabian prince.' As he had intended, this drew an audible gasp. 'Yes, I spent three months in the desert with his entourage, living in a tent made of goatskin. Oh, indeed, I can ride a camel as easily as a horse, sir. They have mouths every bit as sensitive as a thoroughbred, you know—though an unfortunate tendency to spit, which I confess takes some getting used to. The other end is also best avoided. No, I do not plan on expanding the stables here at Elmswood at present, though if I do I will be sure to take a look at the matching pair you speak of.'

'Lord Elmswood!' The cut-glass voice penetrated the general hubbub, followed swiftly by the statuesque woman it belonged to. 'Lord Elmswood, I am Eveline Hartford—though you will know me as Marlow.'

'A pleasure to meet you, Mrs Hartford, though I'm afraid I don't recall…'

'I was your sister Gillian's best friend when we were girls. I must say I'd never have recognised you had you not been pointed out to me. Who would have thought that sickly little boy would have turned into such a—? Well, let me just say you have improved out of all recognition.'

'Thank you,' Daniel said through gritted teeth. 'May I introduce my wife, Kate?'

'How do you do, Lady Elmswood? I confess I expected someone more… Your father was estate manager at Elmswood, I understand?'

'Yes he was. But I hung up my clogs and started taking regular baths when Lord Elmswood condescended to marry me,' Kate said with a sweet smile.

Though Daniel snorted, the sarcasm was quite

lost on the other woman, who was barely listening.

'Surely you remember me?' she said, turning to Daniel. 'Gilly and I were inseparable, and *you*,' she said, with a gusty laugh that set Daniel's teeth on edge, 'you were forever begging to tag along.'

'I'm afraid I don't recall much of those days,' Daniel said, though even as he spoke he did remember—with distaste. Realising the woman was not to be easily fobbed off, he turned to the rest of the fascinated onlookers. 'If you will excuse us? I would like to catch up with an old family friend.'

'Not so old, if you don't mind,' Eveline Marlow tittered as he ushered her off to one side.

'Let me see… My sister was nine years older than I, which would make you—'

'There is no need to bring arithmetic into it,' the Marlow woman snapped. 'I can't believe how many years have passed since we lost dear Gillian…taken far too young. Though she was happy enough with her charming Irishman, and that must have been a consolation to you, Daniel—I'm sure you won't mind my calling you Daniel, since we go back such a long way… My goodness, I really am finding it difficult to reconcile the strapping, handsome man you have become with that little boy. But I can see the family resemblance, especially around the eyes. Yours are a very different colour from Gillian's, and there is no trace of her crowning glory of Titian hair in yours, but I will grant you you have turned into a very striking man. But, oh, your sister was a genuine beauty, was she not? I was far from plain myself, in those days, but she put me in the shade. It was a tragedy…a true tragedy…losing her so young and in such a terrible manner. She had promised to pay me a visit—for I was happily married myself by then, and by a stroke of good fortune I was living quite close to the school their darling little boy was due to attend. Did you know that?'

'I'm afraid I did not. I was—'

'Oh, yes, you'd have been off on your travels by then. You see,' Mrs Hartford said, with an arch rap of her fan, 'I have been keeping track of your progress. Not through Gillian, of course, for she was very much an out-of-sight-out-of-mind kind of person, but I am not without other more *conscientious* correspondents from Shropshire. The Wychams—you were talking to them a moment ago, and I am currently paying them a short visit. Anyway, when we had word that you had returned—well, how could I not make a point of coming along today to introduce myself? Though that should be *re*introduce, shouldn't it? You do remember me, don't you? Surely I have not changed so very much?'

'Not a bit,' Daniel said blithely, for in essence she had not.

'Hermes, Gillian called you—her little joke. For you were always boring on with stories of the Greek gods…and you *were* her messenger, weren't you? Those *billets doux* of hers—do you remember?'

'Vaguely,' Daniel said, aware that his smile was becoming ever more rigid. 'In my defence, it was almost thirty years ago.'

Eveline Marlow's smile faded at this. 'Never say so?'

'Indeed,' Daniel said, 'for the eldest of my nieces is now a mother herself. Gillian would be a grandmother, were she alive. She did tell you, in those letters of hers, that she had given birth to three girls before her "darling little boy"?'

'Well, of course she mentioned the girls. Twins! The poor dear was at death's door, having those two.'

'That would explain her rather distant parenting, no doubt,' Kate cut in.

'Oh, girls… You know, they need none of the attention one must lavish on a boy. I know that from my own brood. Why, girls can practically raise themselves.'

'That certainly seems to have been your dear friend's view. My own experience,' Kate said, 'is that girls benefit every bit as much, if not more, from having a little love and attention lavished upon them.'

'Oh, yes, you took them on, didn't you? Poor little orphans… Yes, I can imagine that they must have missed Gilly terribly. You must have found it so difficult. They would naturally have seen you as a very poor substitute, though I'm sure you did your best.'

'Let me see,' Daniel intervened. 'Eloise, the eldest, is now Lady Fearnoch, and has just given birth to her first child. A girl but, despite that, the apple of her papa's eye. Lord Fearnoch, of course, is very well known in diplomatic circles. Phoebe, the youngest of the twins, is *chef patron* of one of London's most sought-after eating establishments—Le Pas à Pas, have you dined there? No? Well, it is *very* difficult to get a table if you are without influence. And Estelle, the middle sister and eldest twin, is extremely musical. She is off touring Europe at present, but we expect to hear that she has established her own orchestra very soon. So I'd say that Kate has done an admiral job, wouldn't you agree?'

'Gillian's children would be bound to shine, whatever the circumstances.'

Kate gave something very much resembling a snort, but before he could retort she caught his hand, squeezing it in warning.

'You must excuse us,' Daniel said. 'You are doubtless aware, for you seem so very well-informed, that my wife and I are taking a belated honeymoon.'

'I confess I had heard some such thing. Rather an odd state of affairs, though, is it not? For you have been married for years.'

'For years I have dedicated my life to exploring the world, and Kate has dedicated her life to raising Gillian's girls. Fate, in the form of my illness, has contrived to bring us together now, when we finally have time to devote to each other without the distraction of other obligations, and we intend to make the most of it.'

'Indeed we do,' Kate agreed, with a beatific smile in his direction. 'It was a pleasure to meet you, Mrs Hartford, but it is an encounter that I'm sure you'll understand we must curtail now, since we have other plans for this afternoon. What a pity that your visit to Shropshire will be concluded before our upcoming garden party.'

'Well, as to that…'

'If you will excuse us? We really must be off.'

# *Chapter Six*

'I did warn you,' Kate said as they finally left the church for the short walk back to Elmswood Manor. 'As far as the county set are concerned I am and always will be the estate manager's daughter. Clearly eleven years of continued improvement and renovation, providing people with work and making sure their farms are profitable, to say nothing of putting food on their tables, counts for nothing with that lot. I was right to have nothing to do with them.'

'Slow down,' Daniel said, taking her arm.

'Sorry. You are so much improved that I sometimes forget how ill you have been. Are you tired?'

'No, but my jaw is sore from talking!'

She turned, smiling briefly. 'And your ears must be burning. I hadn't reckoned on all those questions about our marriage.'

'Nor I, but I think I managed to deflect them.'

'You are extremely adept at turning the subject. Is that a skill you have honed over years in foreign service?'

'And is interrogation by stealth a skill *you* have honed over years of looking after my nieces?'

Kate was obliged to laugh. 'I should know better than to attempt to use subterfuge against a master of the art.'

Daniel gave her arm a little shake. 'The ordeal is over and we have achieved what we set out to do. So I think we both deserve a pat on the back.'

'Largely thanks to you. No one was in the least bit interested in me. Actually, I'd rather they weren't interested, so I'm delighted that you took centre stage. If I never have to pass the time of day with any of those people again I'll be happy. Save that I will have to. *Must* we hold a party? No, don't answer that. I know we must.'

'What's bothering you?'

'Nothing.'

'Come on, Kate, you're a terrible liar.'

'I suppose it's sour grapes, really. Or wanting to have my cake and eat it. I am not interested in socialising with those people, and I am not interested in their lives, but to see how little they care about all the work I've done is galling. Perhaps I should have made more of an effort to blow my own trumpet.'

'I'd like to understand better what you've achieved so that I can defend you.'

She laughed. 'I can fight my own battles, thank you very much.'

'Oh, I'm very much aware of that. I'm just glad we're on the same side.'

On reaching the manor, they decided to remain outside, heading for the walled garden.

'Do you mind if I take my coat off?' Daniel said as they made for Kate's favourite bench in the wilderness area. 'Even I am finding it hot.'

'Of course not. We can go inside if you'd rather?'

'No, I like it here.'

Daniel threw his coat carelessly over the back of the seat, and Kate decided to follow his lead, taking off her bonnet and gloves.

'That Hartford woman was horrid,' she said. 'I take it you *do* remember her?'

'As I said to her, it was a long time ago.'

Which was his way of saying that he had locked it away, along with the rest of his past history, and didn't want to discuss it. But Kate was getting tired of the growing list of topics which he considered out of bounds.

'Hermes, she said your sister called you.'

'It was Gillian's pet name for me.'

'Hermes was the messenger of the gods, wasn't he?'

'I thought you didn't know anything about the Classics.'

'We're supposed to be getting to know one another better on this honeymoon of ours. How can I do that when you won't even answer a simple question?'

'I delivered love letters,' Daniel said, after a tense moment's hesitation. 'Gillian enjoyed intrigue and she required adoration. I took the letters she wrote to her beaux and hid them in various secret locations, bringing replies back if there were any.'

'Good grief, how many admirers did she have?'

'I've no idea—nor whether the extent of her flirtations before Sean Brannagh began and ended with love notes or extended to assignations. Given what Eveline was hinting at, the latter, I presume.'

Kate took a moment to assimilate this. 'You were a child. Your sister was nine years older than you. Selfish as she was, she must have known it was wrong of her to embroil you.'

'I didn't need much persuading, Kate. I was pathetically eager to please. It was not only my father she had eating out of her hand.'

'That Hartford woman referred to you as a sickly child.' Kate frowned. 'But I don't remember you being anything other than a picture of health.'

'I really don't see what relevance my childhood ailments have now.'

'Don't you think that we are the sum total of our experiences?' Kate asked. 'You have admitted that in every role you have played an element of the real Daniel lurks. I'm interested in knowing *all* of that person. Including what he was like as a child. Go on—indulge me, please.'

He rolled his eyes. 'Very well. My mother died not long after giving birth to me. I know almost nothing about her, my father never spoke of her, but I can only assume, given the large gap between myself and my sister, that there were a number of failed pregnancies in between.'

'Oh, the poor woman.'

'As I said, she died, and since I was born some weeks before full-term I wasn't expected to survive. Obviously I did, but during my very early years I was sickly, and left in the care of a nurse.'

'While Gillian hogged your father's attention, no doubt?' Kate interjected.

'I presume so. As a result of my poor health I was tutored at home. When I eventually grew out of my childhood ailments I begged to be sent to school, but my father insisted that I was too much of a weakling to cope. The fact that I refused to hunt or shoot confirmed him in his assessment.'

'I presume he enjoyed both pursuits?'

'He did—with relish.'

'And I may safely also presume that is why you did not?'

'It was a small enough rebellion, and in fact it stemmed from a very real repugnance. Perhaps if I'd tried from an earlier age to please him…'

'Or perhaps if he had evinced any interest in you…'

'The only interest he had in me was in riling me or thwarting me, and the net result was that I determined not to allow him to do either. But don't start imagining me persecuted mercilessly, Kate. I spent most of my time hiding away—either here, or in the library, the one room in the house that held no interest for either Gillian or my father.'

And the room he still chose as his sanctuary.

Daniel would be repelled by any show of pity, but Kate ached for the lost, neglected soul he had described, though she could not reconcile that boy with the sturdy, self-sufficient youth she remembered.

'So your father starved you of affection,' she said, 'but Gillian—'

'Oh, I was every bit in thrall to Gillian as my father was,' Daniel said sardonically.

'You were a little boy, and she was a beautiful and utterly selfish young woman who even then cared for nothing and no one but herself,' Kate said vehemently. 'She took advantage of you.' A terrible thought struck her. 'Surely your father didn't blame you when she eloped?' Daniel's overly casual shrug was all the answer she needed. '*That* is what you meant when you told me that Gillian didn't give a fig for the consequences when she eloped, isn't it? You were a *child*, for goodness' sake.'

'He accused me of aiding and abetting her since I'd kept the letters secret from him. Regardless of my age, that constituted betrayal for him.'

'What happened?'

'I was summarily packed off to school.'

'But wasn't that what you had wanted all along?'

'The school I'd imagined for myself was rather different from the one I was forced to attend. But in the end it all turned out well, don't you think? If Gillian had not run off with Branagh then your precious girls wouldn't have existed, let alone found their way to you, and you wouldn't have had the chance to raise three such paragons.'

'They are not paragons, but they are fine young women. Despite the fact that Mrs Hartford thinks the only credit due is to your sister, I am proud to have played a part—and so should you be.'

'I've no right to be proud of them. I've done nothing to contribute to their success.'

'You put a roof over their heads, paid their father's debts and provided one of them with the ideal husband—which, in turn, allowed her to set up the other two for life. But apart from that you're quite right—you've done nothing.'

'How did you know about the debts?'

'I didn't. Eloise guessed as much. She was right, then, I take it?'

'I left the Brannagh family to fight between themselves for the right to sell off the house and the racehorses to pay the bank. I paid the tradesmen, for I doubted anyone else would. And now I really think I've had enough of ancient history for today.'

'I don't know about ancient history,' Kate said, acceding to the note of finality in his voice, 'but I thought you made an excellent job of inventing your own more recent past. Though you did stretch credulity a little far with that tall tale you told the vicar's wife about taking a thorn from the paw of a baby lion.'

'Actually, that one was true,' Daniel said, visibly relaxing.

'And the one where you plunged in a dugout canoe over the edge of a waterfall and into a whirlpool?'

'I have been in a dugout canoe. On a very calm river. And someone else was paddling.'

'I'd like to paddle a canoe,' Kate said. 'Or even row a little dinghy. I've never done that. Listening to you today has made me realise how narrow my life has been. By choice, and I've been very happy, but now I think you are right—it's time I broadened my horizons.'

'Then we'll build that into our ending,' Daniel

said. ‘Though I don’t wish to talk about endings now, when we’ve only just begun.’ He turned towards her. ‘I was proud of you today, knowing how nervous you were. No one questioned our story. “We have other plans for this afternoon,”’ he teased, his tone ensuring there was no mistaking the innuendo. ‘Well played, Lady Elmswood. Perhaps you should consider a new life on the stage when you are done with playing this part.’

‘You seem very certain that I was acting.’

His smile dawned slowly. ‘I would be very happy to be proved wrong.’

She ought to be shocked at herself for being so brazen, but being this new, bold Kate excited her. She leaned into him, trailing her fingers down his cheek, then leaned closer again and pressed her mouth to his.

She heard the sharp intake of his breath as their lips met, had time to worry, when he hesitated, that she had been overly forward, then stopped thinking and started kissing.

Her eyes closed and she felt as if her whole body was melting into their kisses. Slow, gentle kisses becoming deeper kisses, the kind of kisses she hadn’t known existed, leading her from gentle pleasure to sweet, drugging delight, and then on to a new place, where kisses were not enough. She forgot where she was, she forgot who she was, only wanting more of this ache inside her that their kisses had triggered.

As if he read her mind Daniel cupped her breast, drawing a moan from her, making her nipples peak. He dragged his mouth from hers to kiss her throat, to kiss the exposed flesh at the neckline of her gown. She moaned again, but it still wasn't enough.

'Kate.' He gave her a tiny shake. 'We can't do this here.'

His eyes were dark, his pupils tiny, his cheeks flushed. *She* had done this to him. And she wanted to do more.

'It's Sunday,' she said, leaning back into him. 'No one will come.'

'I wouldn't be so sure about that,' Daniel muttered, his smile wicked.

'Truly, there's no one around…we are quite alone.'

For some reason her words made him laugh, but when she opened her mouth to ask him what was so amusing he kissed her again. They kissed until they were breathless, until the bench they were sitting on became too much of an obstacle for closeness, and then Daniel pulled her towards him, rucking up her skirts so that she could kneel astride him. And when their mouths met again, and she wrapped her arms around his neck, there was no distance between them, and she could feel him, hard and aroused, pressing between her legs, through his breeches and her petticoats, and the ache inside her became a craving, an irresistible urge to be even closer.

'Kate…' he said, as she wriggled closer. 'Dear Lord, have you any idea…?'

'Yes, I have,' she answered, because she could see the effect she was having, and feel it—both on Daniel and on her—and it filled her with such confidence and such strange, wicked joy to know that she could do this, she could have this. 'Yes…' she said again, in a different tone, with a different smile, and just as she'd hoped he kissed her again.

It was a different kiss, like a change in tone. And then there were more kisses, as his hands worked their magic on her breasts, on her nipples, and she lost herself in the sensations he was arousing, entranced, caught up in craving, in a driving need to reach a pleasurable conclusion.

When his hands left her breasts she moaned in protest—a moan that became a gasp as he slipped his hand between her legs. She swore, shocking herself, using a word she had never uttered, as he found the gap between her pantaloons and touched her.

'Sorry,' she muttered, and she felt his shoulders shake slightly in amusement, which eased her embarrassment, and then his touch made her forget everything again, save the need for completion.

His fingers slid over her. She was wet. And hot. And then they slid into her and she was tight. She could hear herself, panting, begging, rocking against his touch, arching her back, saying *yes, yes, yes*, as he stroked her and thrust into her and teased her. He was taking her to the edge of something, refusing to let her fall and tumble, and she had no idea what he was doing, knew only that she didn't want him to stop, that she couldn't take any more.

And at that point she jumped or fell or flew—she knew not which—crying out her astonished delight, feeling herself tightening around his fingers. She clutched his shoulders, then fell onto him, pressing kisses, wild indiscriminate kisses, over his face, panting his name, until gradually it eased, and then stopped.

Reluctantly, belatedly embarrassed, she eased

herself upright and met his gaze. 'I had no idea…' she mumbled dreamily.

He kissed her softly on the mouth. 'I know.'

'But *you* did?'

'Yes.' He frowned slightly. 'No. Not like that.'

He helped her upright, getting to his feet.

'What are you doing? Are we—? Shouldn't we—? What about…?'

He kissed her again, shaking his head. 'I think that's more than enough. It is for me. That's what's different.'

'You don't want to continue?'

He laughed at that. 'You must know perfectly well that I do. So much that I'm going to have to go for a swim. But—no, that was enough.'

'But…'

'Why rush towards the end when we can enjoy the journey?'

'That sounds to me like a quotation.'

'It is—very roughly translated, and from a very old book full of very interesting suggestions that I am hoping we can both enjoy in the weeks to come. If you like.'

His smile was wicked.

'I have no idea what you're talking about, but I am already pretty sure that I will like whatever it is,' Kate said.

Daniel laughed again. 'My wife is a temptress!'

'Am I? I rather like that notion.'

'And I am certain that you'll be very good at it.' He kissed her again, then turned her around, adjusting the neckline of her gown. 'But I really don't think we want anyone else to see how tempting you have been. Let me see if I can make you look a bit more respectable and myself a bit less like I have a limp.'

Daniel was just finishing his swim when Kate watched him from her bedroom window two days later, completing two more lazy laps before pulling himself onto the bank and draping his dressing gown around him. Looking up, he saw her, smiled and waved.

She tried not to spectate every morning, but she made no attempt to hide it when she did, and he always waved. Was he disappointed when she wasn't there? He seemed quite unembarrassed by his nakedness. But then he'd nothing to be embarrassed about.

Oliver appeared, wheeling his barrow on his way to either the rose garden or the walled garden, but Daniel, padding barefoot across the lawn, seemed not to notice him. She thought that she'd agreed with Oliver that he would start the week making the quarterly maintenance checks on the cottages at the east of the estate, but perhaps it was too early for him to make a start.

He wasn't wearing his shirt, but she didn't for a moment think, as Daniel did, that it was for *her* benefit. Not at this time in the morning. It was very hot, that was all. He was tanned, and there was no doubt that he had a very impressive physique, but, studying it objectively, Kate decided she preferred Daniel's sleeker, lither form.

If only *she* had a sleeker, lither form. Turning away from the window, Kate stood in front of the mirror, studying herself dispassionately. Her face was too tanned, and there were crows' feet at the corners of her eyes, but she could still pass for twenty-six—or seven at a push. She had none of the girls' carriage-stopping beauty, and she'd have liked better cheekbones, but on the whole it was a very acceptable face.

No, her face wasn't the problem.

Taking a deep breath, she pulled her nightgown over her head, and forced herself to look at her naked body. This was not something she had ever done consciously before, and it came as something of a shock. She was so pale. And very far from sleek! Without her corset, her breasts bounced! She hadn't realised that her hips flared out quite so much, and—dear heavens—were those dimples at the tops of her thighs? She leaned closer, and a soft roll of flesh appeared at her waist, so she stood up again immediately, pulling her tummy in, distracted by the way the action made her bosom stick out and made her waist seem much smaller. But that in turn made her hips look bigger.

Deciding that now she'd come this far she might as well know the worst, she turned sideways to look at her rear and was pleasantly surprised. A couple of dimples there, but actually quite a pleasing shape. At least she thought so.

What on earth would Daniel think?

She flushed all over—or so it felt—at the notion of Daniel seeing her naked. Would they have to be naked to make love? Even if they were, it would be dark, wouldn't it? People didn't make love in broad daylight. Or did they? So far every single kiss they had shared had been in broad daylight, and even in the walled garden, where they'd shared a great deal more than a kiss, she had remained fully clothed!

Kate turned from the mirror, pulling on her dressing gown. She didn't want to be fumbling about in the dark when they made love—*if* they made love—she wanted to see everything. Not only all of that sleek, muscled body, she wanted to see his face. She wanted to see the effect she was having on him. Seeing the effect she had on him was one of the most exciting aspects of making love. So far, at least.

She sank down on the bed, wrapping her arms around herself. Her body had started to—to thrum! Had it been a mistake to kiss Daniel at all? Before she had kissed him she'd had only vague notions of what she had been missing. Now she knew, what was she going to do when he was gone?

'For heaven's sake, Kate!'

Startling herself by speaking aloud, she laughed, gave herself a shake, and got up to set about finding some clothes. They had more than two months more to spend together. What she was feeling was far too urgent to last. She'd probably have had enough of him long before he left, though right at this moment she couldn't imagine that.

The more she knew of him, the more she wanted to know. Was it the fact that he was so determined not to be known that intrigued her—a question of her wanting what she couldn't have? They were married until death parted them, but he was her husband only until Sir Marcus summoned him. By autumn he would be gone, maybe even before. And then what would she do?

She would be alone at Elmswood for the first time in her life. How would she cope, going back to the previous incarnation of their marriage, writing Daniel tedious little summaries once every couple of months and getting a few lines back in return, if she was lucky? No, that was impossible. But what, then? There was no question of Daniel doing anything other than returning to foreign service—it was what he lived and breathed for—and no question, either, of her wishing any different, was there?

She would miss him. He was not easy company, but he was very good company. He had brought out a side of her that she hadn't known existed, and she liked the Kate she'd become. Unlike Daniel, she had no intentions of sloughing off that particular skin and starting again. But that was what she'd have to do, wasn't it? She couldn't imagine herself taking a lover. But nor could she imagine a life without any sort of lovemaking.

So what, then? So nothing—yet, she told herself impatiently. She and Daniel hadn't even made love properly. She might well be disappointed. Though, frankly, it was more likely he would be. And, even more frankly, after yesterday she doubted either of them would be, in which case she would spend the remainder of their faux honeymoon making hay!

Once she'd done that, then she would worry about the future. In the meantime, if she must worry about anything, she would think seriously about what Daniel would make of her thirty-three-year-old body…

Kate stopped in the act of pulling open her stocking drawer. Maybe a darkened room in the middle of the night wasn't such a bad idea after all.

'We should probably start to think about this garden party we're going to host,' Daniel said, pouring Kate's tea and passing her a plate of bread and butter. The bread was thinly cut, the butter spread carefully right up to the crust, just as she liked it. 'Make a list of people to invite,' he continued, 'think about hiring extra help, that kind of thing.'

His hair was damp from his swim. He was wearing one of his tunics and loose-fitting trousers, not silk this morning, but linen and, by the looks of it, undyed. He looked cool and comfortable and she was already hot, even though she was wearing one of her lightest muslin gowns. With a chemise and pantaloons and corset and petticoats—no wonder she was hot! Did Daniel have anything at all on under those two items of clothing?

'What is it?' he asked, looking amused.

'I don't know anything about men's undergarments,' Kate said, immediately covering her hand with her mouth, appalled to have spoken her thoughts. 'I mean—I was thinking that they are very different from the female kind.'

'I know.'

'Daniel!' Kate set down her teacup, spluttering with laughter. 'This is not a fit topic for the breakfast table.'

'You brought it up, and now that you have I have lost all interest in making lists for a garden party I'd rather not host in the first place.'

'I brought it up only because I was thinking how delightful and cooling it would be to dress as you do, without all my petticoats and such.'

'It's the "and such" that interests me.' He propped his chin onto his hand, smiling mischievously. 'Tell me more.'

She folded her lips together, trying not to laugh. 'I will do no such thing.'

'Then I suppose we had better get on with drawing up a guest list.'

'Must we? I'm not in the least bit inclined to spend my day planning a party that no one is much interested in my attending. You're the one they're interested in. I think I'll affect a headache that day.'

'Kate, you don't imagine for a moment that I *enjoyed* all that fawning and naked curiosity at church, do you?'

'No, of course I don't, and I am certainly not saying that I wanted to be fawned over and interrogated either, but it has made me think quite seriously about the future. I have never had only myself to consider, and I want to be able to do just that. I don't want to be alone, but I don't want the kind of company who cares only for my position in society—or for the man I'm married to, for that matter.'

'Which would be pointless, since I won't be here.'

'I know that, but they don't yet. And that's another thing. I like you being here, Daniel, and I'm not sure I'll want to remain here when you're gone.'

'Kate, you know…'

'I know you're going. Don't worry. I am not

going to fall on my knees and beg you to stay just because we have shared a few kisses, delightful as they were. We've lived apart for eleven years perfectly happily. Unlike you, I have no idea what the next eleven years hold for me, but I do know that the last thing I want is to chain you to my side here at Elmswood. I'm not even sure I want to remain chained here myself all of the time—and don't ask me what I mean by that, because I've no idea.'

'Very well, I won't ask you. Shall we be self-indulgent and forget all about the world and the future for today?'

'I think that is a capital idea. I would like that very much.'

'What would you like to do?'

She pretended to consider this, but in reality indulged in the pleasure of simply looking at him and enjoying the effect she had on him when she looked at him in a certain way. His wife the temptress, he'd called her. She liked that.

'I've been thinking about what you said yesterday,' Kate said. 'About enjoying the journey.'

He inhaled sharply as she leaned closer, so that their lips were only inches apart. 'I do hope this means you're going to indulge me by returning to the subject of your underclothes.'

She gasped, laughed, leaned closer. 'In a way. This journey…does it take place in daylight or under cover of darkness?'

'An intriguing question. There's certainly a place for darkness. When you can't see, you are forced to rely on your other senses,' Daniel said, taking her hand, running his fingers over her knuckles. 'Touch, obviously.' He turned her hand over, pressing a kiss to her wrist. 'And taste. But when you're just starting out on the journey, as we are, I think it's best to be able to see.'

'That's what I thought, but—but I'm not sure I want you to see me naked.'

'That's a bit rich, given you have been sneaking a glance at me most mornings in just such a state of undress.'

'It's not a subject I enjoy being teased about.' Kate pulled her hand away.

'I'd just like to understand what it is that you're worried about,' Daniel saud gently. 'I haven't had the pleasure of seeing very much of your delightful body, Kate, but…'

'No one has ever seen it,' she snapped. 'Not even me, not really…until this morning. And I wish I hadn't looked now, because—oh, this is too embarrassing. You are so—so—and I am so— I wobble! Don't laugh at me.'

'I'm not. I am fascinated by the idea of you wobbling.'

Despite herself, she laughed. 'Well, I would prefer not to. I wish I looked more like you.'

'I am extremely glad you do not.'

'Daniel! It is the swimming, I suppose, that makes you so…'

'Lacking in wobble? The swimming helps with my stamina, but it's my daily yoga practice which keeps me fit in mind and body.'

'Your daily *what* practice?'

'Yoga,' Daniel said, enunciating the word carefully. 'It's a discipline I learnt in India—a system of poses and stretches, combined with breathing exercises which are supposed to keep the body and mind in balance.'

'I've never heard of such a thing. I don't think I even understand what you mean.'

'Would you like to learn?'

'Are you teasing me?'

'I've never tried to teach anyone. In fact I don't think I've ever discussed the practice with anyone before,' Daniel said, sounding defensive.

'Are you sworn to secrecy?'

He laughed. 'No. You don't have to join one of those pathetic secret clubs that men are so fond of, if that's what you are imagining. It's private, that's all, and something I choose to keep to myself.'

'Then I'm honoured. And I would like to try, though I'm not sure I'll be any good,' Kate said. 'Or what I should wear.'

Daniel grinned. 'Ah, that brings us back nicely to the subject of your undergarments. You cannot practice yoga in a corset, and I am not at all sure that a dress would be a good idea either. Would you like to try a tunic and trousers?'

'Wear your clothes?'

'Well, not these precise ones. Sylvia will be in to collect the dishes in a moment, and I don't think I want to risk her finding me naked.'

'Daniel!'

'Kate!' He got up from the table, holding out his hand. 'Well, are you up for the challenge?'

She let him pull her to her feet. 'Where shall we go?'

'We need somewhere with a good amount of space, where Sylvia isn't likely to disturb us.'

'There's the music room,' Kate said. 'You probably remember it as the billiard room, but I'm afraid I had the table dismantled and removed to the village hall, where it has proved very popular. I have never played, and the girls showed no interest, and for some reason the acoustics in that room are perfect for the pianoforte, or so Estelle says. I hope you don't mind?'

'Why should I? I'm not in the least bit interested in billiards. It sounds ideal. Come upstairs and I'll find you some suitable clothes. You can change and then I'll meet you there.'

# *Chapter Seven*

The billiard room faced out to the working gardens of Elmswood, with a view to the stables, the kitchen garden and the outhouses, behind which lay the Estate Office. Daniel pulled the shutters over, having no desire to have Kate's precious gardener witness their actions. The man was doubtless a green-fingered genius, but he had the irritating habit of being a constant presence, appearing on the lawn every morning at precisely the time that Daniel was either preparing to swim or finishing his swim.

There was enough sunlight filtering in through the shutters to make the room dim, but not dark. Estelle's pianoforte stood against one wall, with a circle of chairs around it for her audience. She was shy about her music, he remembered Kate saying in one of her letters, and never played for strangers, though she could occasionally be tempted to play the organ in the church.

The chairs he now moved aside were an odd assortment, chosen for comfort. Aside from the oak panelling, there was none of the gentleman's club type of furnishings he vaguely recalled from his father's day, and not a trace of that distinctive smell of snuff and brandy which lingered after he had enjoyed a game of billiards with friends. The room smelled of roses—a scent he traced to an onyx dish of dried petals on the mantelpiece. He picked up a handful, inhaling the heady fragrance, reminded of a *hamam* he had once visited and the scented oils they'd used there.

The door closed gently. He let the petals fall and turned round. Kate was standing just inside the room, her arms wrapped protectively around herself. She had rolled and pinned his white silk trouser legs, revealing her bare ankles and dainty feet. She had tied a wide blue sash around her waist and rolled up the sleeves of his tunic to her elbows, making his austere clothing look absurdly feminine and Kate herself, with her hair down and tied back, distractingly alluring, as if she were dressed for bed.

'I managed to avoid being seen,' she said, still hovering at the door.

Realising that any compliment would make her even more self-conscious than she already was, Daniel concentrated on making her feel at ease. 'Lock the door, just to be on the safe side,' he said, 'then come over and join me. I'm glad you dispensed with your shoes. You can find your balance better without them.'

'I feel odd. I'm not used to wearing so little, or to being so unconstrained.'

Manfully, he refused to allow his eyes to wander to her un-corseted bosom. 'Forget about what you're wearing. Concentrate on being able to move freely. Now, stand very still, shoulders back, arms at your side, and we'll start with some simple breathing exercises.'

'Enough,' Kate said, flopping onto her tummy and gasping for breath. 'I can't do any more.'

Beside her, Daniel was still in that odd pose, his body held in a rigidly straight line by his elbows and his toes, and not in the least out of breath.

'Well done,' he said, pushing himself upright to sit cross-legged in one fluid movement. 'You have a natural balance. It took me days of practice before I could hold some of those poses.'

'You're being kind.' She heaved herself up,

and managed with some ungainly floundering to place herself in approximately the same pose. He looked relaxed and comfortable. She, on the other hand, felt awkward and sore.

'Did you enjoy it?' he asked.

'I did—though I suspect I would give you a different answer if you asked me tomorrow morning. I will almost certainly feel as if I have been stretched on a rack. Who would have thought that balancing and breathing could be so difficult? Is my face red? And my hair—I must look a fright.'

'You look delightfully rumpled.'

Kate giggled. 'You look as if you've barely been tested.'

'I've been practising for more than ten years.'

'So what can an expert of ten years do that I cannot?'

'A handstand?'

'Will you show me?'

Daniel rolled forward onto his hands, then slowly, and with complete control, raised his legs over his head. Kate watched, enthralled, as he held the pose for a few seconds, then moved into a series of other moves which flowed like a dance, each one controlled, deliberate, graceful. His face was quite blank, his eyes focused inwards. His tunic rolled back, exposing a taut belly, and the muscles clearly defined beneath his smooth, lightly tanned skin. He ended the sequence on his feet, taking one of the controlled breaths he had taught her, then opened his eyes, smiling sheepishly.

'That was like a ballet.'

Daniel laughed. 'It's supposed to be fluid. I have to confess to showing off a little.'

'I have to confess to enjoying every moment. How have you managed such a transformation in a matter of weeks since your illness?'

'Hard work, and the fact that I managed to maintain my practice routine for much of the time I was in captivity.'

'But you were manacled. I saw the marks.'

'Where there's a will there's a way.' He dropped onto the floor beside her.

'Are you really as fully recovered as you seem to be? I thought it would take you much longer to regain your strength. You were as weak as a kitten a few short weeks ago.'

'I realise that. And I'm not entirely free of the effects of my ordeal. I get severe attacks of pins and needles in my feet, and there are times when I wake up convinced that I still have manacles around my ankles. I expect I'll suffer from occasional bouts of the ague for the rest of my life, but it won't kill me. I'm lucky to be in such good health, and I'm extremely lucky to have had you as a nurse.' He reached for her hand. 'I owe you a great deal.'

'You've said thank you, and I've told you there's no need. I only did what any wife would do.'

'No, you seriously underestimate yourself. I have had a very brief account from Sir Marcus of what you went through. He praised your resourcefulness and your courage, which amounts to an admission that you were tested above and beyond the call of duty—wifely or otherwise.'

'I did what was necessary, that's all, Daniel.'

'You're uncomfortable with praise. Your little toes are curling. So I won't say any more, except that you are an extraordinary woman and I'm very lucky to have you as my wife.' He kissed her hand. 'Thank you.'

She had never heard him sound so sincere. For a moment, when their eyes met, she caught a glimpse of a very different Daniel, a man who cared, and, oddly, she wanted to cry. But then he let her hand go, getting effortlessly to his feet, pulling her with him, smiling at her in quite a different way.

'I didn't know my simple garments would look so good on you.'

She dropped a mock curtsey, then groaned. 'Ouch.'

'You need a hot bath,' Daniel said. 'I don't suppose that's possible?'

'Only if I divert both the kitchen maid and chambermaid from their other tasks and commandeer all the hot water from the kitchen for the next two hours, thus preventing Cook from doing her work too. Shall I go and jump in the lake instead?'

'It would be the perfect solution—if you could swim. Why are English country houses so primitive? It should be possible, in this day and age, to have hot water more readily available.'

'I have seen some patented bathing apparatus advertised, which claims to be able to fill a bath at the turn of a valve.'

'In Arabia and in Turkey they have something called a *hamam*, which is a steam bath—or rather a series of baths, rather like the Roman model. There are different days set aside for men and women, and you can spend the entire day there.'

'An entire day devoted to bathing!'

'Bathing in hot and cold water, steaming,

having a massage, taking tea, having your body oiled. Don't wrinkle your nose—it's extremely relaxing and it would ease all the aches and pains in your poor muscles.'

'So you've been to Turkey? Would Sir Marcus add a week to your sentence if he knew you'd admitted that to me?'

'Sir Marcus thinks you are eminently trustworthy. I wouldn't be surprised if he didn't try to recruit you, he thinks so highly of you.'

'If he sent me to Turkey then I would try one of those *hamam* baths. I like the sound of them. I feel as if my body has toothache.'

'Would you like a massage? I could give you one.'

He was not quite smiling, but there was that wicked look in his eyes that dared her to accept and made her body throb in a very different way.

'Would it make me feel better?'

'I think it would help us both.'

One of the benefits of living in a house with so few servants, Daniel thought as he rummaged through his travel trunk, was knowing their routine. Sylvia, for example, always made the beds first thing, straight after collecting the breakfast dishes, and would have no reason to come upstairs for the remainder of the day.

Kate knew that as well as he did, but she was perched nervously on the single chair in his room, eyeing the door as if the maid might burst through it at any moment.

He found what he was looking for and set it down on the bedside table before turning the key in the lock. 'Now we won't be disturbed.'

'But what if she has forgotten something? She'll think it very strange...'

'That Lady Elmswood is in her husband's bedchamber while the pair of them are on their honeymoon?'

'Lady Elmswood would not have spent the last two hours contorting her body into poses it is not designed to contort into while wearing her husband's clothes.'

'No, that was most definitely Kate. I infinitely prefer Kate. She is decidedly unconventional.'

'I'm not, Daniel. I am tediously conventional.'

He laughed softly. 'So tediously conventional that you asked me to marry you.'

'That was different.'

'No, *you're* different. You still have no idea how extraordinarily brave you were, coming to rescue me...'

'I didn't rescue you. I simply nursed you, and then dragged you back here against your will to recuperate.'

'There you are—that alone is evidence of how extraordinary you are.'

'You were too weak to resist.'

'It's true. I do find you quite irresistible.'

'When I am red in the face and my hair is a tangle and I'm wearing men's clothes?'

'Especially then.' He pulled her to her feet, wrapping his arms around her, resting his chin in the wild tangle of her soft blonde hair. 'You see, you're not the only one who is unconventional.'

She put her arms around his waist, nestling closer to him, and his body responded instantly. He didn't remember ever being so responsive to a woman, but it had been so long—perhaps that was why his desire for Kate was so strong.

It was suddenly urgently necessary that he kiss her. He said her name and she lifted her face, smiling up at him in a way that left him in no doubt that she wanted to kiss him too. He moaned softly as their lips met and their tongues touched. Only two thin layers of fabric lay between them. He could feel the press of her breasts against his chest, the heat of her skin as he slid his hands down to cup her bottom, feel how hard he was already, pressing against her belly.

Dragging his mouth away, taken aback by the strength of his desire for her, putting that too down to abstinence, Daniel was distracted by the corresponding blaze of heat in her eyes. Also due to abstinence—a lifetime of abstinence, he reminded himself. She deserved better than a hard, quick—

*Dear God, don't think like that.*

'Ready?' he asked her.

Her laugh was husky. 'I think I have made that clear enough.'

Which made it impossible not to kiss her again, cupping her breasts this time, feeling her nipples harden at his touch, feeling himself get painfully hard as she slid her hands under his tunic to touch his bare skin.

He undid the sash she had tied around her waist and then started on the row of buttons, aware of her watching him, tensing as he undid the last button, but making no attempt to stop him when he pulled the tunic apart. Her skin was so pale. Her nipples were dark, hard peaks begging for attention. He took one in his mouth, heard her soft, delightful sigh, and it almost overset him—hearing her breath catch in her throat, knowing that if he touched her now, slipped his hand between her legs, she would climax quickly and he could be inside her…

It took a Herculean effort to stop. They gazed at each other, breathing heavily. Half-dazed, he led her over to the freshly made bed, over which he had spread a fresh bathing sheet, indicating that she lie crossways on her tummy, helping her to remove the tunic when she did.

'Kate…' He whispered her name simply for the sake of saying it.

There was no one like her—this combination of trust and innocence and experience. She wanted him, she made no attempt to hide that, and she trusted him completely to please her and to do her no harm.

He longed to please her. It almost stopped him in his tracks, the strength of his longing, and set alarm bells clanging. But he stilled them. Because he didn't want to listen, and because he had already reassured himself that it was nothing…nothing more than the sum total of their current circumstances.

Their circumstances were extraordinary, and soon they would change. But he didn't want to think of the time when it would be over. All he was interested in right now was Kate. Pleasing Kate. Who looked so delightful, spread half-naked on his bed. With the curve of her spine, the indent of her waist, the swell of her bottom barely concealed in his own silk trousers.

He picked up the glass vial of oil and warmed it between his hands. He swept the fall of her hair away, leaned over, and began the massage, working along her shoulders first, which would be painful from the poses he'd led her through. His own tunic was an unnecessary barrier. He cast it off, then spread her legs very slightly so he could lean closer, his bare chest brushing her back. Her hands were stretched up, under his pillow. He kissed the nape of her neck. She whimpered.

He put more oil on his hands and began to work down the knots of her spine, then over her sides, up to the flattened curve of her breasts, down, shaping the indent of her waist, feeling the softness of her belly, which she tensed at his touch.

The trousers were held in place by a cord. He undid it.

'Kate?'

There was a second's hesitation, and then a muffled 'yes'. He eased the trousers down, pulling her towards him so that he now stood between her legs, his breath coming fast as he feasted his eyes on her bottom, dimpled, begging for his touch. The soft, yielding flesh set him on fire. The responsive arch of her back when he stroked her made his member throb. He worked the oil into the creases at the tops of her legs, working down one thigh to her calf, her ankle, her foot, then back up the other leg.

She was moving restlessly on the bed. He would slide so easily into her, and she would welcome the release of their bodies finally uniting, but this was Kate and he wanted to give her more.

Easing her onto her back, he was once again almost overset by the sight of her, eyes dark with passion, her nipples hard nubs, the curls between her legs so much darker than her blonde hair, revealing the hot, wet, inviting centre of her. He used the bath sheet to pull her towards him, then leaned over to kiss her, his mouth on her mouth, his chest brushing her breasts, the aching hardness between his legs sheathed only in his trousers, pressing against the hot dampness between hers.

She wrapped her arms around him, tilted instinctively against him, but he gently disentangled himself to kiss his way down her body until his mouth covered her sex.

'Daniel!'

He licked her, aroused even more, if that was possible, by the scent of her and the taste of her and the heat of her.

'Daniel…' she said, but now it was a plea, and he had reached the limits of his own self-control.

Using his tongue and his hands, relishing every moment, he was urgent, in an agony of needing, wanting, lost in a way he never had been, in the need to be inside her.

She came quickly, crying out, panting his name, bucking under him, then pushing herself up on the bed to wrap her arms around his neck, kissing him feverishly with abandon.

'Hurry,' she said, and he didn't give a damn whether she knew what she was asking or not.

Yanking at the cord which tied his trousers, kicking them away, he was panting and groaning like a wild beast as his agonisingly engorged shaft brushed the damp heat between her legs.

'Daniel…' Kate said, twining her legs around his waist.

If he hadn't known better, he'd have thought she knew precisely what she was doing, but he did know better, and he found it in him—just—to stop himself from thrusting hard and deep.

'Kate?'

'Don't stop.'

'No. Yes. Kate, are you sure?'

She laughed, pulling his face towards her for a deep, slow kiss. 'What do you think?'

He stopped thinking. He pushed into her and he was lost. Pushing higher, he let his eyes clash with Kate's and their gazes held. It was written clear on her face, every move he made, and when he reached the top and held her, and she tightened around him, he knew that his feelings for her were written on *his* face, and he didn't give a damn about anything except this perfect, silent communion of two people truly becoming one.

He began to move and she followed him, so that they quickly found a rhythm, his thrusts and her tightening matched by their breaths, becoming frantic as he thrust harder, faster, their gazes fixed on each other, their bodies locked, until she cried out, a warning he only just heeded, pulling himself free of her just in time before his own climax took him, shaking him to the core, racking him with pleasure.

Clinging to her, heedless of anything save the need not to let her go, he was soothed by her hand on the back of his head, by her saying his name, by the soft kisses she pressed to his mouth, by the feeling, when it was over, that the world had been turned inside out.

For long, timeless moments afterwards Kate was utterly lost in the pleasure of what had just occurred. Nothing had prepared her for this feeling that she was floating blissfully, that she was alone in a world that contained just herself and Daniel.

He rolled over onto the bed, pulling her with him, and they lay completely naked in broad daylight. Her head was on his shoulder, their legs were tangled together, her hand was flat on the expanse of his chest. The hair was rough, but his skin was smooth. She could feel his heartbeat slowing, feel her own doing the same. In the shaft of sunlight coming through the open window she could see dust motes dancing. She felt alive, her blood zinging in her veins as if she could do another hour of yoga and hold every pose. She was energised and yet completely at peace. This was what had been missing in her life.

At the exact moment this ominous thought made her heart skip a beat Daniel sat up. 'This was a mistake.'

'What?' Kate pushed herself upright.

Daniel was already off the bed, grabbing his crimson dressing gown and throwing it at her. 'Put that on.' Turning away from her, he pulled on his own tunic and trousers.

Bewildered, every bit as much by the change in him as by the clamouring of her own feelings and the warning bells in her head, Kate wrestled with the folds of fabric, stumbling from the bed and pulling the dressing gown around her as Daniel turned away.

'Why are you being like this? Are you saying you regret what happened?'

'I don't know what we were thinking, behaving like a couple of love-struck newlyweds,' he snapped. 'No! Kate, I didn't mean that. I'm so sorry.'

Tears smarted in her eyes, but when he made to touch her she pushed him away. He immediately took a step back.

'You felt it too,' he said bleakly.

'I don't know. Yes, if you mean that we were—as if I had been waiting for you all my life, I suppose—isn't it always like that?'

'No.'

'What happened, Daniel? Could it be that we have not—I mean because I have never made love and you cannot have made love for a long time—could it be that?'

'It's what I thought at first.'

'It felt perfectly natural…as if we were made for each other, Daniel.'

'Don't!' He paced over to the window, leaning his shoulders against the shutters. 'Perhaps it's a bit like the effect of yoga. Our minds and our bodies are attuned to each other. We've spent a great deal of time in each other's company, almost exclusively in each other's company, and we have been through a—a traumatic experience. I've had a close brush with mortality and you witnessed it. That combination would certainly explain the strength of our feelings. But it can't be allowed to happen again.'

He made no pretence of not having felt something profound, Kate noted bleakly. If he had pretended, would it have been worse or better? She didn't want this to be her one and only experience of real lovemaking, but her instinct told her that it would be a huge mistake to make love to Daniel again.

'Do you agree, Kate?'

She did, though she wasn't entirely convinced by his explanation, and it irked her, his determination to deny feeling anything for anyone.

'You don't think that it might be a simple case of us having inadvertently fallen in love? Fiction becoming truth?'

She had the small satisfaction of his looking as if she had slapped him. But only for a second.

'This is not a time for jokes. For a start, a person doesn't just fall in love without realising it.'

His dismissive tone served to rile her. 'I don't believe it's something one can make a conscious decision about, Daniel.'

'One *can*, however, make a conscious decision not to fall in love. Ever.'

'Or not to love at all. Ever. As you have.'

He flinched, but did not look away. 'As I have. And you know why.'

The fight went out of her. She shivered, unable to believe that only a few moments ago she had been in the throes of ecstasy. She would be a complete fool to allow any feelings she had for this cold-hearted man to rule her—and she wasn't even sure what those feelings were. She had her whole life before her, and it was entirely hers to do with as she saw fit. She was not going to spend it pining for a man who refused to give a damn about anything. Save his work.

'We have just over two months to get through,' Kate said, 'and, thanks to you and Sir Marcus, we have a party to host and a role as the honeymooning Lord and Lady Elmswood to play out. Perhaps we should have our quarrel sooner rather than later.'

'Don't be like that, Kate.'

'What would you prefer me to be like, Daniel? I'm not like you. I can't just close the door on one life because it's served its purpose and walk away. I'm not playing a part.'

'I was not acting when we— You can't imagine *that* was acting?'

'No, I don't. I think it was one of the rare occasions when you were yourself. But it's over now, isn't it? We don't want any feelings that Daniel or Kate might have to get in the way of your marvellous career and your wonderful other life.'

'This isn't worthy of you.'

'No, it's not. But I've never been in this situation, so you'll have to bear with me.'

'I'm sorry.' Once again he moved towards her, but he took only one step. She had no need to ward him off. 'We both need some time to restore our equilibrium.'

'If by that you mean we both need time alone to reflect, then I agree. I'll see you later.'

Kate unlocked the door and made her way

hurriedly to her own room. Only when she threw herself on the bed and caught herself listening did she realise she was waiting, hoping for him to come after her.

She rolled over, pulling the pillow over her head, and burst into tears.

In the library, later that day, Daniel could not concentrate on any of the books he had picked out to read. Dammit, why had he not foreseen this eventuality? But why should he have? It had never happened before.

Because he'd never met anyone like Kate before.

Distracted, he fell into a reverie, replaying every moment of their lovemaking that morning. It was the way she looked at him, looked *right* at him, as if she saw something no one else ever had. That was the worst thing. And also the best thing.

'Dammit!'

His instinct was to run, but he couldn't run. He was trapped here until Sir Marcus released him. And he didn't want to go—not yet. Somehow, without realising, he had started counting on having three full months with Kate, and he still wanted every day of them. Though at the same time he wanted to close the door on what had happened, forget about Elmswood, make a fresh start.

Without Kate? Without ever seeing Kate again?

The thought actually made him feel physically sick.

Decisive action—that was what was required. He would write to his lawyer, find out who, if he died today, would inherit all Kate's hard work, and then make sure that they did not. That ought to make him feel better, but it didn't.

Pacing the room, he stubbed his toe on the library steps. His own fault for not folding them up. After Kate had moved them here from the morning room he'd found them neatly folded every morning, for the first two or three mornings. Just to be contrary, if not downright petty, he'd made a point of unfolding them. So she'd stopped folding them away. Now she had inadvertently made her point. He'd tell her so. She'd appreciate that.

No, perhaps not.

He tried to picture Kate in a half-made gown, standing patiently on the top step while her gown was pinned, though he couldn't picture the niece doing the pinning. Eloise? She was the dressmaker.

They all had red hair, Gillian's girls, and according to Kate they were beautiful. As their mother had been.

He had not thought of Gillian in years—until he had become imprisoned here. She had already effectively been dead to him when news of her drowning had reached him. Now, once again, despite his best efforts, he was being dragged back into the past, to the life he had walked away from, and to the person he was determined he'd never be again.

Exasperated, Daniel pulled the steps over to the corner bookshelf. There was a book somewhere on the top shelf, he dimly recalled, about Ancient Egypt. It might inspire him to invent some artefacts for his explorer alter ego to boast about at the garden party they had not yet arranged. It was a folio edition, so it must be one of those lying in a stack on their sides.

He ran his finger down the spines. The Egyptian book was at the bottom. He tried to pull it out, but the other books came with it and went crashing to the floor. Instinctively, he moved, almost overbalancing, clutching just in time at the shelf.

And then he remembered it happening before—just like this. Save that *he* had fallen that time, tumbling to the floor along with the books. He could see his much younger self right there on the floor, laughing despite the jarring thud of his landing. Leo was there, laughing too, dusting him down. And then the door opened and his father came in.

Daniel frowned over at the door, but he couldn't remember what had happened next. Picking up the volumes, he set the Egyptian book down on a table and returned the rest to the top shelf.

It was nothing more than a stray memory, triggered by the act of retrieving a book, but it had decided him. What happened today had been a warning. No matter how he tried to disguise it, attribute it to compatibility or blame it on his brush with mortality, his feelings for Kate already ran too deep—and, even worse than that, he knew she felt the same for him.

No wonder his prosaic explanation had hurt her. A person could choose not to fall in love, he'd said, and he believed that. They were not in love, the pair of them—not yet. And he had to ensure they didn't tumble over the precipice.

A brief trip to the past would cure him of any inclination to do that. It would be painful, but it would be well worth it.

## *Chapter Eight*

It was late afternoon when Kate returned from the Estate Office, where she had singularly failed to distract herself with work and had spent most of the afternoon gazing into space, alternately reliving that morning's encounter and trying to imagine how she and Daniel were going to navigate the next two months.

En route to her bedchamber, to freshen up, she reached the top of the stairs—and gave a squeal of surprise when Daniel appeared at the door of the master suite.

'Kate. I've been waiting for you. Will you come in? I'd like to talk to you.'

'What about?'

'Myself,' he said, drawing from her a wry look.

She allowed him to usher her in, then made

for the window seat, which stretched across the embrasure of the three central windows, where he joined her, though he did not sit down.

'I'd forgotten how much better the view is from up here,' he said. 'You can see into the kitchen garden and the rose garden as well as down to the lake.'

'It's because it's built out above the drawing room, while the rooms on either side are set slightly back.'

'I know.'

'Yes, of course you do.'

'You're wondering what I'm doing here.'

'I can only presume you have finally decided to view your sister's portrait. Is it a good likeness?'

She waited for him to shrug, but instead he sat down beside her. He was wearing a fresh tunic and trousers in black silk.

'It has captured her very well,' he said. 'It used to hang in my father's study. After Gillian ran off it vanished. I assumed he'd destroyed it. Are the girls very like her?'

'Phoebe is her image. Estelle's beauty is even more striking, if that is possible, though she'd hate me saying so. And Eloise is a…a slightly muted version—though that doesn't mean she is not extremely beautiful. But it can't be denied that when she is beside the twins, it is easy to overlook her.'

'Gillian would not have appreciated her daughters outshining her. She had to be the sole focus of attention in every room she walked into. Even I fell under her spell.'

'You were a little boy and, from what you've told me, starved of affection. So I'm not surprised.'

'You make me sound like a stray kitten.' Daniel grimaced. 'I suppose that is an apt description. The runt that no one wanted, that everyone thought too weak to survive.'

'Don't say that.'

'It's the truth. When she eloped, my father purged this place of any trace of her. I was forbidden to mention her name, all her possessions were destroyed—it was as if he had never had a daughter—and I was banished, for my part in her fall from grace. I was sent to school—which should have been a small victory for me, but was an absolute disaster.'

Daniel had been gazing at his sister's portrait, but now his expression was quite blank, his tone equally so. It made Kate's spine tingle. She had no idea why he was confiding in her like this, volunteering such deeply personal and painful memories, but she sensed the reason was ominous.

She wanted to comfort him, to hold his hand, to tell him to stop, because she knew it hurt him, but she didn't dare interrupt. So she waited, silently, until he spoke again.

'I was ten years old and Elmswood formed the boundaries of my world. I'd never had friends, I'd no experience of what they call the rough and tumble of life at such a school. Can you imagine—? No, I don't suppose you can. In plain terms, I was bullied, ostracised and humiliated. No, don't, Kate. Let me speak.'

With difficulty, she did as he bade her, biting back her indignant exclamations and protests. 'Go on.'

'I could either sink or swim. I chose to swim—though against the tide, not with it. I threw myself into my studies—Classics and languages—and I took up athletics. But I wouldn't play their stupid ball games, I wouldn't acknowledge the strict hierarchy that matters so much in those places, and I duly paid the price.'

'Daniel! I'm sorry, but that is awful.'

'It served to toughen me up. I relied on no one but myself. I learned how to put on a front.

I learned not to care. All lessons that stood me in good stead later. I got by for the better part of four years. I was lonely, but I grew accustomed to that too. I thought I preferred being alone. And then Leo arrived at the school.'

'The Classics tutor you mentioned?'

He took his turquoise amulet from his pocket and began to turn it over in his hands. 'He was my tutor, but he also became my friend—my only friend. For that last year at school I was happy. Leo and I planned to visit the ancient sites of Greece and Italy one day. He was as eager as I was to explore the world of antiquity. Then I made the mistake of inviting him to Elmswood for the summer, and my father hated Leo from the first. He saw that I was happy, and he set about destroying that happiness. Leo left suddenly one day, under a cloud, and I was removed from school—presumably so I couldn't have any further contact with him.'

'What happened to provoke such an extreme reaction in your father? It had to be more than jealousy or a desire to thwart you.'

For the first time Daniel looked agitated. 'I can't remember.' He jumped to his feet. 'My father must have had serious words with Leo—some sort of argument, I presume. He refused to discuss it with me, so I don't know what triggered it. All he would say was that he wouldn't tolerate my having such a friend. And as for Leo—he didn't answer my letters. I never saw him again.'

'And that's when you joined the Admiralty?'

Daniel sat down again and put his turquoise back in his pocket.

'My father decided I needed to pay a suitable penance for blotting my copybook a second time and proving to be a sore disappointment to him. He reckoned consigning me to shuffle papers closeted away in Admiralty House for a few years might teach me a bit of a lesson. But after two years I was thoroughly bored, and I had worked out that no matter how many papers I shuffled I'd never be good enough for him. So I volunteered to sail with an expedition sponsored by Joseph Banks and the Royal Society. The perfect opportunity, you'd have thought, to make a man of a so-called insipid eighteen-year-old with no experience of the world. But naturally my father objected. Having lost one child to foreign climes, he wished to keep the other close to home and under his wing.'

'That implies protectiveness, but it sounds more like wanting to control your every move,'

Kate said. 'I can't believe all this was playing out while I was growing up on your doorstop. I had no idea.'

'Fortunately for me Sir Marcus stepped in, persuading him that my duty to King and country required me to sail, and so I sailed. Though I had no idea at the time, he'd been keeping an eye on me, and had seen evidence of the particular qualities he required in anyone serving in his field. He wished to test my suitability, without either myself or my father being aware that he was doing so. When I returned, three years later, I had clearly passed the test, since he offered me my first active role. And the rest, as they say, is history.'

A great deal more history than Daniel had ever revealed before, Kate thought, struggling to assimilate all that he'd told her.

'Did your father know, then, that you were not really an explorer?'

'Oh, yes, he knew. And he knew too, that when I left I had no intention of returning.'

'You wished him to disinherit you. You told me that when I proposed. But he didn't.'

Daniel smiled grimly. 'Between us, you and I thwarted his plan to put me back in my place. By then I'd found my own niche, and I was determined, as you know, not to give it up. Not ever.'

Her stomach sank. This, then, was the point of his confession. 'It means everything to you, your work? More than anything?'

'I'm sorry, Kate, but it does.'

'Don't be sorry. You have made it clear from the start—when we married—and consistently since you arrived here. This morning gave me no expectations.'

His hand sought hers. 'I know that. What happened this morning took us both by surprise.'

'But it changes nothing. That's what you're essentially saying, isn't it?' Kate shifted out of his reach.

'My missions tend to last a year—sometimes less, rarely more. I have no time to make friends, no time to become embroiled with anyone, and I like it that way. I prefer it that way. That last mission was the longest time I've ever spent in one place. Looking back, I see that it was far too long. It left me open to becoming more embroiled than was healthy.'

'So you are determined not to get "embroiled", as you put it, with me,' Kate said.

'I'm choosing not to. It would be a mistake. I know myself very well. I know that I thrive on being alone, being my own man, answerable to no one. I don't want to settle down. I doubt I *could* settle even if I wanted to. I am trying to be very honest with you. The life I have chosen for myself is the only one I want, and one perfectly suited to me. There is no room for anyone else in that life. Do you understand now?'

'Perfectly.'

'I know I've hurt you…'

'You give yourself too much credit. I am not in love with you, Daniel, and nowhere close to falling for you. I am not going to waste my time or my affections on a man who has made it crystal-clear he doesn't want either.'

'Kate…'

'No, you've had your say, now let me have mine.'

She took a breath, trying to quell her outrage and hurt, to think logically, to speak rationally, knowing that he would discount anything else.

'I am touched by what you've told me, and honoured that you have confided in me, and I do understand, fully, how much the life you have chosen matters to you. Your sister— Oh, who knows, Daniel, if she ever thought of you or considered getting in touch with you? Did she know you had been sent off to school? Probably not.

Would she have written to you there? You were ten…she was nineteen, recently married, in a strange country, cut off entirely from her family. I reckon she'd have had more than enough to contend with, don't you?'

She waited, receiving a non-committal shrug in response, but she was not fooled. He was listening.

'And as for your father—the man you knew doesn't square with what I remember of him, which admittedly is very little. If he really did adore Gillian, martinet or not, he must have been devastated by her elopement, and likely he saw it, rather than as her staking a claim to her own life, as trampling on the one he had given her. The purge of all her belongings—that's not the act of someone who doesn't care. Did she write to him? Probably. Did he forgive her? No. There were no second chances with him.'

Her fists clenched involuntarily.

'But that's not his biggest crime, as far as I am concerned. What is worse by far is that he punished the innocent for his own selfishness and terrible indulgence. He punished *you*, sending you away, and he punished his grandchildren, by refusing to acknowledge them, denying them a family and the sanctuary here that they were in dire need of.'

She unfurled her fists and made a conscious effort to mellow her tone.

'And he kept them from you too, Daniel. He didn't even tell you that you had a nephew and three nieces.'

'If you are imagining that I would have leapt at the chance to play uncle, you're mistaken.'

'You don't know that. If you had known where Gillian lived, you would have written to her. He kept that from you.'

'Kate, you are imagining a rose-coloured past that never happened. I could have sought out my sister and her offspring when my father died. I chose instead to have my lawyer draw up what was fair and equitable, what was glaringly absent from my father's will. But I did not deliver it in person. It would have been a simple matter then, to make the trip from England to Ireland. I chose not to make it.'

Was he truly so cold, or was he intent on hurting her? It didn't matter. She would be a fool to ignore the implications.

'I understand why you hate this place. I understand why you are so determined never to walk in your father's shoes. But I don't understand why you are following his example in other ways.'

'What the hell do you mean by that?'

'You are punishing your nieces for your father's crimes. I don't care what you say about not wanting to hurt them, not having time, or it being positively dangerous for you to take the time to write the occasional letter, the fact is that you are hurting them. You're their nearest blood relative. You are right here in England, but you are refusing point-blank even to meet them. You are simply too concerned with your own life and your own business to give a damn about theirs. Does that sound familiar?'

'Are you suggesting that I am selfish?'

'You've fought to be the man you are, and I admire you for it, but now it's your way or nothing. I'd call that selfish, wouldn't you?'

She felt sick. Her chest was heaving. Her face was flushed with anger. Kate, who almost never lost her temper, was almost as furious with herself as Daniel. She glowered at him.

'Are you finished?' he said, in a carefully polite tone. 'May I speak?'

'Be my guest.'

'We have two months more to maintain our fable of being Lord and Lady Elmswood. I suggest that you take tonight to calm down and we start afresh tomorrow.'

Kate stared at him incredulously. 'Is that it?'

'What more is there to say? We are clearly utterly incompatible in our views. This morning must have been, as I suggested, a peculiar combination of circumstances that we need have no fear will happen again. I am glad we had this conversation, Kate. There's no room for misunderstanding now.'

'There most certainly is not.'

She studied him for a moment, but he met her gaze blandly. The man she had shared such life-changing intimacy with this morning was nowhere to be seen. Life-changing! She almost snorted. It certainly had been.

She turned on her heel and left him without another word.

'We are going to High Farm,' Kate said. 'If you take the first turning on the right and then—'

'I know where the High Farm is.' But instead of taking the turn Daniel pulled the pony and trap over to the side of the road. 'We're supposed to be on our honeymoon. I don't think we're going to convince anyone if you won't even look at me.'

She looked at him. She forced a travesty of a smile. 'There—that is the best I can do. I'm afraid I don't have your vast acting experience.'

'It's been two days and you're still angry with me.'

She sighed heavily. 'I'm angry with myself. You made your feelings—or rather lack of them—crystal-clear from the start. Then you did me the honour of explaining why you behave as you do a couple of days ago, and I threw it back in your face. I'm very sorry for that. You won't change, and I don't want you to change, but I—I have not your ability to simply forget what happened between us.'

'I have not forgotten! What happened between us was…' He met her gaze, and the longing to touch her, to reassure her, to tell her how much he ached with longing, was almost irresistible. 'I have not forgotten, Kate, but it doesn't help to dwell on it.'

'I am not dwelling on it, nor begging for a reprise. I am simply saying that I am finding it difficult to find a way to be at ease in your company. I hadn't realised how tactile we had become. I am having to be constantly on my guard not to—not to touch you.' This last was said in a whisper. She was blushing painfully. 'It makes me snappy, and most unlike myself.'

He *hated* seeing her like this. He felt so damned guilty, and at the same time so damned relieved, for he was exactly the same. Even now he was having to work hard not to take her hand. He hadn't noticed how often he took her hand until he'd forced himself to stop.

'Perhaps we shouldn't put a complete embargo on touching—not immediately.' He gave in to the need, taking her hand between his. 'We took things too far and it's given us a craving for more. We both know that would be a mistake, but to give it up immediately—no, we should try for a gradual retreat.'

'So you're suggesting we wean ourselves off each other slowly?'

There was a glint of humour in her eyes that had been absent for the last two days. Immensely relieved, Daniel nodded. 'Hand-holding. A few chaste kisses. Nothing more.'

'I don't think we have ever kissed chastely.'

He kissed her cheek. Lavender. His body responded enthusiastically. Dear God!

'Like that,' Daniel said, stalwartly denying himself a second kiss. Not even on her cheek.

'You don't think that would be to stretch our powers of self-discipline to breaking point needlessly?'

'I don't. But if you would prefer to continue being on slightly frosty terms…'

'Neither of us wants that. I've missed your grumpy face at the breakfast table.'

'I'm never grumpy.'

'You are, but I put up with it because you butter my bread so nicely.'

'And don't forget I know just how you like your tea. Milk first, but only a tiny splash. And you like your morning kiss not on the nape of your neck, as I first thought, but on the lips. Like this.'

It lasted only a few seconds. The simplest of kisses. A brief meeting of lips, no lingering. But they both felt it. He saw it in her eyes. The longing, and the sure and certain knowledge that it was not going to be a simple matter to wean themselves from each other.

Not simple, but it could be done. Kate was like the opium which he had occasionally been obliged to consume for form's sake while on that mission to Hong Kong, posing as an English trader exporting Indian opium to China. He had witnessed its effects on those who fell under its spell first hand.

'A gradual retreat, a measured dose,' he said. 'If we persevere, it can be done. What do you say?'

She hesitated, biting her lip, but then shrugged. 'I have grown accustomed to you making my tea.'

The pony was cropping happily in the grass verge at the side of the road. Daniel released Kate's hand to pick up the reins again.

'Good. Now, let's go and pay a visit to this model tenant you've been telling me all about.'

'Are you sure you want to do this?' Kate said as they resumed their journey. 'I can easily call myself another day. You'll probably find it very boring.'

'I think Lord Elmswood should show some interest in what his wife has been doing with the land all these years, don't you?'

'You're not in the least bit interested, Daniel.'

'No, but Lord Elmswood is, and, actually, it may surprise you to know that I am intrigued.'

'It would surprise me a great deal. In all the years I've been writing to you I don't recall your once evincing any interest in the estate.'

'I had no idea until I came here that your improvements would be so radical.'

'How do you know I've been radical?'

'You've forgotten—I'm a spy… I know everything. I really haven't appreciated you nearly enough. All this work you've done—you should be featured as a shining example of estate management in some journal for landowners, if there is such a thing.'

'I can't imagine anything more embarrassing. Besides, all the work has actually been carried out by others. All I've done is supervise.'

'You know that's nonsense. You are far too modest.'

'Would you like me better if I was forever boasting about my achievements?'

'I like you exactly as you are.'

She smiled uncertainly. 'If you hadn't married me I'd probably be eking out a living in a cottage, with a cat to keep my company.'

'And I would be— Oh, Lord knows. It doesn't bear thinking of. Our marriage has made everyone a good deal happier—me, you, and the people of Elmswood.'

He turned the pony into the farmyard and Kate brushed aside the question of whether or not she was actually happy.

'You can tie up at the gatepost here,' she said, jumping out of the trap.

Daniel followed her, looking around him with a slight frown on his face. He was dressed in country clothes today, boots and breeches, with a coat and hat, though no gloves. A cow lowed in a big new barn. Chickens were scratching in a desultory way in the caked mud.

'English chickens are so much fatter than African or Indian chickens,' Daniel said. 'And they seem to have a great deal more feathers.'

'They need them here in the winter. I suppose they can make do with less in the tropics.'

'I hadn't thought of that. I can't get used to the countryside being so green, or the way the fields here are marked out so clearly and the hedgerows are awash with colour. I'm used to a palette that consists of shades of brown beneath a stark, blinding blue.'

'Be careful, Daniel, you're sounding almost as if you prefer the English countryside.'

He secured the reins on a gatepost. 'I've never had anything against England. At this time of year it's quite beautiful. Here comes your farmer and his wife.'

'Edward. And Emma. How lovely to see you.' Kate smiled reassuringly, for the couple emerging from the farmhouse were eyeing Daniel askance. 'May I present my husband, Lord Elmswood? This is Mr and Mrs Styles, Daniel.'

Emma dropped a deep curtsey. Edward—reluctantly, it seemed to Kate—was about to make a bow when Daniel held out his hand.

'How do you do, Mr Styles? It is a pleasure to make your acquaintance.'

'My lord. A pleasure.'

Though his face said otherwise, Kate thought, surprised.

'May we offer you a cup of tea, my lord, or a mug of ale?' Emma asked, casting her husband a reproving look.

'His Lordship will be wanting to inspect the farm,' Edward said. 'Doubtless you'll be wanting to be reassured that our modern methods are not compromising your profit, my lord. I did not have the pleasure of meeting your father, but I believe he had a reputation for being conservative when it came to the running of the estates'

'I am not—'

But Edward gave Daniel no time to say what he was or was not. 'I know that Kate here—that is, Lady Elmswood—has been investing heavily, but I think you'll find we are reaping the benefits of her foresight—quite literally. It would be a shame—no, it would be a tragedy—to return to the old ways.'

'Edward, my husband doesn't—' Kate began.

'Her husband has no intentions of interfering with the management of the estate,' Daniel said tersely. 'I am here only as an interested observer, I assure you. I take a natural pride in my wife's achievements but she, as I'm sure you already know, is extremely modest. So much so that she has generously attributed those achievements to you.'

'Oh.' Edward's cheeks turned a dull shade of red. 'I beg your pardon, Lord Elmswood. Only I thought—all the tenant farmers were worried, you see—that with your being absent for so long you might have inherited your father's rather outmoded view of the way things should be done.'

'I admit to being largely ignorant on the subject—which is why I'm interested in hearing about the changes.'

'Well, now…' Edward's brow cleared. 'I'd be more than happy to tell you, if you really are interested, though I'm not sure where to start. Would you like to hear about the wheat?'

'Very much,' Daniel said, to his credit looking enthusiastic.

Kate bit back a smile. 'Edward is a scientific

farmer. He has been experimenting with different types of fertiliser over the last five years, using guano, which is— Actually, it is the deposit left by seabirds, which is imported from Peru.'

'Peru!' Daniel exclaimed, seemingly genuinely startled. 'In South America?'

'Have you been there on your travels, my lord? No? Well, perhaps you'll go exploring there next and see if you can get a deal for us with the guano. We've been comparing it with potash, which is the ashes of elm, and also with bone meal.'

'Where, dare I ask, does that come from?'

'The knacker's yard,' Edward told him, grinning. 'There's some don't like it, ploughing the ground-up bones of horses into the soil that those same horses might have ploughed, but for me it's a natural cycle.'

'And what has this to do with wheat?'

'Simple, my lord, it's all about yield. Of course it's not only down to the fertiliser we put in the soil. Scientific farming is a whole combination of things. There's crop rotation…'

Kate watched, amused, as Edward launched into a lengthy explanation of what was obviously a subject very close to his heart, though she was soon drawn in, reminding him of failures and successes, of comical misunderstandings, and of the resistance they had met with some of the neighbouring farmers, who had worried their own crops might be contaminated.

'But Edward's success speaks for itself,' she finished, with a glowing smile. 'Though there are still a few die-hards, stubbornly sticking to traditional methods, there are more who have started to follow where he leads and to see the results too. He is an acknowledged leader in the field now—if you'll pardon the pun. He has even been asked to speak at agricultural fairs as far afield as Somerset. We are very proud of him here at Elmswood.'

'Thanks to you, for giving me the opportunity, Kate—and for letting me have the farm. I'm not from these parts, my lord, and there were several men wanting this tenancy when it became vacant. But your good wife had the foresight that other landowners lack, in being keen to encourage experimentation. My Emma and I never forget how lucky we are to have been given the chance. You must be very proud of her.'

'And grateful,' Daniel agreed, slanting her a smile, 'I am more than happy to leave the running of the estate in her capable hands, for I have neither her expertise nor her passion.'

'Well,' Edward said, smiling shyly, 'I'll be honest, my lord, and tell you that I'm very glad to hear that.'

'I'm so sorry,' Kate said two hours later, as they sat together on the bench in the shade of the terrace. 'I didn't intend for you to have to listen to a lecture on modern farming techniques. How tedious for you. I shouldn't have suggested we call. I should have known that Edward would get carried away.'

'I wasn't bored—though the subject doesn't hold quite the level of fascination for me that it does for you.'

'There is a limit to how much discussion even I wish to have about ground-up bones and sea-bird droppings. Just between ourselves, I'm not hugely interested in the day-to-day business of farming. I enjoy the challenge of planning a strategy and implementing it—just as I have enjoyed the challenge of restoring the gardens here, and the house, but now it's over…'

'Don't tell me you're finding your precious Elmswood tedious?'

'Not tedious, exactly, and it's not as if I don't have enough to do, but…'

'You need a fresh challenge. Is that what you're saying?'

'What I'm saying is that you have unsettled me. I don't mean our—what we…' Kate took a sip of her iced lemonade. 'I am not referring to our making love. I mean that your presence has made me look at myself and Elmswood in a different light.'

'You would probably have started to do so regardless. Estelle would have fled your little nest of her own volition sooner or later, even if I had not been forced to play the cuckoo who usurped her.'

Kate giggled. 'You say the strangest things sometimes, but you're right. Estelle would have left. Being here alone might not necessarily suit me, but it would have taken me a good deal longer to recognise that possibility—or at least to admit it to myself—if I'd been alone and not had you for company.'

'Temporarily, remember. This comfortable nest you have made for yourself is yours for as long as you want it.'

'Into my dotage, you mean? I could grow old and fat…'

'And possibly adopt a few cats for company.'

'Cats adopt people, not the other way round.

I would certainly be comfortable...but would I be happy, do you think?'

'You have been up until now, haven't you?'

'Yes.' She drained her glass. 'Yes, I have. And I shall be happy again, I'm sure.'

'You don't sound very convinced.'

Kate shrugged. 'It doesn't matter.'

'You mean it's none of my business?'

'I suppose I do. That's what you want, isn't it? For us to go back to how we were? Exchanging polite notes every other month that say next to nothing?'

'No.' Daniel poured himself another glass of lemonade. 'I know we can't do that.'

'What, then? Do you think our marriage has served its purpose?'

'Kate!'

'It's an obvious question, wouldn't you say? Elmswood doesn't need me. I could easily hand the management over to Oliver.'

'No, not him.'

'Why on earth not? Why don't you like him?'

'I don't have any feelings at all for him.'

'That's not true. You don't even like to pass the time of day with him in the morning.'

'That's one of the things I don't like about

him. He's always there…hovering in the background!' Daniel exclaimed.

'Oh, for goodness' sake! He's our head gardener. He works in the gardens. Of course he's always there.'

'No, I mean— Oh, I don't know. There's something about him that unsettles me. But you know him, and I don't, so if you want to train him up as your replacement, go ahead. No one is forcing you to stay here if you don't want to, least of all me. You've more than fulfilled your side of our bargain. And if it's a question of divorce…'

Kate's glass slid from her hand and broke on the terrace paving. 'You want a divorce?'

Tears sprang to her eyes. She leaned over to pick up the shards of glass, but Daniel put a restraining hand on her arm.

'Leave it. I'll clear it up in a minute.'

'A divorce! Won't it be expensive? To say nothing of the scandal?'

'I don't give a damn about either. Look at me, Kate.'

'No.' She sniffed. 'I don't know why I'm crying.'

'I don't want a divorce.' He put his arm around her shoulders, pulling her towards him.

'I thought you did. And if it's what you want, then—'

'I don't. I know that our marriage is—well, it's unconventional, to say the least, but I've always considered myself married to you, Daniel, for better or worse. For always.' She was too comfortable, nestled against him, so she pushed herself upright. 'But whether I remain in Elmswood or not is a different matter. You married me to be caretaker for your heir, whoever that may turn out to be. I've done enough to ensure that Oliver or whoever you choose to employ can do that job now. When you return to foreign service I don't want to remain here.'

'You sound very certain about that.'

'I do...' she said, much struck. 'It's one of those occasions, I think, when you don't know something is true until you say it. I am certain I don't want to remain here. I'm sorry.'

'You've no reason to be sorry. *I* am sorry. I thought you loved this place.'

'I do, but— Oh, I don't want it to be my entire world any longer. And that is your fault. Or rather Sir Marcus's, for plucking me from here and opening my eyes. Must we talk of this now?'

'We'll need to discuss it in a lot more detail at some point. I have written to my lawyer, asking him to track down my heir. If only Eloise's child had been a boy it would have been an simple matter. Perhaps her next offspring will be the appropriate sex.'

'She's only just had little Tilda, and her son—if she has one—would inherit his father's title.'

'Well, whoever it turns out to be, once the lawyer has found him I can make a will and sort out a settlement for you.'

Fresh tears sprang to her eyes. 'I don't want a settlement.'

'Now you're being quite ridiculous. You've earned it.'

'But won't we—? Are you saying that we—? When you go, Daniel, will I never hear from you again?'

'I don't know.' He reached for her, and then changed his mind. 'You might meet someone else you want to marry, in which case my lawyer will need to do whatever it takes to rid you of me.'

'Stop that! I have one husband already. I don't need or want another. Please can we stop talking about this now? What we really should be discussing is the garden party.'

Daniel heaved a theatrical sigh. 'I think I'd rather talk about making a will.'

'How much notice do you think we will need to give?'

'As little as possible. Then we'll kill two birds with one stone—there are bound to be people who won't be able to make it, and Sir Marcus will not have to write to me to remind me of my obligations.'

'Oh, my goodness, do you really think he's keeping an eye on us? How?'

'Perhaps that damned St James is his man on the inside,' Daniel said. 'It would explain why he's forever appearing out of nowhere.'

'You don't really imagine…?'

'No, I don't. Come on, let's start with a list of guests. What about your Mr Styles and his wife?'

'Isn't the party intended for the local gentry?'

'All the people you don't mix with, you mean? I see no reason why we shouldn't do a little mixing of our own. We shall be the radical Lord and Lady Elmswood.'

'Are you serious? I rather like the idea, but there are some who might take offence.'

'I doubt they'll be offended enough to refuse, however, and miss out on the opportunity to inspect us in our own environment, so to speak.'

'You make us sound like specimens in a jar.'

'Not a bad analogy. But at least we'll be specimens floating in our jar together.'

'How lovely. I shall look forward to that.'

'I wonder if we could ask Phoebe to put together a menu for the buffet?'

'Won't it be easier if you don't tell my nieces about the party? Then they won't feel left out.'

'But what if they hear from someone else? Then they'd be hurt. Whereas if I let them know and explain— Though what I am to say, Daniel, that won't be hurtful, I have no idea. It will look as if you are choosing to meet anyone and everyone save your own flesh and blood.'

'That is because I don't give a damn about anyone and everyone,' he snapped.

'So you *do* give a damn about them?'

Daniel pushed his chair back, draining his coffee as he stood. 'The only thing I give a damn about is reassuring Sir Marcus that I am playing ball. The details I am happy to leave in your more than capable hands. Excuse me.'

# *Chapter Nine*

Two weeks later, Kate stood staring out of the window at the early-morning sunshine. The rain which had been falling incessantly for the last week, perfectly matching her gloomy mood, seemed finally to have lifted. It looked as if it was going to be a lovely day for their garden party.

Her spirits refused to lift at this welcome development.

She and Daniel had tried, since that last difficult conversation, to find a compromise which would allow them the comfort of physical contact, the tenderness of fleeting kisses, without the risk of it leading to lovemaking. It was a compromise intended to wean themselves of desire, but it was not working. Every seemingly innocent touch, every chaste kiss, fed the embers they were so valiantly trying to dampen.

Worse, as far as she was concerned, it set both of them on edge, making them acutely aware of their feelings for each other without allowing them any outlet.

Daniel, a man accustomed to denying himself any feelings, was finding it a battle. Kate, accustomed to being entirely open, was on the brink of declaring defeat.

Breakfast had become a tense affair, as they both girded their loins for whatever mood the day might bring. Sometimes they both managed to maintain a certain calm demeanour, co-conspirators in the pretence that all was well, but usually one or other of them was unable to maintain the facade. They were both brittle, wary of each other, and though neither deliberately set out to start the day on a sour note, that was often the net result.

For the most part, save for the welcome oasis of their yoga practice, they avoided each other, kept busy by their respective tasks relating to the organisation of the garden party, prolonged discussion of which made dinner painless enough, if tedious. Neither of them was happy with the situation, but they endured it, for they could not envisage doing anything else.

Today, Daniel's smile was forced, but at least he was smiling.

'It looks as though the weather is finally co-operating,' Kate said, relieved, as he began to set out their breakfast. 'Thank goodness. I'd really rather not move the party indoors.'

'Come and have your tea.'

She sat down, waiting while he poured her tea and his own coffee, smiling her thanks when he passed her a slice of bread and butter. Today, she was determined, was going to get off to a positive start.

'Mrs Chester has promised to come in early, which is good of her.'

'She's already here, and so is Sylvia, supervising the small army of helpers already gathering.'

'I should go and…'

'Sylvia is in her element, ordering everyone around. And Mrs Chester is happily assembling ingredients and consulting the very detailed receipts Phoebe so kindly sent. The stables, I have no doubt, are another hive of hired-hand activity. Leave them all to it and enjoy your breakfast, Kate. It's going to be a long day.'

'I'm dreading it.'

'I'm not exactly looking forward to it myself, but we'll get through it together.'

She smiled wanly. 'Aside from the annual harvest dinner for the tenants, I've never hosted a party before. What if it's a disaster?'

'The only disaster I can think of would be a sudden cloudburst, but I reckon Shropshire is all rained out for the moment.'

'What if no one comes?'

'Ah, that is the one thing we needn't worry about. The first party hosted by any Lord Elmswood in—what? Fifteen years? It's bound to be a massive draw.'

'More like twenty. Your father had already withdrawn from society some years before his death.'

'They'll also be curious to see the restored gardens. You know how nosy folk can be.'

'You know that's not true, Daniel. They are coming because of you.'

'We shall both be on display and under scrutiny. But we'll be together—don't forget that.'

'Specimens in a jar…' she murmured.

'Very toned and agile specimens, thanks to our daily practice.'

'"A demonstration by Lord and Lady Elmswood of the ancient practice of yoga will be held in the music room. The couple will be attired in silk nightclothes. Those of a sensitive disposition would be advised not to attend,"' she said.

'That would certainly ensure that word of our party reached Sir Marcus's ears.'

'Oh, I have made sure he knows about the party. I sent him an invitation, knowing he can't possibly accept it—for how would he explain his presence to our neighbours? Who are, as you have already pointed out, an inquisitive bunch.'

'As the sponsor of my next exploratory trip?' he suggested.

'Would that be to Peru, to explore the source of guano?'

Daniel gave a bark of laughter. 'Don't tempt me.' He poured her second cup of tea. 'It has required a lot of hard work over these last few weeks, but once today's party is over we can relax.'

It was the kind of bland remark that anyone would make in the course of a conversation, but under the circumstances it seemed to Kate that Daniel was being deliberately obtuse.

'Once it's over we will have nothing to distract us.'

He made no pretence of misunderstanding her meaning. 'We are almost halfway through the three months. We can do this, Kate.'

'I am not sure that I can. I have not your ability to delude yourself.'

'I am not deluded. I am determined.'

'Determined to deny how you feel! I *know* you want me.'

'Don't do this—not now, not today of all days.'

'And I haven't stopped wanting you either.'

'Kate, for pity's sake.'

He leaned over to touch her hand, but she snatched it away.

'If not now, when? This halfway house is torture for both of us—and I *know* it is the same for both of us, so don't deny it. After today I think it might be best if we put an embargo on any contact at all between us. Do you agree?'

'I've told you, this is not the time to discuss it.'

'Fine.'

Furious, frustrated, knowing perfectly well that she couldn't possibly have chosen a worse moment, Kate pushed back her chair, getting to her feet.

'I have a hundred things to do today. I'd better make a start.'

She was at the door when he caught her.

'You're right. It's the same for me.'

'Oh, Daniel, I know that. It's one of the things that makes it so—so damned hard to bear! Do you think it would be easier if we simply gave in to our feelings?'

'All that would happen is that we'd become addicted to each other—and how would that help make it easier to part at the end of it?'

'You don't think that we'd grow tired of each other, then?'

Daniel groaned. 'What is the point in us discussing this?'

But the last two weeks had been such an endurance test of restraint that Kate couldn't stop herself. 'So you don't think that? How long, then, do you think it would take? Six months? A year?'

'What the hell does it matter?'

Shocked, Kate took a step back. Daniel, white-faced, fists clenched, was staring at her as if he hated her.

She knew why it mattered—she had known for two weeks why it mattered. Though she'd never permitted herself to admit to it, and she most certainly wasn't going to do so now.

'You're right,' she said, her voice not much above a whisper. 'We shouldn't be discussing this now. I'm sorry. I'm very nervous about the party.'

He drew a shuddering breath. 'I apologise. If you will excuse me? I'll go and make sure that everything is in hand at the stables.'

Kate had spent the last two hours bathing and dressing—an inordinate amount of time for her, which she wasn't entirely convinced had been well-spent.

Her hair was curled and pinned, threaded with a wide turquoise ribbon acting as a bandeau. The underdress of her gown was the same turquoise colour, with an overdress of white dotted Swiss cotton. It had a round neck, and the full sleeves which were currently in fashion, and was trimmed with white cotton lace. It was new, freshly arrived from a London modiste, thanks to Eloise, who had included a pair of turquoise slippers and a pair of long white gloves with the gown.

With only fifteen minutes before their guests were due to start arriving, she had no option but seek Daniel out.

She found him in the morning room, standing at the window, watching the buffet being set out on the terrace, supervised by Mrs Chester. He was dressed formally, in a dark blue tail coat and fawn trousers. His hair was closely cropped at the back, an effect she knew now was achieved with a tiny pair of scissors and two mirrors.

The scissors were silver. He had bought them in a bazaar in Arabia, in a country whose name she couldn't recall, where he had met Lord Henry Armstrong's oldest daughter, who was married to an Arabian prince. Daniel had liked Lady Celia. He'd said that Kate reminded him of her.

He'd told her all this one morning when they had been resting after their yoga practice—the only times in the last fortnight when they had been relaxed in each other's company. They hadn't practised this morning. She was trying very hard not to see this as significant.

She mustn't think about that conversation at breakfast this morning. She mustn't think about all the implications and the heartbreaking consequences. Today's party was vital to Daniel. It would make Sir Marcus happy, that they were seen to be obeying his instructions, and if Sir Marcus was satisfied he would permit Daniel to return to foreign service. And that was all Daniel wanted.

So Kate closed the door, allowing the latch to click, alerting him to her presence. He turned. His waistcoat was fawn-coloured, to match his trousers. His necktie was white, and tied in a very elaborate knot. The high points of his starched collar showed off his tanned face.

His illness had etched fresh lines in his face, but otherwise he was the picture of health. The weight he had lost due to his illness was still making his cheekbones sharper, but he had lost that initial gauntness, and was now quite simply a very striking, very masculine and slightly intimidating man.

Kate hovered in the doorway, unsure of her welcome. 'I have run out of things to check. I think we might be ready for our first guest. You look extremely smart. I don't think I've seen that coat before.'

'I have definitely not seen that dress before.'

To her relief, Daniel smiled, holding out his hand.

'Let me take a closer look.'

She joined him, making a self-conscious twirl. 'Do you like it?'

'You look lovely, Kate.'

'Eloise organised it for me, but I specified the colour.' She smiled shyly. 'To match your amulet.'

Daniel took the turquoise stone from his pocket and held it against the ribbons at her neckline. 'It's a perfect match. Are you planning to be my lucky charm for the afternoon?'

'I was rather hoping that we could share this one,' she said, daring to touch the stone.

'It will be here, in my trouser pocket. Any time you feel the need to touch it...'

'I will ask you if I feel the need.'

'I was going to suggest you slip your hand in...'

'Daniel!'

'Do you want to try it out, as a sort of rehearsal?'

She had almost forgotten what it was like to tease like this, to see that wicked glint in his eye.

'Let me see,' Kate said, rising to the challenge. 'I think it would be easier if I stood behind you, like this, and that will be my signal for you to make sure your arm is in front of you...'

'Like this?'

'Just like that, to cover the fact that my hand is slipping into your pocket.'

'Oh, dear God.'

Daniel whirled around so quickly that she was thrown off-balance. He caught her hand as she pulled it back out of his pocket and crushed her against him. Their lips met in a starving kiss that left both of them breathless. Then slowly, he released her.

'Probably best if you ask,' he said, his voice not quite steady.

'As long as I know it's there,' she answered, following his lead, though what she wanted was to hurl herself back into his arms and kiss him until neither of them could resist. 'I've been dying to ask where you got it and what its significance is ever since I first saw it, but I didn't want to pry.'

'The stone was given to me by Joseph Banks, from his own collection.' Daniel had moved over to the mantel and was checking his necktie in the mirror.

'The famous botanist who sponsored the expedition you sailed with?'

'He was an old man when I met him. He invited me to his home when I returned. There had been an incident when we were at sea. One of the men fell overboard and I went in after him. It was nothing—the sort of thing that happens all the time—but the man turned out to be some sort of cousin of Banks.'

'So the turquoise was a thank-you.'

'No. He'd had a silver cup engraved, which he presented me with. The turquoise was something I took a fancy to in one of his cabinets, and he gave it to me. It's not worth anything, but I've always thought of it as a—a symbol.'

'Of your new life?'

'And the new me. Of which there have been many versions since,' he added wryly, turning away from the mirror. 'I reckon it's time for me to put this latest incarnation on display. Are you ready to face our guests, my lady?'

*'Nice little mare...she'll do as a hack—though of course you'll want something with more range when it comes to the hunting season.'*

*'As I was saying to Wycham only the other day, you'll be rightly taking your time to find your feet before plunging in to society. Good to see a man finally back in the Elmswood saddle, so to speak. With the greatest of respect to Lady Elmswood, all this modernisation lark has given your tenants some very peculiar ideas. Time they were reined in a bit. We're very glad to have you back in the fold.'*

*'Surprised to see some of the lower orders here today, mind. Thought at first you was as radical as your good wife, but I can see now it's a subtle way of teaching them their place. Look at them—couldn't get any more uncomfortable.'*

*'Glad to have the chance to have a word,*

*Elmswood. Wanted to let you know about a little club we have. Meet up once a month, play some cards...you know the kind of thing.'*

*'If I might just have a word in your shell-like, Elmswood? We've been looking for another man to sit on the board of the workhouse in...'*

*'Good to see a man's hand on the tiller here at Elmswood again. You'll be keen to make your mark on the county, no doubt. Luckily we've a free governor's position on the board of the boys' school at...'*

*'Nothing onerous. All you have to do is attend a meeting once a quarter. It's more of a social event than anything...'*

Daniel's head was spinning as he stood at the window of his bedchamber, gazing down at the throng of people in the gardens below. Almost three hours since the first batch of arrivals. Three hours of tedium, of being importuned, of having unwanted invitations pressed upon him.

In despair, he'd tried to drag the conversation around to his travels, only to discover that the only stories they were interested in, once separated from their women folk, were warm tales of exotic women and their habits.

From the beginning there had, it seemed to him, been a concerted effort by each new arrival to separate him from Kate. Looking down at the throng on the south lawn now, he could see that it wasn't a singular attack, though that was how it felt. The sexes were clearly delineated and, looking closer, he saw that it was clear that within each group the classes were equally clearly separated.

As an exercise in levelling, the garden party had failed, but in every other aspect it was a triumph. Save that it was one he and Kate had been forced to endure apart.

He couldn't see her. She was doubtless taking yet another party of women on a tour of the rose garden. Or perhaps, like him, she was hiding in her bedchamber. He wasn't hiding. He was having a respite from being Lord Elmswood. A much-needed one. His head really was aching, and he had at least another two hours of this torture to endure.

It shouldn't be difficult. All he had to do was return to the fray, find Kate, and pin her to his side. Then he'd be spared the male camaraderie and false bonhomie.

He'd made an attempt to mingle with the tenants. He'd played men both high and low-born in the past. He had the knack of fitting in and a habit of seeing others in terms of those who were useful to his current goal and those who were irrelevant. But he'd forgotten just how ingrained was the habit of sticking to one's own here in England.

Standing in the midst of a group of farmers, trying desperately to engage them in a conversation to alleviate his monologue, he'd been reminded, horribly, of those early days at school. He didn't know the rules. He didn't understand the customs, the terminology, the in-jokes. He didn't want to belong to the county group who claimed him as one of their own. But the group he was attempting to infiltrate didn't want him.

His necktie was too tight. He was sweating. His eyes were gritty. And his *head*! The last thing he needed was a recurrence of the ague.

He rummaged in his travelling case for a glass vial, mixed and then swallowed a dose of the precious bark, then wiped his face with a cold flannel and quit his bedchamber. This was a mission, like every other. He'd see it through to the end and, even though he felt as if one more hour as Lord Elmswood would kill him, he knew better. Besides, somewhere out there was Kate, lady to his lord, in need of him.

'Daniel!' Kate hurried up the stairs to meet him on the half-landing. 'I've been looking for you everywhere. We have an unexpected guest, and— Are you feeling quite well?'

'Why? What do you mean? I'm fine.'

'You are quite flushed.'

She tried to put her hand on his forehead, but he brushed her away. 'A headache, that's all, nothing to worry about. Who is this unexpected guest?'

'Sir Marcus. I left him in the drawing room, but—'

'Ah, you have found him, Lady Elmswood. I was beginning to think you had deserted your own garden party, Fairfax. That wouldn't do, now, would it?'

To Kate's utter relief, Daniel tucked her arm into his, cast her a quick smile, and led the way down the stairs.

'This is an honour, sir. How do you do?'

'I am very well. Bigger question is how do *you* do, Fairfax? You look a little hot under the collar.'

'Too much sun. I should have worn a hat. Shall we retire to the drawing room?'

'No, no. This is a garden party, is it not? Excellent. Then I'd appreciate a little tour of the garden, if you would oblige. Will you be so good as to lead the way, Lady Elmswood?'

'I shall be honoured,' Kate said, her heart sinking. 'We are very proud of our gardens here at Elmswood. I can offer you a walled garden and a rose garden. We can also take a walk down to the lake. Or, if you would like to see a more practical aspect, we have an excellent kitchen garden.'

'Roses,' Sir Marcus said decisively.

'That is the most popular part of the garden—it will be very busy.'

'Yes, that's what I thought. Lead on, Lady Elmswood.'

She did—out through the drawing room and onto the terrace, where Sir Marcus was happy to embroil them in a discussion about the disgraceful state of country roads before moving on.

He was inspecting them, testing them in their roles.

Fixing a smile on her face, and throwing in the preposterous suggestion that the new railways would very soon make the state of the roads irrelevant, she edged closer to Daniel.

'Don't forget the turquoise,' he whispered to her. 'Do you want to check that it's still there?'

Kate spluttered.

'You find the subject of transport amusing, Lady Elmswood?' Sir Marcus asked.

'It was my suggestion that in addition to a horseless carriage there might one day be a horseless plough that my wife found amusing.'

'Really? And yet you have quite a reputation for advocating all that is modern in farming,' Sir Marcus said. 'I have been hearing a great deal about your innovative methods.'

'You have?'

'Shall we continue on to the rose garden? If you will excuse us…ladies, gentlemen?'

Sir Marcus led the way down the terrace steps, turning right.

'I see you already know the lie of the land,' Kate said.

'I am merely following the crowd. Am I taking you in the wrong direction?'

'No, you have surmised perfectly correctly.'

'And how are you enjoying having your husband at home after all these years, Lady Elmswood?'

Sir Marcus's face was shaded by the brim of his hat. She could detect nothing from his voice. 'Why, I have to confess to being quite delighted with his company,' Kate said. 'With the girls gone now, I have all the time in the world to devote to him. It is proving a most rewarding exercise.'

She felt Daniel shake with laughter, and knew that she had hit the right note.

'As you can see from our guests, we have been welcomed into Shropshire society with open arms. The vicar tells us that his church is never so full as when we attend. If we wanted to, we could fill our days with social events.'

'But we don't wish to do that, do we, my love?' Daniel interjected, with a doting smile. 'I have explored the far corners of the globe alone, Sir Marcus, as you know, but I must say exploring this little…' His pause, and the look he gave her, almost overset Kate. 'This little corner of Shropshire,' he concluded, 'is proving an unexpected delight.'

'No need to overdo it, man,' Sir Marcus muttered.

'Forgive us,' Kate said, pleased to see that the usually imperturbable gentleman was looking distinctly uncomfortable. 'But to discover the joys of marital bliss when one is well past the first blush of youth is such a delight.'

'Indeed it is,' Daniel said. 'You should try it yourself, Sir Marcus.'

They had reached the rose garden, but instead of taking one of the many paths leading through the beds Sir Marcus continued on.

'Don't you wish to inspect the roses?' Kate asked him. 'Despite last week's rain, they are quite at their best.'

Sir Marcus, however, ignored her. 'Enough of this charade, Fairfax. We'll go back to the house. I need a word in private. With both of you.'

He led the way at a pace, round the side of the manor and in through the front door, which he closed behind them, shaking his head when Kate indicated the drawing room door.

'I will make this brief. Firstly, Fairfax, I am pleased to hear of your return to health in such a short time. Your efforts to regain your strength have been noted.'

'Have they indeed?' Now that the three of them were alone, Daniel's tone was very different. 'May one enquire who noted them?'

'Second,' Sir Marcus said, 'I am also pleased to note that you have had the sense to do as I bade you, and make yourself at home here. The party, Lady Elmswood, is a master stroke. I presume it was your idea?'

'Actually, it was—'

'Thirdly—and I am afraid you must forgive my bluntness, Lady Elmswood—I wish to remind you that the goal is for you to return to active service, Fairfax.'

'That, Sir Marcus, is the one and only reason I am still here at Elmswood.'

'Is it?' The man from the Admiralty stared pointedly at Kate. 'Are you absolutely sure of that?'

'We are acting,' Daniel said evenly. 'We are doing exactly as you instructed us to do.'

Sir Marcus sighed theatrically. 'Daniel, I have known you since you were sixteen years old. You are that very rare creature, a man who thrives in his own company, and it is one of the key reasons why you have been so successful.'

'I am perfectly aware of that.'

'Frankly, Lady Elmswood, your husband is a bit of a cold fish. He is also an excellent actor, however. I admire you very much, madam. I would not like to see you hurt.'

'I am not sure what you mean, sir.'

'I am aware that you put on that little display for my sake, madam. Laying it on thick to try to embarrass me. But I am an old hand at this business, and sadly more than able to read between the lines. I sense that your affection for your husband is genuine, Lady Elmswood, and that concerns me greatly.'

'Sir Marcus, I have understood from the moment Daniel walked through this door that he would be leaving after three months.'

Daniel, she reminded herself, was standing rigid by her side, and he wanted this and only this.

'Of course I have come to—to care for him in these last weeks we have spent together—at your behest, I would remind you—but it is a natural affection, grown out of enforced intimacy, and will I am sure fade equally naturally when he departs.'

Kate, longing for the comfort of Daniel's hand, forced herself to move out of his reach and to meet Sir Marcus's penetrating gaze.

'I am flattered that you were taken in, but I assure you that you have no need at all to be concerned. Daniel belongs to the foreign service heart, body and soul. What's more, after eleven years of ruling the roost here at Elmswood, the reality is that he is getting in the way. People expect Lord Elmswood to take over from his lady, but this lady, I assure you, has no intention of allowing that to happen.'

'In fact,' Daniel interjected, 'we were discussing just this morning how to effect our parting of the ways. Having fooled someone so perceptive as yourself, sir, I reckon we should start working on that sooner rather than later.'

'A quarrel?' Kate said, but her voice faltered.

'No, you are too easy-going for that to be believed. I think I should be the one to cause the estrangement. I shall take agin' modern farming, and your Farmer Styles will lead a band of men armed with pitchforks and hound me out of Shropshire.'

Kate giggled. 'If only I had had the foresight to invent a horseless plough I could have chased you with that myself.'

'Now, that is a sight I'd pay a large amount of money to see. What do you think…?'

'What I think is that it might have been a mistake to send you here, Fairfax.'

How could they have forgotten Sir Marcus, even for a few moments? Dismayed, Kate opened her mouth to protest on Daniel's behalf, but he shook his head.

'As you pointed out, it has given me the opportunity to restore myself fully to health, and we have ensured that the cover story you concocted has been well and truly established.'

'I do not need to be reminded of my objective. It was, as I am sure you have deduced, in some measure a punishment for your failure to observe protocol. Yes, I thought you'd have worked that out. But it seems to me you are enjoying your respite here, Fairfax, far too much. And it seems to me that the pair of you are enjoying each other's company far too much.'

'Are you suggesting that I leave?'

'No. If I do that you'll resent me, and I would rather you didn't, Daniel. I don't want you going back into service with regrets, as Sinclair did.'

'Alexander?'

'It's not my story to tell. Not his either. But if you let him know I've given permission, it might benefit you to talk to him.' Sir Marcus nodded. 'Yes, I rather think that might be for the best. I will leave you now. I am very glad I took you up on your invitation, Lady Elmswood. This has been a most helpful visit. Your husband is one of our most valuable men, and I would be extremely sorry to lose him, but— Well, as Sinclair will tell you, and as you already know, Fairfax, it is all or nothing. The King and I expect no less. Good day to you both.'

Bright sunshine filtering through the gap in the curtains woke Daniel. His head was woolly, his eyes gritty. He didn't remember going to bed. What *did* he remember? The party. Sir Marcus.

He grimaced. Sir Marcus.

His head had been aching. Yes, he'd left the

party and come up here to take some medicine. But that had been before Sir Marcus. What had happened after? He couldn't remember.

He wriggled his toes to rid himself of the usual pins and needles, but his legs and arms seemed to be free from aches, and his head no longer felt as if it was being penetrated by hot knives. Whatever had ailed him yesterday, it couldn't have been a recurrence of the ague. If the party *had* only been yesterday.

He lifted his arm to flex his fingers, and realised he was naked.

'You're awake.'

Nor was he alone in his bed!

Daniel turned his head to find Kate peering anxiously at him. 'What are you doing here?'

'I fell asleep.' She sat up, rubbing her eyes. Her hair had come undone and formed a wild, matted tangle around her head. She put her hand up to it, groaning. 'Is it a bird's nest? No, don't answer that. I can see by your face that it is. Never mind my hair—tell me how you are feeling?'

'Naked.'

'You were drenched in sweat, and it took me such an effort to get you out of your clothes I simply didn't have the energy to get you into your nightshirt.' She leaned over to place a cool hand on his brow. 'Your fever seems to have gone.'

She was still wearing her party gown, but she had loosened the ties and the respectable round neck was now gaping, giving him a distracting view of her breasts only just contained by her corset.

'Kate, if you don't move, my fever is likely to return with a vengeance.'

'Oh, I'm sorry. Am I making you hot?'

'Yes.'

'You were so restless I was afraid you'd fall out of bed, so I lay down beside you and talked to you, and— As I said, I must have fallen asleep. But I can see you're better now, so I'll get up.'

He caught her wrist. 'Don't go yet.'

'But I'm making you hot…'

'You are, but it's not fever.'

'Daniel! You are supposed to be ill.'

'I'm feeling much better now, but if you wish to reassure myself by taking my temperature again, Nurse…'

'You are outrageous.' She sat up cross-legged on the bed. 'I was worried about you.'

'I am worried about myself. You stripped me naked and I don't remember it.'

'You put up much more of a fight than the last time I took your clothes off.'

'How strange, when for the last fortnight one of the things I've wanted more than anything is to be naked with you.'

'Daniel…'

'She said, with a warning note in her voice,' he teased, though his smile quickly became a frown. 'I know we agreed that we would not make love again—that it would be a mistake, that we should wean ourselves off each other. I know all those things, but I can't make myself believe any of them. You were right yesterday morning, though I still think your timing was appalling. And now my timing is equally appalling.' He pushed himself upright, knuckling his eyes. 'Though Sir Marcus's timing was worse, damn the man.'

'Do you have any idea what he meant when he said you should talk to Alexander Sinclair?'

'Not a clue, but I intend to write to him today.'

'He thinks I'm in love with you—Sir Marcus, I mean.'

'But you reassured him, didn't you? You have developed a natural affection for me that will fade naturally when I leave. That hurt.'

'It was painful to say.'

'It's all or nothing, Kate. You heard it from the horse's mouth.'

'For both of us.'

There was something in her tone that made his stomach lurch. 'What do you mean?'

'I love you.' Kate's mouth trembled. 'But you already know that, don't you? You probably guessed it before I did. I didn't want to face up to it. I've been refusing to even let myself think the words, let alone say them. But I finally faced up to it last night, lying here beside you, remembering how close to death you were only a few months ago, worrying that it might happen again.'

'Oh, Kate!'

'Don't look so stricken. I'm not telling you to make you feel guilty. I'm telling you because I'm tired of pretending—to myself, as much as to you. I love you, and whether you want to admit it or not I know you're in love with me. It's the only explanation for what happened between us when we made love. You know… "My face in thine eye, thine in mine appears, and true plain hearts do in the faces rest."'

'Donne,' Daniel said, with a lump in his throat. 'One of my favourites.'

'Is it? It's one of Eloise's favourites too. I

never understood it until that morning. "For love, all love of other sights controls, and makes one little room an everywhere." I understand that too now—but you don't, or won't. You would never be content with me, with my world, would you? You only want to live in your own world. Alone. So, you see, you don't need to pretend that you don't love me any more, Daniel. Whatever you feel for me, it doesn't make any difference. I will never be your first love, and I'm not interested in second-best. I love you, but I'm keeping my heart safely to myself. I've no intention of letting you crush it.'

He felt as if the breath had been knocked out of him. He felt as if his heart was soaring, racing, and at the same time was about to plummet. Kate loved him. Of course she did. And he loved Kate. Of course he did. The two things were the perfect halves of one whole, an elemental truth.

'I do love you.'

But the words he had never uttered, had never believed he would utter, made Kate's eyes fill with tears.

'I know,' she said, her lip trembling.

'I don't want to leave you. When Sir Marcus hinted yesterday that he might recall me immediately I should have been delighted, but all I could think of was you.'

'It didn't occur to you that you could stay, though, did it? Be honest, Daniel.'

'I can't bear to think about leaving you, but if he'd had insisted I would have gone, yes.'

She flinched, but forced a smile. 'I did ask you to be honest.'

He reached for her hand, twining his fingers around hers. 'Try to understand, Kate. Sir Marcus won't tolerate any insubordination, but he is not a martinet. If he recalled me it would be because he truly believed it was in my best interests—and those of the country, it goes without saying. It's so much more than a job. It's who I am. But for the first time in my life yesterday I was torn. The fact that he saw through both of us, saw what we had not yet admitted to ourselves, made it impossible for me to ignore what you, brave Kate, were trying to tell me yesterday morning.'

A tear trickled down her cheek. 'But it has to be all or nothing, doesn't it?'

'I can't stay here. I hate this place.'

'You don't think you will ever be able to make it your own, Daniel?'

He shuddered. 'There's something about this place that spooks me. I can't put my finger on it, but it's there. I could never live here. But it's not only Elmswood, Kate. It's the life—all the trappings of being Lord Elmswood. I'm a fish out of water.'

'You were the biggest fish in the pond yesterday.'

'I must be a better actor than I thought if you believe I was enjoying myself. I don't want to be a member of that exclusive little band who consider themselves the elite. I don't want to be fawned over nor looked up to.'

'Though you don't take kindly to anyone looking down on you.'

He gave a snort of laughter. 'The ones doing the looking up now are the very ones who looked down on me at school.'

'Those exclusive boys' schools that the great and the good attend are supposed to ensure that all the boys end up in the same little elite club when they grow to be men. Your school had the very opposite effect on you.'

'It instilled in me a lifelong disgust of clubs and an equally fierce determination to live life my own way. Neither of which were what my father intended. Nor indeed the school.'

'But it inadvertently moulded you into the perfect spy,' Kate said with a sad little smile.

'Which brings us full circle. You must be your own man, and I must be my own woman. I want you to be happy, Daniel. So you are free to go and you must go, when the time comes, without looking back. It's what I'm planning to do.'

'You are set on leaving Elmswood?'

'Unlike you, I have nothing but happy memories of this place, but I can't spend the rest of my life living vicariously through the girls. I want to create new memories for myself. So, yes, I am set on leaving.'

'Then I must hurry my lawyer up. It might be a good idea to take a trip to London. I could arrange to meet Alex there too—kill two birds with one stone.'

'He may be reluctant to leave Eloise and Tilda so soon after the birth.'

'I'll sort something out.'

'Yes, you're right…not now,' Kate said, reading between the lines of his impatient comment. 'And, if you don't mind, I'd rather not discuss how we are to part just yet.'

'I think we've talked more than enough about everything for the moment.'

'You must be exhausted. I'll leave you to sleep.'

But she made no move, and Daniel gave in to

temptation, pulling her towards him. 'Stay with me for a moment.'

'Just until you fall sleep.'

Kate stretched out beside him, on top of the sheet. He slipped his arm around her and she rolled closer. Her hair tickled his nose. Her cheek rested on his shoulder.

'I've never spent the night with anyone before,' he said.

'You didn't even know I was here.'

'I am very much aware of you now.'

She laughed softly. 'Go to sleep, Daniel.'

He kissed her hair. She burrowed closer. They drifted off to sleep.

Kate awoke for the second time that day in Daniel's bed, but this time she was also in Daniel's arms. The sun was shining directly through the window, which meant the day must be considerably advanced. She was lying on her side, with Daniel curled into her back, his arm draped over her waist. Still half-asleep, she ran her hand over his bare forearm, feeling the muscles ripple in response. She inched one foot to the edge of the bed, and he shuffled closer.

There was something pressing against her

bottom. Oh, dear heaven, something that set her pulses immediately racing.

She should move. She should move right now.

Kate wriggled cautiously. Not the kind of move she had intended, but the kind of move that Daniel most definitely appreciated. His obvious appreciation set up a clamouring ache inside her.

She really should get out of bed now, but somehow, when she rolled over, it was not towards the door but towards Daniel, and he was so warm, and his smile so sleepily wicked, that she couldn't help but smile back. And their smiles met and became a kiss. And Kate lost what little ambition she had to be anywhere save right here in the arms of the man she loved.

Who would have guessed that sleepy kisses could be so delightful? Or that making love to the man you loved, who loved you, could be so blissful? A communing of body and heart and soul? They savoured each kiss and each touch, murmuring incoherently, stroking, smoothing, soothing and at the same time rousing.

Her clothes seemed to discard themselves as they kissed, clinging to each other. She was on her back and Daniel lay over her, his erection pressing into her belly. And then he was on his back and she was astride him. And then she was on her side again, with Daniel spooned against her, and he was stroking her, teasing her, drawing out her pleasure. And then she rolled towards him, wrapping her hand around him, stroking him, teasing him, making him groan with pleasure.

And then their lips met again, and their kisses became urgent, and then she was on her back and he was inside her, and the first thrust sent her spiralling out of control. She wrapped her legs around him, tilting herself up to take him higher, surrendering to the utter delight of their joining, pulsing around him as he thrust, trusting him completely to protect her. But in the instant when he came, pulling himself from her, she wished that he had not.

And then they lay together, spent and sated, and their kisses became tender, and then gradually they stopped.

This time when Kate moved Daniel made no attempt to stop her.

There was nothing to be said. They both knew that. And so they said nothing.

# *Chapter Ten*

Their lovemaking had removed all the built-up tension which had made the lead-up to the garden party so taxing. And in the days that followed, Kate and Daniel achieved a kind of calm which allowed them to enjoy each other's company once more. They were careful with each other, mindful not to talk about the future or the past, determined not to mention their feelings or to tempt passion.

Though their disobedient bodies defied them, cleaving towards each other, brushing hands, bumping knees, seating themselves as closely together as possible, whether on a bench in the garden, on the terrace, or on the floor of the music room after their yoga practice.

It was a strain, but a very different kind of strain, Kate found, having to bite back the *I love you* that she longed to blurt out every time Daniel walked into a room, and seeing him having to make a real effort not to do the same. Not that they needed to speak the words aloud. Every time they allowed their eyes to lock it was there between them.

She loved him so much, and though she knew it was hopeless there were times when she railed at her own decision. Times when she wanted to beg him to stay, or to go but come back soon. Times when she wanted to do exactly what she knew would be utterly wrong—to tell him that she'd wait, for however long it took, for him to change his mind.

He wouldn't change his mind. And she was not going to waste her entire life waiting. But in the middle of the night, as she lay alone in her bed, wondering if Daniel was lying wide awake on the other side of the house, Kate questioned both these things.

A week after the party she was in the morning room at her desk, staring helplessly at the stack of invitations and calling cards they had amassed, when Daniel appeared.

'What on earth am I to do with these?' she asked.

'Ignore them.'

'I can't do that. It's so rude.'

'We made it clear that we weren't going to be socialising.'

'For a short period. Most of these occasions are miles away.' Kate flicked through the cards and letters. 'A gathering to celebrate the start of the hunting season in October. A party to celebrate the coming of age of the eldest Miss Forbes—who are the Forbeses?'

'I think he's the chap who wanted me to invest in his railway company. Member of Parliament for somewhere or other, so he assured me that getting the legislation through would be no problem.'

'A railway company!' Kate exclaimed. 'In Shropshire?'

'Progress,' Daniel said, grinning. 'It will come—even to rural Shropshire.'

'Not this century.' Kate returned to the cards. 'Another coming of age…and at least two of these are for Christmas balls, for heaven's sake.'

'Kate, you don't even know if you'll be here at Christmas.'

'You're right.' She set the bundle down and joined him on the window seat. 'It will be the first of August on Monday. Should we talk about what happens—how we will handle things at the end of the month?'

Daniel grimaced. 'I have had a letter from my lawyer. Unless one of my nieces has a son, the title will go to whichever is the eldest of my father's first cousins. I've no idea what relation that makes them to me, but it's far too distant for me to hand them Elmswood. Do you think Eloise will have more children?'

'Goodness, Daniel, Tilda is not even two months old. Though she has started smiling already, Eloise informed me in this week's letter. Clearly a most advanced child.'

'The lawyer has sent me a draft settlement for you, but I want him to ensure that you retain the right to live here in perpetuity. No, I'm not changing my mind on that point. Even if you don't want it now, it would make me happier knowing that you will always have the option.'

A lump rose in her throat. She almost never cried—tears were so pointless and such a waste of time, she felt. But of late she found herself constantly on the brink of them.

'So you'll have your lawyer monitor my movements? Will he keep me informed of yours?'

Daniel cursed, taking her hand, pressing a fervent kiss to the back of it. 'I don't know. We'll talk about it another time.'

'We can't keep putting it off.'

'Are Eloise and Alex set on staying in Lancashire for the time being?'

'I think so,' Kate said. 'Travelling with such a small baby is problematic, and Eloise would never abandon Tilda to a wet nurse.'

'Unlike her own mother,' he said bitterly. 'I'm not changing the subject, but before we talk about what happens after I—after the end of August—I need to speak to Alex.'

'Sir Marcus's suggestion? I'd forgotten. Can't you simply write to him, Daniel? If you go to Lancashire you'll have no option but to meet Eloise and Tilda, and you said...'

'I know what I said. And I heard what you said too.'

'When? I say a lot of things. I don't necessarily remember them all.'

Daniel grinned. 'But I do. Will we go for a walk around the walled garden? The sun looks as if it's trying to peek through, and I saw St James heading for the kitchen gardens this morning when I had my swim, so we should be alone.'

'He has estate business in town today. You have to admire his dedication, Daniel, to work in the gardens in the early mornings before he goes.'

'I assume he isn't married, since you've never mentioned a wife? Don't you pay him well enough?'

'More than enough!' Kate said indignantly as Daniel pulled the front door behind them. 'And if he does take on the management of the estate he will be quite a catch. Perhaps he hasn't met the right woman. Or perhaps he simply prefers to live alone. You of all people should understand that.'

Daniel pushed open the door of the walled garden and Kate stepped through, stopping immediately, as she always did, to close her eyes and let the garden work its magic.

When he kissed her, she kept her eyes closed. For if she kept her eyes closed it wouldn't end, and they could also pretend it had never happened. She kept her hands firmly by her sides and their lips clung. She could feel his breath on her face. She could sense his yearning to pull her into his arms. Their kiss deepened. Then their tongues touched and they sprang apart.

Out of habit, they proceeded clockwise around the garden, her hand tucked into his arm, their legs brushing as they walked.

'I think we should both go to Lancashire,'

Daniel said, breaking the silence as they came to the wilderness.

Kate stopped in her tracks. 'Both? You mean you and I together?'

'Well, I certainly don't see the point in us travelling separately. It's about a hundred miles, isn't it? We could do it over two days in two stages.'

He ushered her over to their bench, dropping down beside her, stretching his legs out in front of him as was his habit.

'It makes perfect sense. I urgently need to speak to Alex. *You* are desperate to see this wondrous child—and Eloise too, of course. It would kill two birds with one stone.'

She stared at him, astounded, but he kept his gaze resolutely ahead. 'Sir Marcus said that you were to remain here.'

Daniel shrugged. 'Sir Marcus told me I must speak to Alex.'

'You could arrange to do that without visiting the Fearnoch estates.'

'I could, but I don't want to.' He turned towards her. 'You told me it was selfish of me to refuse to see my nieces. You told me I was punishing them for my father's crimes. I hadn't thought of it that way. It's taken me some time to accept that you're right. But don't go planning a big family reunion just yet. Aside from anything else, Kate, you don't know whether or not Eloise will even want to meet me.'

'Oh, there's no question that she will.'

'You haven't posed the question because I've asked you not to. But I will pose it now, if you will enclose my letter with yours. I can make absolutely no promises to her, but I see now…' he slanted her a smile '…that it was wrong and selfish of me to make up her mind for her.'

'What about you, though, Daniel? You have been so adamant that you cannot have emotional ties.'

He shrugged. 'It's a small risk. I'm doing this for you, because there's not much else I can do for you, but I'll make it clear to Eloise that I can make no commitment to keep in touch.'

'She of all them will understand, being married to Alexander.'

'Precisely—that's why I think the risk can be managed.'

The risk to himself of caring, Kate thought sadly.

'I am sorry,' Daniel said, taking her hand again. 'It's little enough, but it's all I can offer.'

She gave herself a shake, forcing a smile. 'I'm going to see Eloise for the first time in over a year and I'm going to meet Tilda for the first time ever. That means the world to me Daniel. Thank you.'

*Fearnoch Estates, Lancashire,*
*one week later*

'I had no idea that Alexander's domain was so extensive,' Daniel said, peering out of the post chaise window. 'We passed the gatehouse lodge about half a mile back and there's still no sign of the house.'

'He and Eloise have placed much of the estate in trust for the people who work there,' Kate said. 'Alexander was never comfortable with the vast amount of money he inherited. A great deal of what they haven't already signed away has been invested in the coal mines, and building the villages where the miners and their families live.'

'Perhaps we could do that with Elmswood. Set up some sort of trust…give the lands over to the people who work them.'

'That's a radical idea. Are you serious?'

'Entirely. We should talk to Alexander about it.'

'It was actually Eloise's idea.'

'Really? Though I suppose I shouldn't be surprised. She is her mother's daughter—by which I mean you. But her aunt's niece doesn't sound quite right.'

'Are you nervous, Daniel?'

'No, Alex and I are acquainted, remember?'

'You know full well that is not what I meant,' Kate said with a wry smile.

'At least I know from Eloise's reply to my letter that she'll let me through the door.'

It was a poor answer, and Kate deserved better, but how could he admit to what he was feeling without raising false expectations?

He made a show of staring out of the window, because he was incapable of lying to her face and she always knew when he was prevaricating.

He wasn't nervous—there was nothing to be nervous about. They were to stay only two nights. He would find out from Alexander what Sir Marcus's cryptic comments meant—though he still had no idea what difference Sir Marcus thought it would make. Kate would spend time with Eloise and the child. Then they would return to Elmswood and the countdown to the end of August would begin in earnest. But he didn't want to think about that.

'Look, you can see the house now.'

Kate leaned over his shoulder to point. Her

travelling dress and pelisse were azure-blue, perfectly matching her eyes. He was wearing country dress, which was stifling in the heat of the carriage. There were too many clothes between them—far more than usual. Probably just as well.

The house came into view, a huge, sprawling pile that he couldn't imagine Alex living in. His heart began to thump uncomfortably. But he had no need to be nervous. He was worried about what Alex might say, that was all.

Kate's hand found his, pressing it. She thought he needed reassurance. He didn't, but it was a comfort. It occurred to him far too late that they hadn't talked about how they would present themselves to Alex and Eloise. Alex, of course, knew that the marriage was strictly one of convenience, and that was what Eloise had always believed too, but conveniently married couples didn't hold each other's hands. Or gaze longingly at each other. Or…

'Daniel, I've only just thought… Eloise thinks that we are—goodness, I suppose *indifferent* is the word.'

Conveniently married couples didn't read each others mind either, Daniel thought ruefully.

'We'll only be here a couple of days, and she doesn't know me at all.'

'Yes, but she knows *me* extremely well. And Eloise is one of those people, Daniel, who *notice* things. You know…notices the kind of things people would prefer not to have noticed. She's going to notice that you and I— What am I to tell her?'

'You're like her mother. She would not question you on such a personal matter.'

Kate looked quite incredulous. 'You really don't understand how things were between us, living at Elmswood. I'm only five years older than Eloise. She was as much a mother to the Twinnies as I was, having stepped into the breach left at their birth by their real mother. We are very close, Daniel—more like sisters than aunt-by-marriage and niece.'

'Yet you were astonished when you heard about Tilda. She clearly doesn't tell you everything. Do you really know her as well as you think?'

Kate's face fell. 'Perhaps she didn't confide in me because it was a subject I know nothing of. She has a good deal more experience of love and marriage than I.'

'Then she'll have the sense to realise that the

precise nature of your marriage is your own business.'

'Yes.' Kate bit her lip. 'But it goes against the grain with me to pretend, Daniel.'

'I'm not suggesting you pretend. I'm saying that the subject won't come up. Eloise is a besotted new mother. She'll have no interest in any other topic of conversation.'

Kate opened her mouth, no doubt to remind him that he didn't know Eloise, then closed it again. 'I *am* looking forward immensely to seeing her and Tilda.'

'And Alex?'

Kate laughed. 'Oh, yes, him too. Look, we're here.'

The post chaise came to a halt at the imposing front entrance, where a wide semi-circle of shallow steps led up to a huge set of double doors.

Even before the carriage steps were unfolded a young woman carrying a white bundle came rushing out of the house. She was dressed in an elegantly simple green gown. Her hair was auburn, not the bright Titian that Gillian's had been, but she was unmistakably his sister's daughter. That smile, and those eyes… A lump formed in his throat. It had been almost thirty years since he'd seen Gillian. If she was alive she'd be nearly fifty. Gillian at fifty! How she'd have hated that.

'Ready?' Kate looked at him anxiously.

Outside, his sister's child was holding her own child up to the carriage. Both of them were smiling, and Eloise's smile was generous, warm, loving. Not a bit like Gillian's.

Daniel turned away to kiss Kate briefly on the lips. 'Ready as I'll ever be,' he said.

'Now that she's settled she'll sleep soundly right through the night until six,' Eloise said proudly as she joined the after-dinner conversation.

'Truly the most perfect baby that has ever been born to woman,' Kate said. 'Seriously, though, she is absolutely adorable. And motherhood suits you—you look radiant.'

'I don't feel radiant,' Eloise replied. 'I feel fat and overly bounteous.'

Alexander gave a snort of laughter. 'Nothing I can say will persuade her otherwise, but I'm working on it.'

The pair exchanged a look that Kate, astonished, could only describe as lascivious. Beside her, Daniel was gazing fixedly at the drawing room carpet. He had been silent for most of dinner, just listening to the conversation—which, admittedly, even Kate was beginning to find just a little tedious.

She could well believe that Alexander and Eloise were able to interpret the many and varied gurgles their child made. She was equally sure that to Tilda's parents the imminent arrival of a first tooth or a first attempt to sit up was of major import. But, frankly, she could think of at least a thousand more interesting things to discuss. Such as that look Eloise had just given her husband, though that would have to wait until they were alone.

'But that is more than enough about Tilda,' Eloise said, with a rueful glance at Kate, which reminded her that her niece was as observant as ever. 'We've not even asked Uncle Daniel how his recuperation is progressing, though that is partly because it is obvious you are in excellent health, sir. No one looking at you would imagine that you had been so seriously ill.'

'Yes, I'm fine now,' Daniel said. 'Thanks to Kate.'

'It must have been quite an adventure for you,' Eloise said, turning to Kate. 'You hate to leave Elmswood, even to visit me.'

'I enjoyed it. Actually, it's made me think about…' Kate hesitated, but Daniel was still studiously staring at his feet. 'We are thinking of establishing Elmswood as a trust—along the lines of what you have done here, only on a much smaller scale.'

'What a wonderful idea!' Eloise exclaimed. 'Then, with all the extra time you'd have on your hands, you could expand the gardens—open them up to the public, perhaps?'

'Kate has dedicated more than enough of her life to Elmswood.' Daniel said firmly, finally meeting Eloise's gaze. 'She's only thirty-three. She has her life ahead of her. It's time she stopped devoting it to others and thought about herself.'

'Daniel, now is neither the time nor the place—'

'Are you saying that she has wasted her life on us?' Eloise demanded.

'No, your uncle doesn't mean that…'

'No, I definitely don't mean that,' Daniel said, putting a restraining hand on hers. 'I am extremely grateful that she took on you and your sisters on my behalf…'

'To say nothing of your estates.'

'To say nothing of my estates,' Daniel agreed. 'But her work is done on both counts. It's not my idea for Kate to leave Elmswood, it's hers. And, contrary to what you think, Niece, there is no one who understands better than I how fortunate I am to have married her.'

'And there is no one who understand better than *I*, Uncle Daniel, how fortunate we girls were to have Kate to look after us. I am afraid that we all leap too readily to Kate's defence. She would be the first person to tell us that she can fight her own battles, but we love her so much, you see, and we are terribly aware of how much we owe her for what she has done for us. And now, to make matters worse, I've made her cry.'

Eloise jumped to her feet, throwing herself at Kate in an embrace that almost toppled the pair of them over.

'You know that I don't regret an instant spent with you three, silly girl,' Kate said, laughing.

'No, but Uncle Daniel is right,' Eloise said. 'You have more than earned the right to indulge yourself. I thought that he was putting you out to grass.'

'Charmingly put,' said Daniel. 'Kate warned me that you had a peculiar way with words.'

'Did she? You have the advantage over me, for I know almost nothing about *you*. And before you tell me that I am not permitted to ask questions,' Eloise said, re-joining her husband,

'I will remind you that I understand that better than most.'

'Have you always known that Alexander was in the foreign service?' Kate couldn't help asking. 'All these years and you've said not a word.'

'I guessed early on in our marriage. I've said nothing because there's nothing to say now. Alexander served his time, doing his duty to his country, just as you have served your time doing your duty to Elmswood. Are you thinking of retiring too, Uncle Daniel? Is that why you are here? To ask Alexander how he copes with the tedium of it?'

'Yes, every day I wake up beside you, my love, and I think, *If only I was alone in a makeshift tent in the pouring rain, with cold rabbit stew for my breakfast, looking forward to a day spent crouched behind a fence, watching a house through a spyglass.*'

'*Are* you retiring, Uncle Daniel? Will you and Kate—?'

'No!'

'No, Eloise, there is no question of…'

'You're making Kate and Daniel uncomfortable with your questions,' Alexander said.

'And I promised I would curb my curiosity and make him feel at home,' Eloise admitted ruefully. 'I do beg your pardon. I've done neither. Shall we go back to talking about Tilda? It's much safer ground.'

'You really are nothing like your mother. I mean there's no question but that you're Gillian's child, but my sister didn't have a compassionate bone in her body—and as to her caring about anyone's feelings but her own…'

'No, she never did. I didn't mind for myself, but when she ignored the Twinnies it made me so angry. She would come home after months away and they would have made a little banner, saying *Welcome Home*, and she wouldn't even notice. Estelle wrote a tune once— Oh, but I don't like to talk of those unhappy days.'

'I think Estelle gets her musical talent from Gillian,' said Daniel.

'I never once heard my mother play the pianoforte.'

'She could play anything. Not particularly well, and she had no interest in applying herself or taking lessons, but she could pick out a tune, and she had one of those singing voices that send shivers down your spine.'

'You've never mentioned that before, Daniel,' Kate said.

'I'd forgotten. No, not forgotten—put it to the back of my mind, I suppose.'

'I don't suppose I inherited my talent with a needle from her?' Eloise asked.

Daniel burst out laughing. 'No, she'd no more set a stitch than bake a cake. She couldn't even be bothered to read a book for herself, though she did occasionally enjoy my tales of Ancient Greece.'

'Doubtless on account of the affinity she felt with the goddesses,' Eloise said.

Daniel grinned. 'I never thought of that.'

'It was good of you to bring Kate to see Eloise,' Alex said the next day, as they settled themselves in his study. 'She's been desperate to show Tilda off, though understandably a bit nervous about accounting for her presence. Eloise was as certain as I that she didn't want children. It's a bit of a turnaround…not to say a shock for both of us.'

'Though clearly a welcome one.'

Alex grinned. 'I've never been happier.'

'You don't miss the service?'

'Is that what you want to talk to me about? *Are* you thinking of giving it up?'

'No—God, no. Unlike you,' Daniel said, 'I

enjoy being alone in a makeshift tent in the pouring rain. Not that it often rains in the part of the world I tend to be assigned to.'

'So Eloise got it wrong, then?'

'That I am retiring? Yes, completely wrong.'

Alex drummed his fingers on the arm of his chair. 'She thinks that you and Kate— Lord, I'm sorry…have I touched a nerve?'

Daniel shook his head, wishing he had a cup of coffee. 'Do you really not miss the life?' he asked.

'Never. The last time we met all those years ago in Egypt, when you suggested I marry Eloise—and now that you're here I'd like to thank you for that from the bottom of my heart. No, don't brush me off, Daniel. I mean it. Eloise has quite literally changed my life. For the good, as if there's any question about that. I had no intention when we married that it would anything other than something similar to the arrangement you and Kate have, and that was all I wanted or needed. All Eloise wanted too.'

'What changed your mind?'

Alex laughed. 'Apart from the obvious, the fact that we fell in love! Isn't that enough?'

'Was it?'

'Actually, no, it wasn't at first. I take it we're coming to the nub of this conversation now?'

'I need to understand, Alex. You know that favourite phrase of Sir Marcus's?'

'It's all or nothing.' He rolled his eyes. 'I know it only too well. He warned me off too, you know, when he saw that I was becoming far too fond of Eloise—and he spotted that before I was ready to admit it to myself.'

'The old fox… There's a bit of me that wishes he'd fall hook, line, and sinker himself, and then we'd see if he changes his tune.'

Alex snorted. 'Does the woman exist who'd take *him* on? She'd have to be a female Machiavelli to have even a fighting chance of reeling him in, far less domesticating the old trout. But I've not answered your question, have I? What made me choose Eloise over the work I'd devoted my life to? Especially since I loved the danger of it, and the excitement. Until that point I was never so happy as when I was on a mission—the more dangerous the better. But when I returned to duty that last time, after I was married, I was miserable. I'd spent most of my life since I was recruited out of school serving my country. What changed? I suppose it's simple, really. I realised my job had filled a big gap in my life. A gap now completely filled by Eloise. There wasn't room for both. All or nothing, remember?'

'You make it sound so simple.'

'It didn't feel like it at the time, believe me. I spent weeks trying to persuade myself that I was wrong, that what had always made me happy *would* always make me happy, that being in love with my wife changed nothing. But it did. It changed everything.'

'You never thought that Sir Marcus might be wrong?'

'That I could have both? A happy marriage and my career? But my marriage wouldn't have been happy, Daniel, with Eloise on tenterhooks, waiting for one of those dreaded official communiques. You know: *Sorry to inform you...in the line of duty...blah-blah. Can't tell you anything about how or why...can't acknowledge his work...can't pay a pension or award a medal... sure you'll be comforted by knowing he served his country.* Firstly, I would not subject Eloise to that pain. Secondly, I wouldn't want Eloise simply marking time, waiting for me to come home in between assignments and wondering if I even will. Thirdly, it's a damned dangerous life. You know what it's like when you're careless with your own life—the risk is irrelevant. When you do care, the odds are raised. I didn't want to die, Daniel. I wanted to be with Eloise. And, last but by no means least, Sir Marcus is right. You can't do what you do, what I did, half-heartedly. You lose your focus and you risk everything—and I don't mean your own neck, but others. You have to make a choice.'

'And you don't regret the choice you made?'

'Never. But…'

'What?'

'It's different for me, Daniel. We were in the same line of work, but we're not the same. Forgive me for being blunt…'

'I need you to be blunt, Alex.'

'Very well, then. Sir Marcus recruited both of us, and he has an eye for the kind of man ideally suited to our unique business. We are self-sufficient, we're coolheaded in a crisis, we have an ear for languages, we have a facility for adapting ourselves to the situation. But I never immersed myself in work the way you do—mind you, I was never required to. I was always the man of action. You, though… You are whatever they want you to be, for however long they need you to be it, and then you're someone else. I don't know if what I'm saying makes sense…'

'You were always Alex first, but I've never been Daniel?'

Alex laughed nervously. 'Obviously Daniel Fairfax exists, but...'

'But what?'

'But no one knows who he is.'

'Fortunately I know myself very well,' said Daniel, and got to his feet. 'I appreciate you being so frank.'

'To hell with that—have I helped?'

'I think so. Now, if you don't mind, I think I'll go and get some fresh air.'

'You're very quiet,' Kate said. 'You've barely said a word since we left Lancashire yesterday.'

'We'll be back at Elmswood in an hour, I reckon. I'm sorry it was such a short visit.'

'Are you? That first night you seemed to be getting on so well with Eloise, but the second evening you seemed distracted.'

'I had a lot to think about.'

'So it was your conversation with Alexander that has made you so morose?'

'Not morose, contemplative. I like Eloise. She's very much her own woman. No prizes for guessing who she takes *that* from. I would like to know her better.'

'But you won't,' Kate said, discovering to her surprise that her heart had yet further to sink.

'Alex is very much his own man too. I never thought he'd be happy, settled into domesticity with a wife and a child, but he clearly is.'

'You don't think domesticity could make *you* happy?'

'I have itchy feet—but it's not only that. Alex said the strangest thing to me, Kate. "Obviously Daniel Fairfax exists," he said, "but no one knows who he is."'

'It would be more accurate to say that Daniel Fairfax exists in many forms.'

'And which one do you love, Kate?'

'This one. The real one. Because Alexander is wrong, Daniel. I know you.'

'Then you'll understand why I can't stay. Alex does agree with Sir Marcus that our work has to be all or nothing. That's why he left…because he wanted a different life.'

'With Eloise.'

'It's not that I don't love you, Kate, it's that I can't envisage a different life. It is what I am and who I am. Sir Marcus knows that—it's why he sent me to talk to Alex.'

'I thought Alex might convince you to stay.'

'I hoped he would too.'

She stared at him, almost wishing that he hadn't told her. Such a bittersweet thing to know—that she had come so close to being first in his life. But not close enough.

'Clever Sir Marcus.'

'Yes.'

She wanted to howl, but she could see his throat working, had heard the ragged pain in that one word. So she reached for his hand, forcing it to unfurl, twining her fingers into his.

'We can do this, Daniel.' She touched his cheek, gently forcing him to face her. 'We can do it.'

# *Chapter Eleven*

Daniel completed the last length of the lake, then lay on his back, allowing himself to drift out to the middle while he brought his breathing back under control. Every day in the week since their return from that pivotal visit to Alex and Eloise he'd tried to push himself further, determined to be at peak of fitness when Sir Marcus summoned him. Though he wondered sometimes, as he forced himself to swim one more lap, and then one more, if he was actually trying to make himself ill again and unfit for duty.

It was raining, though only that light, inconsequential rain that verged on being mist, as if it were hedging its bets. He had grown accustomed to the coolness of the English summer now. He'd have to acclimatise himself again when he returned abroad. Though there was no guarantee that they would send him to his usual stamping ground, he supposed, in case his face was recognised. He didn't give a damn where he was sent. He didn't want to go anywhere. He had to get away from here. But he didn't want to leave Kate.

Kate… Was she watching him from her bedroom window, as was her wont? She certainly hadn't been there when he'd dived in. If only she would weep, or beg him to stay, or even ask him to reconsider. Then he'd be forced to explain himself, and in stating his reasons aloud he might find them more convincing. But she was resolutely silent, and he couldn't stay. And he didn't want to go.

If only Kate could come with him. If only he was more like Alex. But he wasn't *like* anyone. For the next two or three weeks he would continue to be Lord Elmswood. And then—what the hell did it matter? And then he would be someone else.

A violent shiver shook him. He swam to the bank, struggling to get a grip on the muddy grass, hauling himself out with difficulty. Grabbing his dressing gown, he pulled it on. Looking up, he was sure he saw Kate at her window. He waved, but she didn't wave back. He turned, only to see Oliver St James appear with his wheelbarrow. The man lifted his arm in salutation, and something clicked in Daniel's mind.

He looked up. Not to Kate's window but to the master suite. His father had been watching. His heart began to beat very fast. His mouth was dry. His father had been watching what? Had he been swimming?

Still looking up, he headed for the terrace, but his foot slid on the muddy grass bank and he lost his balance, landing with a painful thud on his backside.

'Let me help you up, sir. That was a nasty fall.'

*That was a nasty fall.*

Dazed, Daniel held out his hand. St James took it, pulling him to his feet with such force that he stumbled against the gardener. He put his hands on the man's chest to break his fall. St James put his hands on his shoulders. Their eyes met, just for a moment, but St James's invitation was clear. He knew exactly what it meant this time, but back then…

Daniel shook his head vehemently. 'You've mistaken the situation.'

He stepped back, but St James had already released him, appalled.

'I'm sorry, sir, I…'

'You were helping me to my feet. There's

nothing to apologise for.' Daniel had just enough sense of the consequences the man must be fearing to keep control of the turmoil he had inadvertently caused. 'Do you hear me, St James? Forget about it. I intend to.'

'Sir, I...' The gardener nodded. 'Thank you, sir, I...'

But Daniel pushed past him, desperate to be on his own. On the terrace he met Kate, hurrying towards him.

'I saw you fall.'

'I'm fine.'

*That was a nasty fall.*

'Are you sure you're not hurt? You look—'

'Let me be, Kate. I need to be alone.'

He made it to the master bedroom, where he locked the door and went to the window embrasure. His father would have seen it all, watched it unfolding day by pernicious day, knowing what he was witnessing while Daniel continued to be blissfully oblivious.

How could he have been so blind, so utterly naïve? The memories came tumbling back, unfolding in his head like a play acted out at breakneck speed. He remembered all the way back to school, where Leo had singled him out, had told him they were kindred spirits, had recognised something in him that no one else did.

*'You can turn to me.'*

*'You can confide in me.'*

*'I understand you as no one else does.'*

*'You can rely on me to look after you.'*

*'I'm your friend. It will be our little secret.'*

*'You're not alone.'*

He had never had a friend. He had taught himself not to want or need a friend. Then Leo had made him see how lonely he'd been. And Leo had told him he need never be alone again. They'd had so much in common. They'd had so much to talk about. They'd made so many plans.

*'I want to be an explorer.'*

The shy confession had taken him months.

Leo hadn't laughed. *'We'll see the world together,'* he'd said. Then he'd touched him.

Daniel shuddered. His shoulder. His hand leaning on it a fraction too long. He had known it was a fraction too long, but this was *Leo*, who cared for him, who told him he would protect him, so it couldn't be wrong.

It was the same when Leo ruffled his hair in passing. When he tapped Daniel's cheek. When he straightened his jacket or adjusted his necktie. Innocent everyday touches. Yet he had known.

For he had never said anything. And he'd never returned them.

Then Leo had come to Elmswood, and they'd been alone much of the time. In the library, that day he had fallen from the steps, Leo had been laughing. Then dropping down on the floor beside him, putting his arms on his shoulders. Daniel had gone quite still. Leo's hand had smoothed over his jaw.

*'Poor Daniel.'*

*'I didn't hurt my head.'*

*'Then show me where it hurts.'*

And then his father had come in.

Leo had left.

His father had been furious, throwing accusations that Daniel had felt honour-bound to defend. Until that morning by the lake.

*'That was a nasty fall. Let me look.'*

*'I'm fine.'*

*'Don't play games with me, Daniel. You know what you want.'*

*'I don't want anything.'*

*'You know you do.'*

He had been frightened. Torn. Leo was his friend. He'd stood passively, but at the last moment hadn't been able to help recoiling, so that the kiss had landed on his cheek.

That was when his father had erupted onto the scene. And Leo had disappeared for ever.

Shaking, sweating, Daniel sank down on the window seat, dropping his head into his hands.

Daniel had remained locked away in the master suite for much of the day. Kate, feeling foolish but too worried to care, had stood at the door several times, on the verge of knocking, before creeping away again. If he wanted her, he would find her. But when he'd eventually left the room it had been to retire to his own bedchamber.

He didn't come down for dinner. He didn't go for his swim the next morning. He didn't come to breakfast either. But as she took her tea she heard the tell-tale creak of the front door.

She followed him at a discreet distance and stood at the gate of the manor grounds, watching as he took the road to the village, turning into the churchyard just before the village green. An hour later, after hovering by the gate, keeping her eyes fixed on the road, there was no sign of him returning.

Kate could stand it no longer. She hurried down the road and through the churchyard gate, but the church was empty. Outside, the sun was hidden by a grey haze, the air heavy and damp with rain, clouded with insects. The churchyard was very old. She picked her way through overturned stones and broken urns. The grass needed scything.

The hem of her gown was soaked by the time she turned the corner, and there was Daniel, sitting cross-legged on the ground by the railings surrounding the Fairfax family tomb, staring at the huge stone set into the wall, which listed the Earls and their Countesses and the surprisingly frugal number of their offspring, whose mortal remains were interred here.

Kate stood stock-still, but he must have sensed her presence for he turned his head and to her immense relief beckoned her over.

'There's no mention of Gillian or Diarmuid,' he said.

'They were lost at sea, their remains never found.'

'My father tried to pretend she had never existed, but she did. Her name should be recorded here, and her son's, regardless of whether they are buried here or not.'

Kate sank onto the grass beside him. 'That's easily remedied. If you tell me what you want to add, I'll speak to the stonemason.'

'Thank you. You'll get soaked, sitting on the ground.'

'I don't care. I've been so worried about you.'

His hand sought hers. It was cold. He squeezed her fingers, but then immediately released her. 'I needed to be alone.'

'Do you want me to go?'

He shook his head. He was holding his turquoise in his other hand.

'I remembered yesterday what happened with Leo.'

'Leo?' She had been imagining any number of reasons for his strange behaviour, but all of them had been connected with their visit to Eloise. 'There was a quarrel with your father, you said?'

'That's what I assumed. But it wasn't a quarrel. My father saw something. Something I didn't.' He turned the turquoise round and round in his hand. 'Though, looking back, deep down I knew. But I didn't do anything about it because I thought he was my friend.' He gave an odd little laugh. 'I so desperately wanted to believe he was my friend.'

Kate's skin prickled ominously. She waited with bated breath, watching Daniel turn the stone over in his hand.

'The school I went to was brutal. It was a harsh, cruel and well-established regime that required you to submit entirely to the dominance of the older boys and the prefects, and then to step into their shoes when you've served your time, and take your turn at whipping the next generation into line.'

'That is utterly disgusting.'

'*Fidelitas, veritas, integritas.* Fidelity, truth and integrity. That was the school motto. If you played the game, you'd get your reward. I didn't play the game, so my life was hell on earth, but I kept myself going by thinking that the one thing I did have was my integrity. And then Leo arrived at the school, and at last I had a friend who thought like me. He was an outsider, like me, though he seemed popular enough. But he was simply better at playing the game, he told me. I was making it too hard for myself, he told me. There were ways to make it easier without compromise. He'd show me. I believed him. I thought he was my friend. But he wanted me to be a different sort of friend entirely, if you take my meaning.'

'Oh, God. Oh, Daniel.'

'I knew there was something wrong, that I occasionally felt uncomfortable in his company, but I didn't say anything or report it to anyone.'

Kate's head was spinning. The tale Daniel was unfolding was utterly shocking, and such a complete bolt out of the blue that she could barely follow it, but she was terrified of saying anything for fear of it being the wrong thing. Daniel was clearly still reeling. So she waited.

'Looking back, he was subtle, clearly well-practised at his sordid game,' Daniel said with a sneer. 'There was never anything I could object to. He used to ruffle my hair, like Gillian did. It was much longer then. It curls when I let it grow.'

And now he never let it grow.

'What else?' Kate asked, though she wasn't sure she wanted to know.

'More of the same. Nothing overtly wrong. It never got that far.' His lips twisted into a horrible mocking smile. 'I'd like to think that I would have put a stop to it before—before… But I didn't have to.'

'Your father did,' Kate said, as the pieces began to sink into place.

'That summer he saw what I didn't want to see. I thought he disliked Leo simply because I had chosen him to be my friend. In the same way, I suppose, that I thought he disliked Sean Brannagh—because Gillian had chosen him. He came calling at Elmswood at first, did Sean Brannagh—how odd that I'd forgotten all about that. But my father didn't like him—said he was a wastrel, told Gillian to have nothing more to do with him.'

'Which naturally ensured that she was interested in him and only him.'

Daniel laughed sourly. 'And look how well that ended for all of us.'

He stared at the tombstone for a long time, and Kate sat in an agony of indecision, wanting to throw her arms around him. But he was almost trembling in his effort to sit rigidly, and she feared the slightest touch would overset him.

'To cut a long story short,' he finally continued, 'my father caught Leo in the act of trying to do something that even I could not explain away. And that's why Leo left Elmswood. And that's why I was removed from school and sent to the Admiralty. Not spite. Not hate. He was trying, in his own ham-fisted way, to protect me from Leo. Just as he'd been trying, in an equally ham-fisted way, to protect Gillian from Brannagh.'

'But he—he did succeed in saving you, didn't he?'

'Yes, he saved me. He saw enough from his bedroom window to put a stop to it—though, as I said, I'd like to think I'd have put a stop to it myself if it had gone any further. I'm not like Leo, Kate.'

'I know you're not. I have ample proof that you are— Oh, my God.' She stared at him, her hand covering her mouth. 'But Oliver is, isn't he? And that's why you've been so— That's why you don't like it that he's been watching you! And yesterday… Did he—? What did he do, Daniel?'

But he shrugged impatiently. 'It was nothing. What he did—and it *was* nothing, I assure you—it reminded me, that's all. That's not the point.'

'No, the point is that a man you thought your friend—a man who was older than you, and your tutor into the bargain, a man you trusted implicitly, took advantage of you.'

'No!' Daniel exclaimed. 'That's not the point at all.'

'Then what is?'

'Everything I think I know about myself is false!' Daniel jumped to his feet. 'Through it all—my miserable childhood, my schooling, the Admiralty—the one thing that's kept me going is my determination to do things my way. Not to submit to my father's will or the collective will of that bloody school. To go my own way, be my own man.'

'And you certainly have.'

'But it's not been my way at all.' His voice

quivered. He dashed a hand across his eyes. 'You don't understand.'

Kate finally gave in to the need to hold him, jumping to her feet, wrapping her arms around him. But he stood stiffly in her embrace, quivering.

'You're soaked through, and you're hot. We should go back to Elmswood.'

'No!' He wrenched himself free, stumbling backwards. '*Listen* to me!'

'I am listening.' Kate held her hand out slowly, as she would to a spooked horse. 'We'll sit down here,' she said, gently pushing him towards an ancient tombstone. 'You talk and I'll listen.'

He did as she urged, making a visible effort to control himself, and his hand curled so tightly around the turquoise that his knuckles showed white. When he spoke, it was with his jaw clenched equally tightly.

'I feel as if I don't know myself—who I am. I'm seeing my life through a prism. Everything is warped…not as it seems. My precious independence is a sham. I have spent my life being manipulated by others, shaped by events.' He stopped, breathing heavily. 'Take Gillian. I knew it was wrong of me to carry those damned letters, but I was so stupidly proud of her choosing me to help her to defy our father—because that's what it came down to. I thought we were in it together, she and I. I had no idea that she was using me.'

'You were a child.'

'Yes, you've said that—and I was. But I thought I'd learned my lesson. Then I went off to school and I thought that I was making a stand, staying firmly on the outside, suffering for my stance,' he continued viciously. 'I was determined they wouldn't make their kind of man of me, but they did. They made me exactly the kind of man my father wanted me to be—one who does his duty, one who is unquestionably loyal, a man who can be relied on. I'm the sort of man my father would have been proud of.'

He cursed, then took another couple of breaths.

'And then there was Leo, who did exactly what Gillian did and made me feel wanted, special. I fell for it just as blindly, and I came very close to being exactly what *he* wanted me to be. And then came the Admiralty.'

He had stopped shaking. His voice was cold, clipped, but his jaw was no longer so tightly clenched.

'And finally I became an explorer. It was the one thing I'd always wanted to be, and Sir Marcus arranged it so that I could have it. I knew my father wouldn't like it, so of course there was the added attraction of defiance for me, and off I sailed, ecstatic to have finally have achieved my lifelong ambition. And when I returned home Sir Marcus was waiting to offer me a career in the foreign service that he thought I was uniquely suited to. And he was quite right. I can see by your face that you still don't understand.'

'I'm sorry.'

'Kate,' he said, reaching for her, 'when Alex said that no one knew the real Daniel Fairfax, he was right. When you said there were many Daniel Fairfaxes, you were right too. I thought I knew the essence of myself, though.'

'As I do.'

His hand tightened around her. 'We're wrong—both of us. I don't think there *is* an essence—that's what I've been trying to tell you. The reason I'm so perfectly suited for my work is that I can be anything I choose—or, more accurately, I can be whatever person is required. I acted as Gillian wanted. I nearly became what Leo wanted. I have been countless other men in my years serving abroad. I am not my own man at all, Kate. I'm not only a perfect fit for the work that has become my life, that life is the only one I'm fit for.'

'You're wrong. This thing you've remembered—this terrible, awful thing—has skewed your memories. And, yes, it's changed your understanding of your father, but it doesn't change the fact that he was a terrible father to you and to your sister.'

'No, I'm not sitting here weighed down with regrets, if that's what you're imagining.'

'There *is* a real Daniel Fairfax,' she said fervently. 'He's sitting here with me. He's a man who refuses to run with the herd. He's self-sufficient, and he's brave, and he's funny, and he's infuriating, and he can bend himself in two, and he has a unique dress sense. He won't fight. He won't kill. He breaks the rules if he feels they're wrong. He puts others first. Always. And I love him—so he must exist, mustn't he?'

'Kate…'

Her stomach sank at his tone. There was an agonising air of finality to it.

'I've been playing your husband for the last two months. One thing I can do is throw my heart and soul into any part I take on.'

'All or nothing?' she whispered. 'I won't believe this has been an act.'

'I don't believe it either. I think I love you.

At this moment in time I believe that I love you with all my heart. But when I leave…'

'You'll pack up your feelings and become someone else?'

'I won't have any feelings to pack up. I'll have some lovely memories, but no regrets. I'm sorry.'

'You don't believe that.'

'Not at the moment, but I will.'

'If you wanted to, Daniel, you could be any man you choose.' Her eyes stung with tears, but Kate blinked furiously. She didn't want to be pitied. 'You could choose to be with me.'

It was her last throw of the dice.

He didn't even waver, merely looked at her with such sorrow that he might as well have cut out her heart with a blunt knife. But she was protecting her heart.

'I hope for your own sake that you come to see that what I say is true. You could be anyone, Daniel, and the choice belongs to you, no one else. But I—I am not going to wait for you. I have no idea who I am either, but, unlike you, I'm determined to find out. Now, I think tomorrow we should discuss how we put an end to this situation. I think for both our sakes it should be sooner rather than later.'

## *Chapter Twelve*

*Two months later, October 1831*

Kate sat in the morning room, flicking through the contents of the leather folder that contained the embryonic history of Elmswood which Estelle had started. She was seated at her desk, taking her morning tea. Since Daniel had left she always sat at her desk with her tea. She had packed the Turkish coffee pot and cups away.

Estelle's latest letter had been posted in Paris, where Estelle was relishing her newfound freedom and enjoying practising her languages—which came as a surprise to Kate. She had been studying while Kate was abroad, it seemed, in preparation for this Continental journey of hers. She had an ear for language, it turned out. Another thing she had inherited from her mother's side of the family, since Daniel…

Kate pushed her unfinished tea aside. Daniel was gone. Estelle would never meet him. Daniel was in some far-flung part of the globe, playing some new role, and whatever he was thinking about, it most certainly wasn't Kate.

When they had found Sir Marcus's summons waiting, after they'd walked back in silence from the churchyard that terrible day, it had seemed like a message—fate telling them that their parting was necessary.

Daniel had left the next day, and the intervening hours had been an agony, as he'd packed up both his belongings and the man she'd thought she loved.

When he left, they bade each other goodbye like strangers. He had offered to write—there were practical details still to be sorted regarding Elmswood—but Kate had refused, and since then the only contact she had had with him had been through his lawyer. She knew it was for the best. But it didn't stop it from hurting. A lot.

*Life goes on*, she told herself, her mantra, as she got up from the desk. There was no shortage of tasks to fill her day as she prepared to close up Elmswood Manor for the foreseeable future and to start to hand the estates over.

Oliver, who was finally starting to relax in her company again, after an awkward few weeks when he had clearly been terrified that Daniel had betrayed him, would continue to stay here, to look after the grounds and the house, but he had refused her offer of the estate manager's role. He was a gardener, not an accountant. So it was the farmer Edward Styles who would take over the estate, and who would oversee its transition from Fairfax ownership to the new trust which was being set up.

But Kate was determined she would not be at Elmswood to help. The house was so empty and so silent, so full of memories. She would look back on it with pleasure, but for now there was only pain, for everywhere she turned she was reminded of what might have been.

If only Daniel had believed in himself. She would not and could not accept that his love for her was anything other than real. No one could fake what had transpired between them—that meeting of body and heart and spirit that had happened when they'd made love. At an elemental level they were two halves of one whole.

Kate—practical, pragmatic Kate—would have

scorned such an idea in the past, but she would have been wrong. She'd seen the same bond existing between Eloise and Alexander. She was delighted to see her niece so blissfully happy, but had declined her invitation to return for a longer visit, for it would be bittersweet. Eloise knew that Daniel had left, and had tactfully said nothing of her own feelings. The fact that she hadn't even asked about Kate's told its own story.

Outside, the rain was falling softly and the paths were strewn with newly fallen leaves. The walled garden was no longer her sanctuary, but she forced herself to open the door, to take the clockwise route to the wilderness and their bench.

She would be leaving in less than a week. She had taken a six-month lease on a house in Devon, because she had never lived by the sea. She hoped to give herself time to think through her next steps. Money was not a problem. As Eloise had pointed out, Kate had earned the generous settlement Daniel had made, and she was entitled to a comfortable independence. So she had accepted it, and had started putting it to use. Though Daniel would never know...

The bench was damp. Kate sat down, heedless of her gown. There was a space there...right there…where Daniel should be sitting, his long legs stretched out in front of him, his arm carelessly around her shoulders, his hand covering hers.

But it would never be filled now. Never again.

*Admiralty House, London*

'So, have your bags packed first thing tomorrow and you'll be on your way.' Beaming, Sir Marcus handed Daniel a slim folder. 'No need to tell you to destroy that. You know the drill. Welcome back, Fairfax. We have missed you.'

'Have you?'

Sir Marcus's smile faded. 'Dammit, Fairfax, I had to be seen to be doing something after that debacle. It simply wasn't possible to allow you to get away with such blatant disobedience. You know the rules.'

'And I broke one of them trying to save a man who had risked his neck for a country that isn't even his own.'

'What is the point of discussing this now? It's over and done with. You've served your time, and now there is a new, exciting role here that is perfect for you.'

'It's very different from the last one.'

'A challenge, but I know you won't let us down.

I swear, Fairfax, if I asked you to play Lady Macbeth you'd be able to do it,' Sir Marcus said with a barking laugh. 'Or even Lord Elmswood, at a stretch. And your success there, I have to tell you, surprised even me.'

'In what way?'

'You know perfectly well I was concerned that you were—how shall I put it?—taking the role too seriously? Yes, that covers it nicely.'

'You thought,' Daniel said baldly, 'that I had fallen in love with my wife.'

'Well, I wouldn't have put it quite so forcefully, but I did worry that I might find it difficult to prise you away from her. She's a feisty thing, and though not in the first blush of youth I could see how she would appeal to you. Not in the usual way. Like yourself, in other words.'

'Kate is not like anyone else I know.'

'Precisely, and that's why I thought she'd appeal. Then there was the fact that she'd saved your life too. And the nursing. All that time you were cooped up on various ships together. It was bound to form a bond. It's been a lesson for me, I can tell you. The next time I have to rescue a man from prison I won't send a pretty woman to bring him back to me. However, no harm done, eh?'

'Save to Kate.'

'Ah…' Sir Marcus pursed his lips. 'Still, in the grand scheme of things she's been on her own eleven years, and she had you playing the loving spouse for such a brief time that she'll be content to get back to normality, I'll wager.'

'Actually, you are quite wrong. Kate is leaving Elmswood.'

'Really? I didn't know that. Stopped keeping tabs on the place when you came back here.'

'There was never any need for me to remain there, was there?'

Sir Marcus, wisely in Daniel's opinion, chose not to prevaricate. 'I won't have you deciding which rules to follow and which to break, Fairfax.'

'And when you sent me off to see Alex you didn't worry that I'd see how happy he was and make the same decision he did?'

'I know you better than that, Fairfax. Sinclair served us well, but he ran out of puff, so to speak, and he's happy enough now, settled up north, doing his good deeds. But that's not you. I understand you probably better than anyone else does. I know what makes you tick, and it's not a little cottage with a little wife and a little baby.'

*I understand you as no one else does.*

A shiver ran down Daniel's spine. 'Yet only

a few months ago,' he said, 'you ordered me to enjoy the company of my lovely and very faithful little wife, the fresh country air and my neat and tidy little estate, and to be grateful that I am still alive.'

Sir Marcus tittered. 'Were those my very words? You have a remarkable memory. A positive boon in your line of work.'

'Flattery doesn't become you, Sir Marcus. I did as you asked. I didn't enjoy being on the estate—but then you knew that was impossible, for you knew my father.'

'That man didn't appreciate you, Fairfax, but we do. We have been here for you over the years, haven't we? We've looked after you. No matter where you were in the world, you knew you could turn to us, that we'd take care of you. And we proved it, didn't we, when we rescued you from that hell-hole? I can tell you now, in the strictest confidence, that we'd have left a lesser man than you to his fate.'

*You can turn to me.*

*You're not alone.*

*You can rely on me to look after you.*

'You knew I hated Elmswood. You sprung me from one prison and then put me in another. I fail to see how that is taking care of me.'

'Think of it as an endurance test. Look, Fairfax, I don't know what particular point you are trying to make, but I have always been like a father to you, and—'

Daniel got to his feet. 'That is exactly the point,' he said, staring at the man who had been his mentor for almost twenty years as if he was a stranger. 'Too much like my own father, in fact. Manipulating me into doing what you want me to do. Moulding me, shaping me, pushing me and pulling at me until I am whatever shape it is you require me to be at the time. But you don't give a damn about *me*, do you?'

'You are our best man. I had several other good men risk their necks to bring you out...'

'Spare me the recital. I am grateful, but it's no more than I deserved, considering that I was risking my neck on a daily basis for you, and have been for almost two decades.'

'You don't serve me—you serve your country.'

'Not any more, I don't.'

'What do you mean? Fairfax, I forbid you—'

'You *what*? I think you should reconsider that remark.'

Sir Marcus sank back into his seat as Daniel leaned over the desk. 'Don't threaten me.'

Daniel laughed. 'I'm done with this. Kate was absolutely right. I can be any man I choose, and I choose not to be your man any longer, Sir Marcus, nor anyone else's. I don't know why it's taken me so long to see it, but out of all the people who have used me for their own purposes you are the worst—or should I say the best?'

'I think you are still suffering from a fever. You are clearly not ready to return to service yet. A spell by the seaside, I think…'

'Dear God, I've not got consumption—and the only fever I have is a desire to get back to Elmswood before Kate leaves and it's too late.'

'Fairfax!'

Daniel turned, and there must have been something in his smile that told Sir Marcus he had lost.

'Leave the folder on the desk on your way out, there's a good chap. I hope you don't live to regret this.'

'How can I possibly regret living my own life for the first time ever?'

*Elmswood Manor, three days later*

Kate was in the music room, mid-way through her yoga practice, when she heard carriage wheels on the driveway. Peering out to the hallway, watching for Sylvia to open the door when the bell was rung, she was astonished to see the door scrape open.

Her knees turned to water.

Daniel's lithe figure was draped in a black woollen greatcoat. He was paler than the last time she'd seen him. She felt sick with longing, looking at him, and with dread too. What new hell could this be?

Steeling herself, she stepped into the hallway. 'Daniel. To what do I owe the pleasure?'

'You're here.' He threw himself at her, yanking her from her feet in a breathless embrace. 'You're *here*.'

'Until the day after tomorrow. Put me down, Daniel.'

'Kate.' He was instantly contrite. 'I forgot myself. I have missed you so much. The journey here from London felt interminable.'

'What is it? Why are you here? I thought you'd be in darkest Africa by now.'

'I was supposed to leave yesterday, but I— I can't believe you're still here. I was so sure— I have missed you so much.'

'Daniel!' She took a step back, looking at him properly, and what she saw made her silly heart leap. 'You look strange.'

'I feel very strange—not like myself at all. Or rather, exactly like myself.' He laughed slightly hysterically. 'I think we'd better go somewhere other than the hallway, I don't particularly want Sylvia to hear what I have to say.'

Out of habit, for she was wearing her yoga trousers and tunic, Kate returned to the music room, sitting down cross-legged on the rug.

'You have been keeping up your practice, I see,' Daniel said, yanking off his greatcoat.

'I enjoy it. It makes me able to look at myself in the mirror. Unlike you, I don't cast everything off when I decide to move on to the next stage in my life.'

Daniel pulled off his coat and boots and sat down with his usual annoying fluidity opposite her.

'I'm ready to move on to the next stage in my life too.'

'I thought you already had.'

He shook his head. 'I told Sir Marcus what he could do with his assignment.'

Her heart flip-flopped. 'This particular assignment?'

'And every other assignment that is waiting to be assigned in the history of assignments.'

She was having difficulty breathing. 'Daniel, are you drunk?'

'No, merely intoxicated. By life and its endless possibilities.'

'What endless possibilities? What are you proposing to do now?'

'That very much depends on you.'

'I have no idea what I'm going to do. I've rented a cottage…'

'In Devon. I know. Sorry,' Daniel said, looking not at all apologetic. 'I had to wring it out of the lawyer, but if I had missed you here I needed to know where to find you.'

'*Why*, Daniel?'

'I love you.'

'I know you do.'

'Yes, but I didn't. I thought— Oh, you know what I thought. But I was wrong, Kate. It didn't go away. It got worse and worse, the missing you, with every passing day. And the more determined I was to try and forget you, the more I kept remembering how you made me feel—how you *make* me feel.'

She could feel her smile growing from the inside out. She could feel warmth seeping through her, as if the sun was shining in her tummy.

'And precisely how is that, Daniel?'

'Like I can be any man I choose. And I choose to be with you—if you'll have me.'

She wanted to throw herself into his arms and tell him *yes, please*, but…

'You want to know what has changed,' he said, though she hadn't spoken. 'It's not so much that things have changed, it's more that I see things differently. It's not that there is no Daniel Fairfax—it's that he's never had a chance to find out who he is. I've always been someone else's man. My life has been a constant process of reinvention, or reincarnation—whatever you want to call it—but I have never been myself. *Never.* I have never been happy. Except when I've been with you, Kate.'

'But what does that mean? How are we to be happy?'

'I have absolutely no idea, save that we will be together. And that it won't be here. But those are my only two stipulations.' Daniel grinned. 'What do you think, Kate?'

'I don't want to be Lady Elmswood.'

He snapped his fingers. 'Then we shall dispense entirely with the title and leave it to gather dust until whoever inherits picks it up.'

A bubble of laughter escaped her. 'Do you mean that?'

'Well, I'm damned sure I don't want to be *Lord* Elmswood. No one can force us to use the title. Do you have any other stipulations?'

'Only that you love me—first and foremost and always.'

He leaned towards her, cupping her face with his hand. 'That's the easiest thing in the world to promise. I will always love you. First and foremost and more every single day.'

'Oh, Daniel. I have missed you so much.'

'Then you agree?'

'We will be Kate and Daniel. And wherever we go it will be together. I agree. I love you.'

'I love you with all my heart, my darling Kate.'

He pulled her towards him, falling backwards on the mat, taking her with him, and their lips met and their kiss instantly wiped away the pain and the sorrow of the weeks spent apart.

'I love you,' Kate murmured against his mouth.

'I love you,' Daniel whispered, his words reflected in his eyes.

Their kisses deepened but they made love slowly, watching each other, matching each other, each touch, each kiss, their hands roaming over each other's bodies, remembering and arousing, casting aside clothes when they got in the way, murmuring 'I love you' in between kisses. His hands were on her back, on her bottom, on her breasts. She was stroking his chest, licking his nipples, relishing the hardness of him pressing between her legs.

More kisses. The slide of his fingers inside her. Her hand curled around the hardness of him. Her leaning over to replace her hand with her mouth. The deep groan that kiss drew from him. The surge of passion it evoked. Frantic kisses. The aching anticipation in the seconds before he entered her. The way she moulded herself around him.

And then the frantic rhythm, the thrusts that made her shudder and cling, the way he said her name, the sudden unstoppable jolt of her climax, and his deep, guttural groan as he came too.

And afterwards a new sensation as they lay sprawled together on the floor of the music room. Daniel was smiling, his eyes shining with love, and she had a feeling as if she had cut the tethers she hadn't known were holding her down.

The future was theirs to make. Together.

# *Epilogue*

*Le Pas à Pas Restaurant, London,*
*April 1853*

'The Elmswood Coven, finally reunited,' Estelle said gleefully.

'We're not at Elmswood,' Eloise said. 'We're in London's top restaurant.'

'And we're about to eat a dinner cooked by London's top chef.' Phoebe beamed around the table. 'What's more, our coven has doubled in size. Who would have thought, when Uncle Daniel arranged Eloise's marriage, that we would all four of us make a love match? I think we owe him a huge vote of thanks.'

'Thank you,' Daniel replied, 'but if anyone is due a vote of thanks it's Kate. If she hadn't proposed marriage to me none of us would be here.' He lifted his champagne flute, tilting it at his wife. 'To Kate, who has made all this possible, and who has made me the happiest man in the world.'

'I'll happily toast the first part,' Alexander said, 'but I'm going to have to lay claim to being the second.'

'Actually,' Owen said, kissing Phoebe's fingertips, 'I beg to differ.'

'Lads, lads…' Aiden said, laughing. 'Can we not all agree that we're equally happy? Owen and Phoebe. Daniel and Kate. Eloise and Alexander. And Estelle—my lovely Estelle—and me.'

'I'll drink to that,' Alexander said. 'And Eloise and I have another little celebration to share with you. We are expecting the arrival of a sister or a brother for Tilda in the autumn.'

'Well, now, since we're sharing good news,' Estelle said, when the toast had been drunk and the cheers and the questions had subsided, 'Aiden and I have something wonderful to tell you too.' Estelle's beautiful smile softened. 'We have not one but two new arrivals expected. Only yesterday we had the papers. We've adopted twins. A little boy and girl, just four years old.'

Phoebe jumped up from her seat to throw her

arms around her twin. 'I am *so* happy for you. I am so very, *very* happy for you.'

'And so am I,' Kate said, reaching across the table.

'Oh, Estelle.' It was Eloise's turn to hug her sister. 'Tilda will be so excited. Two new cousins at once. That is wonderful.'

'I hope you and Uncle Daniel will find time to visit us and meet our twins before you go,' Estelle said. 'We are expecting to have them at Cashel Duairc some time next month.'

'We don't set off on our next trip until June,' Kate said, touching the beautiful pendant that she always wore—a very special gift from Daniel, with his precious turquoise as its centrepiece. 'It's a short visit to some of the Spanish islands in the Balearic Sea. The flowers at that time of year are supposed to be beautiful, though I'm not looking for specimens so much as ideas.'

'Kate has ambitious plans for a new kind of wilderness garden—a mixture of desert plants and English flowers.'

'No one wants to hear about my horticultural endeavours, Daniel.'

'Your garden is becoming quite famous, actually,' Eloise said. '"The entrancing gardens created by the explorer Daniel Fairfax and his botanist wife, who travel together to the remotest parts of the globe in search of exotic new specimens…" Or something like that is what I read recently.'

'I wouldn't exactly call Europe a remote part of the globe,' Kate said.

'But we *are* off to India next year.' Daniel grinned at his wife. 'Kate wants to grow tea.'

'My news isn't nearly as exciting,' Phoebe said, when the laughter had once again died down, 'but if you are not all rushing back to your homes tomorrow I was hoping you would come to the official opening of my new restaurant.'

'Another restaurant?'

'Where is it?'

'It's one where no one pays,' Owen said. 'It's near St Giles, actually, and it's more of a free kitchen than a restaurant.'

'It was Owen's idea. I am always saying what a shame it is that so much of the produce at Covent Garden goes to waste. At the end of the day the unsold produce is left to rot.'

'If you can make cakes out of grass, I said to her, surely you could make something tasty and delicious out of discarded fruit and vegetables.'

'Yes, but I couldn't sell it—I mean, who would pay to eat leftovers in a restaurant, even though the leftovers I make are utterly delicious. As you'll see in a moment, when I serve dinner.'

'Now, *that* will be just like the old days,' Eloise said wryly. 'Mouldy cauliflower ice, anyone?'

'That would be rather too much like the old days—which is why I'm only pulling your leg. But I'm serious about my charity kitchen,' Phoebe said. 'We open tomorrow, and it's first come first served. Will you all come and help?'

'An invitation I think none of us can refuse,' Kate said. 'A final toast. Here's to all of us, who each rather conveniently married the person we love without realising it. Cheers!'

* * * * *

# *Historical Note*

There's a veritable patchwork quilt of my past research stitched into this book. Daniel was partly inspired by the renegade explorer and diplomat Richard Burton, whom I read about in Mary S. Lovell's excellent biography *A Rage to Live*, when I was writing about another explorer—Christopher, in *Claiming His Desert Princess.*

Burton notoriously translated the infamous sex guide, *The Perfumed Garden*, and it is this book I have Daniel obliquely referring to—although I do know that the timeline is slightly out! Other previous reading which informed Daniel's life in foreign service include H.V.F. Winstone's biography of Lady Anne Blunt, and Deborah Manley and Peta Ree's biography of Henry Salt.

So what was Daniel actually up to when he was captured?

I'm sorry, I can't tell you that—it's classified!

But just to do a little bit of scene-setting: in Egypt, Muhammad Ali ruled for a huge chunk of the nineteenth century, during which time he did a lot of modernising and warmongering. He established coveted trade links with India, positioned Alexandria as a key world port, and made Egypt pivotal to the cotton trade.

In Daniel's time Ali was involved in the Greek War of Independence (1821), the Ottoman War (1831-1833) and the invasion of Syria in 1831. Britain at this point was on the side of the Turks. So, as you can imagine, there were vast swathes of opportunity for an undercover British agent to do his thing.

But Daniel's activities are not confined to Egypt, and—because I do like to re-use worlds I've already built—he takes a trip to my fantasy Arabia, and thus encounters two daughters belonging to the eponymous Lord Henry Armstrong.

If you're interested in finding out how they ended up married to Arabian princes, you can check them out in *Innocent in the Sheikh's Harem* and *The Governess and the Sheikh.*

Talking of sheikhs… Kate's new career as a botanist is inspired by two people—one of whom is my invention and one real. The Cornish botanist whose book she reads was the work of Daniel Trevelyan—or was it? You can find out the history of that publication in my book *The Widow and the Sheikh.*

Marianne North was an eminent Victorian botanical artist who explored the far reaches of the globe in search of specimens for Kew Gardens, and it is this real-life character whose history I 'borrowed' for Kate and Daniel's happy-ever-after—though I let them precede Miss North in their travels.

What else?

Squire Mytton—or Mad Jack Mytton—was a real character, whose exploits sound wholly fictional.

I've taken a few liberties with Farmer Styles's experimentation regarding different fertilisers, though the agricultural revolution was in full swing by the eighteen-thirties.

And, finally, Donne's *Good Morrow* is not only one of Daniel and Eloise's favourite poems, it's one of mine.

# MILLS & BOON

## Coming next month

### AN UNCONVENTIONAL COUNTESS
Jenni Fletcher

'It's strange, but you might be the only person in the world who *can* understand.'

Anna felt her pulse quicken at the words. It was the same thing she'd thought when she'd told Samuel how she felt trapped, as if they truly *could* understand each other. As if maybe, despite everything, they might be a good match after all, just as the Baroness had said. The way he was looking at her now suggested he thought so, too, but how could that be possible? She was a shopkeeper and he was an earl…*maybe*. Or maybe not. There was an equal chance that he might remain a captain.

'I do understand.' She tried to keep her voice normal. 'Only my mother told me recently that bitterness and resentment weren't very attractive qualities. Shall I repeat her lecture?'

'Did it make you feel any better?'

'No, but it did make me think. Now I want to let go of the past and move on, wherever it leads me.'

*'Wherever…?'* He echoed the word as he lifted a hand to the side of her face, his fingers sliding gently across the curve of her cheek and beneath her chin, tilting it upwards. The touch sent a thrill of heat coursing through her body, making her feel as if every inch of

her skin was blushing. Thank goodness they were outside in the dark. Although they really shouldn't be. Not together and certainly not touching like this. No matter what he said about understanding each other, there were still too many obstacles between them. Only it was becoming hard to hold on to that thought.

'We ought to go in.' She swallowed nervously. 'You said it was time for supper.'

'Did I?' He moved closer, his jacket brushing against the front of her dress. 'I can't remember.'

'Yes. I don't think…'

Her words faltered as his arms closed around her waist, enveloping her in a feeling of strong masculine warmth. She didn't move or resist, too surprised to do anything as he leaned in towards her, his mouth moving slowly towards and then hovering above hers, so tantalisingly close that it was hard to believe they weren't already touching. She could feel the warmth of his breath as it skimmed across her cheek…and then there was a sensation of cold air as he moved to one side, gently grazing the edge of her mouth.